PENGU

THE FURIES

Keith Roberts was born in 1935. He was Assistant Editor of *Science Fantasy* and *Science Fiction Impulse* from 1965 to 1966 and Managing Editor of the latter in 1966. One of Britain's most distinguished science-fiction writers, his other books include *Pavane* (1968; published by Penguin in 1984), *The Inner Wheel* (1970), *Anita* (1970), *The Boat of Fate* (1971), *Machines and Men* (1973), *The Chalk Giants* (1974), *The Grain Kings* (1975), *Ladies from Hell* (1979) and *Molly Zero* (1980).

KEITH ROBERTS

THE FURIES

PENGUIN BOOKS

Penguin Books Ltd, Harmondsworth, Middlesex, England
Penguin Books, 40 West 23rd Street, New York, New York 10010, U.S.A.
Penguin Books Australia Ltd, Ringwood, Victoria, Australia
Penguin Books Canada Ltd, 2801 John Street, Markham, Ontario, Canada L3R 1B4
Penguin Books (N.Z.) Ltd, 182–190 Wairau Road, Auckland 10, New Zealand

First published by Rupert Hart-Davis Ltd 1966
Published in Penguin Books 1985

Made and printed in Great Britain by
Richard Clay (The Chaucer Press) Ltd,
Bungay, Suffolk
Set in Linotype Plantin

PROLOGUE

WE MAY call them the Keepers. The thing they guarded so
jealously was not material in the way that we humans understand the word. It had volume but no shape, mass but no size.
A seething knot of memories, an electric tree of wisdom, it
came burgeoning through space, tossed by gravitic currents,
licked at by the flames of suns in nova. It came to Earth . . .

Maybe the Keepers were tired. To them, Vanderdecken was
an ephemeral creature and the millennia of Ahasueras no more
than the slow blinking of an eye. Their voyage stretched for
ever, into the future and into the past, back, back, back beyond
our Time, back maybe to the Prime Creation. Where they had
come from, even the Keepers had forgotten. How they had
been spawned they had never known.

They could not bleed, they could feel no pain or fear. They
owned no cells that could die, no bone that Time could
vaporize. They were raw, and nude beyond our comprehension
of bareness. Maybe at last they had become hungry. Hungry
for the thick comfort of flesh . . .

It could be they found us by blind chance; or perhaps they
sensed us and were drawn. Maybe the fears of terror-stricken
worlds spread like ripples into unguessable continuums, bringing their own retribution. We shall never know. What we do
know is that the space-things discovered Earth. They saw the
warmth of her sun. They tasted the green of her continents,
the blue-silver skeins of her seas. They sensed her Life with
every ramshackle nerve, and to them all that they found
seemed good. They piloted their burden through meteor-
haunted shells of air. They dropped down to where they could
see cities boiling like the homes of insects. Then lower, and
closer, and lower . . . They hung in the sky, invisible, a focus of
storms and anxieties. They watched and schemed and planned
and observed; and in time, their choice was made.

They turned on the thing they had protected for so long,
ripping it apart, gobbling its essence into themselves. They

swelled with new knowledge and confidence. They readied themselves for their first and only transformation; and somehow, somewhere, the incredible happened. The Word – their Word – became flesh . . .

CHAPTER 1

I'VE SHOWN that opening to three or four people and so far nobody has liked it. They say it's too fancy and in any case it can't be proved. I know it can't be proved, and as for being fancy; well, this is my book and I reckon I can start it any way I want. After all, I was asked to write it; I pointed out at the time I was a cartoonist not an author, but nobody would listen.

I'm Bill Sampson, and as I said I used to draw funny faces for a living. The year all this started, the year of the Neptune Test, I was living in a village in Wiltshire called Brockledean. I suppose I'd done pretty well for myself; I'd got my own house, an XK150, and a Great Dane, I was fairly comfortably off and I wasn't quite thirty. I'd had a stroke of luck of course; I'd done a lot of jobs in my time, from driving lorries to hauling boxes about in a department store, nothing had lasted very long and I'd never made more than a bare living, sometimes not even that. Then I ran into an old contact of mine and managed to weasel my way into a freelance arrangement with one of the big publishing houses just as they were launching a new kids' comic. I was working as a general hack in a seedy little agency at the time; I chucked that when I got a bit more established, and not long afterwards I was worth enough to be looking round for some nice fat chargeable expenses to fool the tax people. A pal of mine suggested I put some money into property. It seemed a good idea; in those days even a lousy businessman could scarcely lose with bricks and mortar. I started looking around.

The choice wasn't easy. I'd sworn I'd never live in a new house; there was something about modern jerry-building that I found infinitely depressing. A Development affected me like a blowsy London pub, it reminded me of the shortness of life. I saw a lot of property; most of it was in the active process of falling down, and the prices conformed to my definition of daylight robbery. Then I heard about the place at Brockledean and drove out to have a look. It seemed ideal. The house had been a pub at one time, and it stood on its own about a mile away from the main village. Not much in sight except a handful of farm outbuildings. The countryside round about wasn't exactly beautiful, but it was undeniably pleasant. There was a room with a north light that would be fine for a studio, and there was a garage. The garden was small and mostly under grass, so keeping it in order wasn't going to be a full-time job. All in all the set-up just about fitted my needs; I got a mortgage without too much trouble and settled down to enjoy a life of rural simplicity.

I developed a routine. Once a week I'd go to London to deliver artwork and collect scripts, the rest of the time including Saturdays I'd work like a bank clerk. There's nothing romantic about art of course, it's just like any other job. You work fixed hours and try to put it out of your mind when you're off duty; sit round waiting for inspiration and you'd soon run out of crusts. My days were pretty full at first because I was catering for myself; cooking the evening meal usually turned out to be something in the nature of a crisis. I got better in time of course, though I'll admit I'd never make a chef. After the smoke had cleared and I'd washed the dishes I'd usually prowl round the house for a while just trying to picture what it had been like in the good old days when it was a pub. That wasn't difficult; it was the sort of place that invited imaginings. The main structure wasn't old as country houses go, but the foundations and cellars were a different thing altogether. The floors were massive, supported by heavy beams, and downstairs there were some round brick arches that looked to me like sixteenth-century work at least. There'd been a tavern here in the times when the loving-cups were passed. Perhaps the place was haunted; there were all sorts of pleasant possibilities.

As you've probably worked out I'm a bit of a melancholic by nature. I love old things; old buildings, old ideas. The house still kept a lot of relics of its pub days; there was a mark on the brickwork of the front wall where a notice of some sort had been fixed, and there was a post that had evidently supported a sign. It was bare now and stuck up beside the gate like a little gibbet. The estate agent was going to have it removed but I wouldn't hear of it.

I settled down quickly enough, but after a few months I got to feeling that something was missing somewhere. I'd lie awake nights and listen to the timbers settling and creaking, and the hundred unidentifiable noises that old houses make, and I'd feel pretty lonely. I'd promised myself I'd never have a woman in the place; I hadn't been able to find anybody to share the hard times, not that I blamed them, and now I was better off I was too crabby to want to split my profits with a wife even supposing I could find one. If I needed company though there was an obvious alternative; I bought myself the Great Dane.

She was a bitch; I'd wanted a dog, but when I saw her sprawling round the run at the kennels I knew I was just going to have to buy her. She was black, like polished jet, and from the time she was a knobbly-kneed puppy there was only one name for her. Sekhmet, Egyptian goddess of darkness, consort of the lord of the underworld. Maybe it was a little high-flown; anyway it soon got shortened to Sek, which was classically unsound but a whole lot easier to yell.

One of Sek's minor advantages was that she seemed inordinately fond of my cooking. I could never resist the temptation to dabble about with fancy recipes; as often as not the results were disastrous, but it seemed to me the more horrible the mess the more she enjoyed it. Maybe she was just being tactful; it was hard to tell with her, she was naturally polite.

When the daily battle was over I usually walked Sek for a couple of miles. We'd always finish up at the *Basketmaker's Arms* in Brockledean. She was a firm favourite there. They kept biscuits behind the bar for her; she'd stretch her neck, push her great dark head over the counter, roll her lips back from her teeth, and take the goodies as if they were made of glass. Then she'd eat them without leaving a crumb. She developed a fair taste for beer as well, though I usually restricted her to a dishful at the most. I felt one dipso in the family was enough.

They were a nice crowd in the *Arms*, farm workers, market gardeners, an old Diddy who ran a one-man scrap business; the type of folk I like. I had one particular friend there. His name was Tod; he was a great character, and as Irish as they come. He was a County Mayo man, an agricultural graduate and a 'grower'. His people had been growers for generations, and although he was a company director, he'd never got round to thinking of himself as someone different. He used to travel the country advising on problems to do with agriculture; his firm specialized in crop spraying and he was an expert on pest control. I did one or two little jobs for him from time to time, copywriting, layouts and visuals for advertising, that sort of thing. I'd never take any money for them, but Tod paid in kind; and they had a sort of exhibition spread just down the road and he was my source of supply for fresh eggs, farm butter and cheese, and the Lord knew what else besides.

It was from Tod that I first heard about the Furies. I walked into the *Arms* one night in late June when Sek was eighteen months old and just coming into her prime. Trade was slack, but Tod was sitting in his usual place at the far end of the bar, nose in the *Daily Echo*. He handed the paper across to me, marking an item with his thumb. By sheer luck I've managed to get hold of a copy of that article; it was headed 'Strange attack in Dorset', and it ran as follows.

FROM A SPECIAL CORRESPONDENT

News was received today of an odd incident involving a man from Powerstock near Bridport, in Dorset. James Langham, a farmhand, was driving a tractor on the property of his employer, Mr Noel Paddington, when he was attacked by what he described as a monstrous wasp. The creature, said by Langham to have been a yard or more across the wings, appeared suddenly over a hedge and dived at the machine at great speed. Langham was able to duck out of the way of the assault, the insect passing over his head and hitting the wheel of the tractor. The assailant then fell to the ground, enabling Langham to kill it with a lucky blow from a spade. The remains were carried in a sack to a nearby barn and Mr Paddington informed. On investigating two hours later he could find no trace of the creature though Langham was most insistent as to the truth of his story. He was much shaken by his experience, and remained at home today. He described the attacker as 'droning like a low-flying plane' and claimed the sting alone, unsheathed in the death throes, was over a foot long.

10

Local police are at present investigating the deaths of three dogs in the vicinity. In each case the bodies were found considerably swollen and each animal appeared to have been killed by a thrust from some sharp-pointed weapon such as a stiletto or bayonet. Asked if the wounds could conceivably have been caused by some such oversize insect, a constable remarked that 'if it was a wasp, he would not care to meet it'. Samples of tissue from the dead animals have been submitted for analysis with a view to determining what if any poison is present, though no report has yet been received.

There was a footnote.

The Curator of the Insect House at the London Zoo said today 'The largest living insect known to science is a beetle, *Macrodontia Cervicornis,* which attains a length of almost six inches. The construction and operation of an insect's body are such as to render any form larger than this highly improbable. A size of three feet or more would be out of the question.'

I put the paper down and shook my head. 'I've heard some tales in my time but this takes some beating. Do you believe it, Tod?'

He took a pull at his Guinness. 'No. It isn't possible. And it's just as well, sonny Jim, I'll tell ye.'

I chaffed him. 'How come? I should have thought you'd welcome it. Look at the trade you'd do squibbing away at whopping great things like that.'

He looked at me queerly. 'You'd be laughing over the other half of your face if it was true, Bill. You think about it. Imagine a wasp. The power of it, the body of the thing packed with muscle and venom. You haven't got an animal there, you've got a machine. All sheathed in with chitin, and that'd be tougher than steelplate. You'd need an armour-piercing bullet to hurt him and all the time he'd be coming on and coming on, and you'd never step from the way of him. And his sting, it would go right through you and come out on the other side, like the paper says it'd be a bayonet. And there'd be his jaws too, snipping away like bolt-cutters. Make no mistake, if

11

a wasp was blown up to a yard big those mouth parts would have off your arm and no bother to it.'

I said, 'Charming, I'm sure . . .'

He said, 'There'd be other things of course. Things like social organization. He's just as smart as we are at getting things done.'

I frowned. 'You're a mine of nasty ideas tonight, Tod.'

He grinned at me. 'There's things that get in a man's mind and won't be driven away, it's the mystic Oirish in me I tell ye . . . I say the next great time will be the Age of Insects. If these big wasps were real we'd have it on us in a jiffy.'

I said, 'That's wrong for a start, insects missed their chance. They've been around for God knows how many years. If they'd been going to dominate they'd have done it before now.'

He shook his head. 'Oh no . . . There were little dinosaurs scuttling and hopping for a good while before Tyrannosaurus sat up and barked. And take mammals, they spent long enough running about like cane rats before one of them built the Pyramids.'

Never argue with an Irishman. He revels in it.

'Take a fly in amber,' said Tod, warming to his theme. 'See the little beast, the hairs of him, and his wings, and the twinkle in his eye. He's a good few times older than the human race, but he's just the same as the ones outside on the muck-heap. Now insects have waited a long time, and some of 'em with a social structure approaching ours an' all, and they haven't changed or evolved, they haven't gone up or down. That means as living machines they're pretty near perfect, which we most certainly are not. We're shedding our poor teeth and claws and we need a whole mess of things to keep us alive and warm, we're fast losing what adaptability we have left and that was bad for the dinosaurs.'

I said, 'But insects aren't adaptable either.'

He opened his bright blue eyes wide. 'Ah now there ye go, dabblin' in what doesn't concern ye once again. Now if ye would just stick to the art of drawing and allow us professionals to know what is going on and what is not . . . Of course your insect is adaptable. If he wasn't, I'd be lookin' for a job. He can live on cyanide of potassium if he wants, we can't. Look, there's people in laboratories with real heads on their

12

shoulders and they're worryin' to death because of running out of things to invent, and the little beggars of insects growing fat on last year's sprays. I tell ye.'

I said, 'Like the penicillin immunity.'

'The very same . . .' Something droned in the darkening sky, and he stopped. He said, 'What do ye suppose the man saw then? Now what could come snapping and buzzing at ye like that, on a nice bright summer day?'

I didn't answer. The noise got louder; then we both saw a plane fly across the window and disappear. Tod laughed. 'I tell ye, I'm nervous already. You give a device like a wasp just this one little advantage of size and he'd be down on us from the air. Like the creatures in the story that tormented the poor souls for their sins, now what were they called?'

I said, 'The Furies.'

He nodded slowly, sipping the drink and rolling it around his mouth. He said, 'Yes, the Furies. Come to think on it now, that would be a good name for a pack of things like that . . .'

For the next few days I kept a curious eye on the newspapers, but there were no more reports, tongue in cheek or otherwise. Of course through most of that year nearly all news was overshadowed by the nuclear test series being run by both East and West. The American experiments were to culminate with the Neptune Project, the forthcoming detonation on the bed of the Pacific of a five-hundred-megaton bomb. It would be the biggest-ever man-made blast, and for nearly six months the Press had been retailing arguments for and against it. The Navy claimed with some asperity that the effects on tides and currents would be global and catastrophic while the fisheries people were worried about contamination; some authorities claimed it would be years before safe catches could be made anywhere near the affected areas. As I remember there were even some doubts expressed about the ability of the Earth's crust to withstand the shock, though they were immediately howled down as alarmist and unscientific. For most of us of course there was nothing to do; we just sat around like saps and waited for the big bang.

From shortly after the signing of the first test-ban treaty it had been obvious that despite the drum-banging of the politicians, the agreement did not mark a new era in human development. For me the proverbial cloud no bigger than a man's hand appeared when an American statesman declared that the signing represented a challenge to the forces of peace. We must keep alert, he said, so as to be ready to resume testing instantly if and when the enemy broke his word. Whether Russia actually did explode a thermonuclear device in the atmosphere is now, of course, of merely academic interest. American experts claimed to have detected a sharp increase in the world level of radiation; notes were exchanged between East and West, the United States protesting that the treaty had been violated, Russia retaliating by claiming the whole thing to be a Capitalist plot designed to shift the blame for what were in fact Western experiments. Shortly after that seismographs recorded heavy shocks which could have been and probably were underground trials in the vicinity of the old testing ground, Novaya Zemla. America, thoroughly alarmed, warned the Kremlin that she would not hesitate to continue her own experiments in the interests of world peace. Great Britain supported her by announcing an intention to 'stand firm', though how, and with what, was never made clear. Russia stayed quiet. Shortly afterwards the West announced the full-scale resumption of atmospheric testing. The event was efficiently publicized and the Russians rapidly followed suit by beginning a new series of their own.

It was rather like a drug addiction; after a temporary abstinence both sides returned to the habit with redoubled vigour. At the beginning of the year radiation levels stood fifty per cent higher than they had done in the scare of the late fifties, and the best was still to come. In Great Britain we saw a boycott of Welsh farm produce, and the Ministry of Health attempted to calm the populace by making a hasty upward revision of all safety levels. The Press began to remark on odd side-effects; one of the most significant was that, as during the London blitz, the churches began to fill.

A couple of nights after talking to Tod I had a visitor. It was about seven o'clock and dinner was well under way. I forget what I was trying to cook, but I'm sure it would have been better not to bother. The kitchen door was propped pessimistically open and Sek was outside somewhere. I heard

14

her bark briefly, then again, then she was quiet. I stopped operations and called her. When she didn't come I walked round the side of the house to find out what was the matter; a Dane never speaks without a reason. When I came in sight of the front lawn I stopped. I was a little taken aback.

The girl had already come through the gate and she was on her knees in the drive, Sek's head towering above her. She was rubbing the great animal on the chest and Sek was standing there soaking it up and looking as sloppy as possible. The youngster straightened when she saw me; she was tall, she might have been fifteen or sixteen. It was hard to tell. She was neatly dressed in blue jeans and a check shirt; her face was round and rather serious with a straight, stubborn little nose and wide-spaced, candid blue eyes. She had a superb mane of dark hair, sleek and well brushed, caught up behind her ears with a crisp white ribbon. Altogether, a surprising vision. I said, 'Well hello, who are you?'

She said, 'Jane Felicity Beddoes-Smythe. How do you do?' She held out her hand.

I said, 'Bill Sampson, and I'm pleased to meet you. But that wasn't very wise you know.'

She was bending down again, calling the dog. 'What?'

'Walking in like that. Sek might not have taken to you.'

'Pooh, what rot. What did you call her?'

'Sek. It's short for Sekhmet. Go on girl, it's all right.' That to Sek; now that I'd arrived she had become more officious and she was avoiding the outstretched hand. She went forward instantly and allowed herself to be petted. I said, 'What can I do for you, Miss Smythe?'

She looked at me blandly. She said, 'Beddoes-Smythe. I don't care, but Mummy likes to hear both barrels go off. It isn't important though, I respond very well to Jane.'

I shook my head slightly. Her voice was beautifully modulated; it struck me she came from the sort of family who're so wealthy they can afford to be polite. I said, 'All right then, what can I do for Jane?'

She waved a well-thumbed exercise book. 'I'm on vacation, we came down last week. I've got a holiday task that rather leaves me gasping, so I thought I'd bring it down and get the scientist to help me with it.'

15

I was baffled. 'I'm afraid you've got it wrong. There's only me here and I'm not a scientist.'

She giggled suddenly, tossed the book down, and started to wrestle with Sek, who was only too willing to play. She said, 'That's an alibi, I thought it was quite ingenious. I told the housekeeper you were a scientist and a friend of Daddy's. Actually I just wanted to come and see the dog.'

I started to grin. I said, 'Where do you live, Jane?'

She pointed briefly. 'Over there. Brockledean House. Mummy and Daddy are away at the moment, they're not expected back for some time. What's that smell?'

I said, 'God, the dinner . . .' I pelted back to the kitchen. Smoke met me. I groped my way inside and got the pan off the stove. On the way out I nearly collided with Jane. She started to cough. She said, 'What a terrible mess. Do you always get in a state like this when you try to cook?'

I finished scraping the remains on to the garden. 'It isn't usually quite as bad as this. But sometimes people call at the crucial moment. Then I forget, and things go haywire.'

She said, 'Gosh, I'm terribly sorry. Can I help?'

'No, it's all right. I can cope.'

'Please, I should feel much better. After all, it is my fault. Don't worry, I'm quite good in a kitchen.'

'I wouldn't hear of it . . .'

She was quite the most determined girl I'd ever met. Half an hour later we both sat down to a first-rate mixed grill, far better than anything I could have cooked. I complimented Jane and she lowered her eyes in false modesty. 'There's a trick to it,' she explained. 'It's very simple really. You get all the things you know are going to take longest and put them in first. Then the others, sort of by stages. That way they all come ready at the same time.'

She insisted on helping with the washing-up. As we were stacking plates she said, 'What do you do for a living, Bill?'

'I draw silly pictures.'

She said, 'You need some more soap-flakes by the way . . . do you mean you're a cartoonist?'

'Yes . . . Look, Jane, this is very sweet of you, but won't your people worry?'

16

She shook her head decisively. 'There's only the Carters. They live in, he does the gardens and she's a sort of general help. They're not really with it, I doubt if they'll miss me till after dark. I'm often out on my own.'

I said, 'All the same it's getting late. Can I run you back?'

She laughed. 'That would cause it. Accepting lifts from strange men ... No thanks, Bill. In any case I go back across the fields, it's quicker that way. You must come and look over the house sometime, it's really rather fine. Can I come and see you again?'

I said, 'But of course, love to have you.'

She said, 'Good. I'll come earlier tomorrow, then we can take Sek for a run. Will that be all right?'

'Yes, if you want.'

She said, 'I'd like a dog. It's difficult though because of term time. Carter would have to look after it and she isn't very fond of animals.' She held out her hand again, formally. She said, 'Goodnight, Bill, thanks for putting up with me. Goodbye, Sek.' She ran to the gate, swung over it, and trotted off down the lane. The last I saw of her in the dusk was the glimmer of her hair ribbon and the twinkle of white ankle socks. I wandered back into the house, lighting my pipe on the way. The kitchen seemed very quiet. I said to Sek, 'Well, old girl, we certainly see life. Or don't you think so?' She bunted my arm with her huge head and walked into the hall. I heard the tinkle of her lead as she tried to pull it off the hook. I said, 'All right, clot, no need for the broad hints. You know I don't lead you at this time of night.' She came back instantly, walked through to the garden, and stood looking alert. I said, 'Go on then.' She cleared the gate with a bound – a favourite trick of hers – and headed up the lane. A few yards on she waited for me and we walked to the pub together.

I half expected I wouldn't see Jane again, but she turned up as arranged. We walked a good way; she chattered a lot about her parents and her friends, her school, her life at Brockledean. Most of what she talked about was new to me; I'd never known much in the way of luxury, anything I wanted I'd had to earn. Jane's father was a stockbroker, and her mother was wealthy in her own right. The girl had her own pony and there was a swimming pool in the grounds of the house. She usually spent the summer with family friends in Sussex but this year that had been impossible. She was an only child and I suppose with her people away she was glad of my company.

The walks became something of an institution. I remember thinking it would be a pity when Jane's parents came back, my place was going to seem pretty empty without her. There was no reason why she shouldn't keep coming over of course, but I had a pretty good idea that wouldn't be allowed to happen. She wanted to come to the pub with me one evening, but I put my foot down there, it would just be asking for trouble. She invited me to tea at Brockledean instead. It was a date that neither of us kept; the Furies intervened.

I first heard about the Berryton massacre from Jane. I was shaving one morning when the phone rang; I went through to the hall yawning, and picked it up. I said, 'Hello?' I wondered who the devil it could be.

'Hello, Bill,' said the handset huskily. 'Bet I got you out of bed . . .'

I still wasn't orientated. 'Er . . . who's speaking?'

'Me, you clot. Jane . . .'

I said, 'Good Lord, I didn't think . . . what's the matter, love?'

A pause. Then, 'I don't quite know. But I sort of had to ring. I couldn't think of anyone else . . . something awful's happened, Bill. It was on the radio a little while ago . . .'

My heart did a few circuits and bumps round my rib-cage. I'd been waiting for World War Three for a long time, but I'd never quite got used to the tension. I said, 'What is it, some fool started a shooting match?'

She said, 'No, not quite as bad as that. But a lot of people got killed in Somerset. A whole village, the man said. I've never heard anything like it. They said it was great big wasps . . .'

I thought of Tod, and the news item in the paper. But it was crazy. I said, 'Look, Jane, is this a gag?' I knew before she answered it was nothing of the sort.

I looked at my watch. About five to eight. I said, 'Tell you what, there's a newscast coming up in a few minutes. I'll listen in and then ring you back, or you can call me. OK?'

'I'll call you.' Her voice sounded very mature on the line. 'I might have to leave it till mid-morning though. Will you be in?'

'Yes, all the time . . . Jane, are you all right over there?'

'Yes, of course . . . I'm just worried because it's all so queer. I'll call you, 'bye . . .' The line went dead.

I put the handset back on the cradle, frowned at it for a moment then shrugged. I went into the kitchen and turned on the radio. I was still finishing my shave when the news started. By the time the announcer had got out half a dozen sentences I'd forgotten the lather on my face. I was leaning over the set to catch every word.

CHAPTER 2

BERRYTON LAY on the border of Dorset and Somerset, a straggling village of some two thousand inhabitants. How many insects took part in the raid was never fully established, but between them they managed to account for nearly a quarter of the population. The first warning of their approach was a deep throbbing that reminded some hearers of a formation of planes. They circled the place at a considerable height, only just visible from the ground. People came out of their houses to stare and point; there was uneasiness but no real alarm. Then the creatures dived, and within minutes the place was a shambles. Some of the attackers went for the pubs, others made for the village hall, where a meeting of sorts was in progress. Some smashed their way into the church, where numbers of refugees had gathered; others simply flew up and down the street hawking at everything in sight.

Only one insect was known to have been killed. It was crawling in the road when a truck driven by the local garage owner hit it, crushing its head. Numbers of wasps gathered at once and according to eyewitnesses the unfortunate man was dragged out and dismembered on the spot. The incident seemed to have signalled the end of the attack. The creatures flew off into the evening sky, taking their casualty with them. They left the village battered and stunned.

Help had been quick to arrive. Ambulances and medical teams had been rushed to the spot from as far away as Exeter while the police and military had thrown a cordon round the entire area. Units of the Royal Armoured Corps supported by Fleet Air Arm helicopters were combing the country round about in an attempt to find the nests; schools had been closed, and all public transport suspended. The newscast finished with a warning to people living in and near the trouble spot to stay in their homes as much as they could and to help the military by reporting any sightings without delay. Above all, they were urged to stay calm. The fullest possible measures were being taken; the menace was local, and could and would be met. Further bulletins would be issued as fresh information became available.

What we didn't know then was that the creatures had managed to establish themselves in nearly every country in the world. In France a village in Normandy had been almost wiped out and the same thing had happened in Belgium and Holland. In America the first sightings were reported from places as far apart as New England and Mexico. The Eastern bloc had their problems too; Czechoslovakia and Poland had been invaded and Russian planes had bombed nesting areas, probably causing more casualties to humans than insects. We were slower to resort to extreme measures, and England was probably one of the first countries to be completely overrun. The things spread out from Wessex, that old melting-pot of alien cultures, to attack every town in the land.

Jane phoned again as she'd promised and we talked the whole thing over. We were a long way from the trouble, but she thought it would be best to stay in for the time being. She said in any case she was expecting her mother to call. After she'd hung up I went into the studio and tried to get some work done, but I couldn't settle. I was glad when it got round to evening and I could go along to the *Arms*.

They'd set up a tube in the public bar and a bigger crowd than usual had gathered to watch. The BBC news teams had had a field day; we saw an hour-long telerecording that covered every aspect of the Berryton affair. A relief centre had been set up in the village hall; the cameras moved from that to show some of the damage up and down the street. It looked as if the place had been bombed; the pavements were strewn with rubble and a lot of houses had lost their windows. Staying indoors was obviously no protection; in many cases the insects had flown straight through the glass without damaging themselves. One of the most disturbing shots had been taken inside the little church. I member it very well; the camera tracked down the nave, turning aside to examine odd details, a pew-end scraped by huge jaws, a statue toppled from its niche. Then up across the altar steps, still covered with glass and flowers, and a tilt to show the gaping hole in the east window where one of the attackers had crashed through. The people must have thought they were being chased by devils, but God's House had been no sanctuary. It was easy to imagine the painted brightness of stained glass bursting, the machine-faces peering down . . .

The search for the nests was still going on. The cameras showed lines of men moving across fields, tanks nosing down narrow lanes. Everything conceivable was being pressed into use; they'd even brought down tracker dogs, and there were mobile radar units engaged in an obviously futile search for tiny flying objects.

The programme closed with some aerial shots of the village. That was where I heard the name Tod and I had coined for ourselves. 'This, then,' said the commentator impressively, 'is Berryton, scene of perhaps the most unprecedented disaster of modern times. An attack as deadly as it was bizarre, an attack by a new life-form that dropped literally from the skies on to this quiet place. Like the Furies of legend they came; and like the Furies, they destroyed . . .'

I thought of Jane sitting up at Brockledean House watching the show with the old people. I'd have liked to see her, but she'd said no, and she knew what she was doing.

They found the nests early next morning, in wooded country some six or eight miles from Berryton, and at lunch-time the BBC announced officially that the menace had been wiped out.

A day or so later I went up to London and when I got back Jane announced that tomorrow I was taking an afternoon off. She said the break would do me good, she'd bring some food over and we could go out in the car. When I looked at the calendar I had a shock. It was the date set for the Neptune Test; all the excitement had driven it out of my mind.

The blast was scheduled for just after two PM, our time. I remember sitting in my kitchen and watching the clock hands creep up to the hour. It was a fine day, with cumulus drifts chasing each other across the sky. I don't know what I was expecting, but nothing happened of course; the clock chimed softly, a breeze moved the window curtains, a bird chuckled outside the open door. A few minutes later I heard Jane coming up the path.

She was wearing a new white dress; she'd put her hair up and she was looking very adult and ladylike. I think the afternoon out was intended to be something in the way of a leave-taking; she'd said her parents were flying back from the Continent at the end of the week. It was a depressing thought, I tried not to let it spoil things.

We drove to the downs ten or twelve miles from Brockle-dean. We walked a good distance then circled back and unpacked the things she'd brought. I don't know what I'd have done if I'd known that earthquake shocks were ripping their way round the globe to us at God knows how many miles a minute. I like to think I'd still have had a picnic...

After the meal we found a little pub. We sat and talked till it was time to head back. I drove slowly; I wasn't in any hurry for the day to end. Half an hour later I swung the Jag into my gateway and killed the engine. Jane got out. She said, 'Well I suppose that's about it. Thanks for everything, Bill, it's been lovely.'

I looked at my watch. Just after eight. 'Like to have coffee before you go, love? It isn't too late.'

She said, 'I shouldn't really, I ought to be getting back...' Then she grinned. 'All right then. It won't take long, will it?'

I said, 'Fix it in a moment.' I walked towards the house. Everything was very still; somewhere a plane was droning, but that was the only sound. Halfway to the front door I stopped. Jane was still standing by the car. I said, 'What's the matter?'

'I – I don't know.' Her voice sounded small. 'Suddenly everything feels wrong...'

The air was tingling as if it was electrified. I felt the back of

22

my neck prickle. I said, 'I'll just check you haven't left anything around, then I'll run you home.' I felt in my pockets for my key-ring. The droning was louder.

I got the door unlocked before I realized. I whipped round again and one look was enough. I yelled at the top of my voice. 'Jane, for Christ's sake . . . run . . .'

She turned back briefly then she was pelting towards me with Sek gathering speed behind. I yanked the door open and they fell through it together. Sek spun in her own length and barked. To her it was still a game; she hadn't seen what was after us.

I got a glimpse of them clearing the hedge on the far side of the road. Six or eight vast insects, converging on the house. I saw black and yellow armour, the blur of wings. I slammed the door and something hit it with a crash that nearly fetched it off its hinges. The wood was stout, it saved our lives. There was another blow; a panel split and yellow legs came reaching and quivering through, and black antennae thicker than the base of my thumb. Sek dived past me and I heard Jane scream. A confused sort of fight developed, the dog leaping up snapping and slavering, the wasp trying to wedge its body through the gap, arching its abdomen to bring the sting into play.

I backed off glaring about for a weapon, anything I could use. There was another crash from behind me and a tinkling of glass. Something landed with a thump on the kitchen floor. I jumped round and had my first real sight of a Fury.

It had come through the window, carrying glass and glazing bars in front of it. The concussion seemed to have stunned it momentarily. It crouched on the floor, quivering; its puppy head with the great bulges of the compound eyes seemed to be staring straight at me. I had time to see the patternings on its body, the veins in the wings thick as knitting-needles. Then the mouth-parts twitched, the wings boomed and it was airborne and coming at my face.

In the hall there was a heavy gate-leg table. I can't remember picking it up and I certainly don't remember throwing it, but I saw it hit the thing full in the mask. The wasp went down in a tangle of legs and I heard a bedroom window shatter, then another. Sek was still baying at the front door; the house was full of noise.

23

Jane was pressing herself against the wall. Her eyes were wide and one hand was on her throat. I grabbed her wrist and dragged her towards the cellar. I opened the door and snapped the light on so she could see the steps. She stumbled past me. Sek was darting at something crawling down the staircase; I yelled at her and she came. I pulled the door shut behind her and locked it. I stood panting with my hand against the wood; I heard drummings and tappings outside then another noise, a sort of steady scraping and crunching. There was no doubt what they were doing; I'd seen wasps on old fence posts often enough, gouging away at the wood. If these brutes set their minds to it they'd have us within minutes.

I backed down the steps. A long splinter fell away from the door, then a hole appeared. It enlarged steadily till I could see yellow mouth-parts working like the beaks of parrots. I put my arm round Jane's shoulders. She half turned; she squeezed my hand almost absent-mindedly then her eyes went back to the door. We both watched the incredible death working its way towards us.

Sek walked forward stiff-legged until she was between us and the steps. She was rumbling a deep threat and her neck hair had risen till it looked like she was wearing a shawl. I saw her shoulder muscles bunching. The first of the wasps that came down stood a good chance of being torn to bits, but the rest would get us easily.

The hole was big enough now for us to see the head of a Fury staring through. I made myself look at Jane. She was white, but she wasn't crying. I tried to speak, but nothing would come.

Her voice was a little tight thread of sound. She said, 'Could we hurt their eyes . . . ?'

It was a tiny hope but it was enough to get me moving again. There was an old rake-handle leaning against the cellar wall. The head of the tool had rusted away, but the shaft was still iron-tipped. I grabbed it and worked my way back up the steps. The door was creaking and bulging and more splinters were appearing near the edge. I braced myself and jabbed the weapon through the hole; the Fury's head vanished, then bobbed back. I lashed out again and felt something grip the pole. I tried to snatch it free, but the opposing muscles were

24

stronger than mine. I heaved and the thing parted abruptly, sheared through by one of those hellish sets of mandibles. I lost my balance and fell back on top of Sek. We hit the floor together. I lay feeling dazed; above me the cellar light started to swing.

I stared at it stupidly. The movement increased; the globe reached the end of its arc, jiggled, and swept back, almost brushing the ceiling. Shadows surged up and down the walls. I realized the floor was vibrating. There was a noise, distant at first but growing louder; a sort of clattering roar, like a tube train coming out of a tunnel.

The light went out abruptly. In the blackness the racket seemed ten times worse. I felt myself tilted first one way then the other. I couldn't think; I didn't realize we were in the meizoseismal area of an earthquake, I just had no idea what was happening. I heard Sek start to howl then even her voice was lost. I shouted to her, but she couldn't have heard. The real Sekhmet was baying too close underneath . . .

I forgot the Furies. All I wanted to do was get out before we were buried alive. I started for the steps on my hands and knees and collided with a wall. I clawed myself upright and tried to walk along it. The bricks slid away from me then came back and hit me in the chest. I cannoned into a pile of boxes and after that I didn't know where I was. I sat up and a fresh shock rolled me into a corner. A weight thumped across my legs and I felt hands clutching. I yelled, 'Jane . . .' She moved convulsively; hair fell across my face. I hung on to her, shouting crazy things she couldn't hear. I felt the earth would split and plunge us down a thousand miles into the mouth of the thing that was roaring. I don't know how long the din went on.

While we lay there a planet was breaking apart. The test did go wrong; it cracked the bed of the sea, raised a volcano the height of Vesuvius where before there'd been a five-mile Deep. The destruction wouldn't have been so bad had not Russia exploded a device of equal power almost within min-utes of the first; some scientists claim the Earth literally wobbled on her axis under the double blow. Ripples from the huge foci spread across the globe, starting secondary slips that in turn set off others and still more. Countries and cities on or near fault-lines suffered most; Lisbon was reduced to rubble,

25

Japan was practically wiped out. Italy, China, and Peru were torn apart; the Chedrang Fault, that had wrecked Assam at the end of the last century, became the centre of another huge disturbance, while in America the San Andreas Rift opened into a maw five hundred miles long and wider than the Grand Canyon. San Francisco slid wholesale into the earth; then the Pacific broke in, changing the shape of the continent for all time. In Britain the Great Glen was convulsed along its entire course from Inverness to Fort William; Loch Lomond vanished overnight, and most of Herefordshire became an inland sea.

The Thames Valley flattened into a flood plain; London was drowned . . .

The noise stopped. I lay still a long time; very slowly, normal sounds began to reassert themselves. Something was snuffling near by and I heard the drip and splash of water. I put my hand out tentatively and touched rough fur. I said, 'Sek . . .'

Jane whimpered and clung tighter. I tried to make her sit up. 'Come on, love, it's over. Don't be scared . . .'

She moaned something. Her head was burrowing against my chest, I didn't hear what she said. I pushed her shoulders. 'It's gone now, Jane. Sek's here.'

She moved at that. Warmth and pressure vanished, leaving a vacuum. She said indistinctly, 'Oh, God . . . Bill?'

'It's all right. Are you hurt?'

'I . . . I don't think so. What about you?'

'I'm fine.' I tried to move my legs and found I couldn't. I tried not to panic. I said, 'I think I'm stuck.' Sek nuzzled at me and I pushed her away. I heaved; something creaked, and the pressure on my ankles got worse. I said, 'Matches. In my pocket. Can you reach? I can't get my arm round . . .'

The air was thick with dust, I could feel it catching my throat. Jane started to cough. Her hands touched me, tentatively then more firmly. She said, 'You're lying on your jacket . . .'

I managed to sit up a bit. There was a fumbling, a flare of yellow light. I saw her face. Two huge dark eyes. Sek towering over her like a spirit from the Pit. She said again, 'Bill, are you hurt?'

'No, just stuck . . . hold the light down.'

The dust was moving in whorls, it was hard to see. There seemed to be a beam across my legs. One end was propped on a pile of masonry and another mass was hanging through the floor just above. By turning my feet sideways I might just wriggle clear. The match went out and I swore; Jane lit another. She said, 'There aren't many left, Bill; they won't last long.'

I was feeling the beam with my hands. 'Try to find a lever. Something you can ram under this thing. For God's sake be careful though or we shall have all that other lot down on our heads.'

The second match went out and Jane spoke in darkness. 'It was an earthquake, wasn't it? The big bomb must have done it . . .'

'Yes, I think so . . . can you find anything?'

She said, 'This might do . . .' I heard vague movements and the weight on my legs eased a little. Something fell with a crash. I lay still again, afraid to move, and felt her working at my ankles. 'What are you doing?'

She said, 'Taking your shoes off.'

Good for her, I hadn't even thought of it . . . I pulled, and one foot came free. The other was still caught. Jane levered at the beam again. It creaked and settled ominously, but I was able to snatch myself clear. She groped for me at once and put my shoes in my hand. She said, 'There may be broken glass . . .'

I stood up awkwardly; Sek rubbed against me and I reached down to pat her. Jane said, 'Can I use another match? I daren't move far because of this silly beam.'

'All right, be careful . . .'

She climbed back over to me. 'Where's that water?'

'Don't know. Hold the light.'

She raised the match over her head. I saw a glint on the far wall. Water was coursing down the bricks; a good-sized puddle had collected already. I said, 'Damaged main . . .'

'Fine,' said Jane disgustedly. 'We shall be drowned next.'

'I don't think so . . . give me the matches a minute.'

She put them in my hand. I said, 'Keep still, going to look for candles.'

'Have we got any?'

'There were some in a box by the steps. It had all sorts of junk in it ... Only saw it the other day.' I was in luck; I uncovered the tin, wrenched the lid off, found a candle. It was broken in a couple of places, but it was still a godsend. I coaxed it alight and held it up. We could take stock of ourselves at last.

We'd been very fortunate; I had a small cut on my hand and a pair of well-bruised shins, Jane had grazed her knee, but apart from that we weren't hurt. We were both filthy of course and Sek's back and shoulders were yellow with dust. We brushed ourselves down as well as we could and started to look round the cellar. I held the candle up under the rent in the ceiling. There were other boards lying at an angle across the hole. I realized after a moment or so I was looking at the back of the big dresser that had stood in the kitchen. My brain was beginning to function again; I said, 'I'm afraid the house must have fallen in. We must be under a pile of rubble or there'd be light coming through somewhere.'

Jane shook her head. 'Perhaps it's dark out there. What's the time?'

I looked at my watch. It had stopped at nine-fifteen. We'd been in the cellar longer than I realized. I said, 'You could be right ... thing is, what are we going to do? We can't stay here for ever.'

She opened her mouth to answer then stopped. She put her hand on my arm. 'Shhh ...'

I listened. Then I heard the noise that had startled her. A shifty, stealthy sort of tapping and scraping. I was reminded of Blind Pew's stick. The sound passed over our heads, moved to where I guessed the kitchen door had been, and died away. Sek rumbled in her throat and I put my hand on her collar. Jane said bitterly, '*They're* still there.'

We listened for a long time at the bottom of the steps. There was nothing else. Jane brightened up. 'I think they've all gone. Perhaps they were killed in the earthquake and that was the last one sort of dragging itself away. In any case wasps sleep at night, don't they?'

I wasn't sure, and didn't feel much like finding out by experiment. I was dubious about opening that door, and said as much. Still, it had to be done sometime. I walked up to it very quietly and peered through the hole the Furies had gouged. There was light outside, blue and vague. Impossible to see anything clearly. I listened, but apart from the water in the cellar there wasn't a sound. I turned the key gently and eased the door open. It moved six inches then jammed. Something had evidently fallen across outside. I took a deep breath and banged the door with my shoulder. There was a grating noise and it gave another foot. After that I couldn't budge it.

Jane was standing just behind me. She said, 'Let me try. I'm a lot smaller than you, I might be able to wriggle out.'

I said, 'Steady, we still don't know whether the things have gone.'

'It's all right, I'll only look.' She edged forward. She was quiet for a moment; then, 'There's a beam wedging it and a great lot of bricks and stuff. I think if I moved some of them you could get through. There aren't any wasps. Everything's in an awful mess though.'

I'd expected that. I said, 'Go on then. But be careful.' She eeled her way round the door and I heard her start to move rubble. As she worked she eased forward until only her legs were in sight. She was gasping and squirming, trying to shift some extra-large obstacle when I saw her stiffen. At the same time I heard a sound I was already beginning to dread. The booming of great narrow wings . . .

I shouted and Jane tried to wriggle backwards. Her dress caught on a nail. I grabbed her round the waist and yanked. She yelped; the cloth tore and we both came down the steps with a rush. Above us the door was driven shut with a good solid crash. I heard tapping and scraping for a moment then silence. Jane clenched her fists. She said, 'Damn, damn, damn . . . They're still there. I saw it flying down.'

I was sweating. I said, 'Are you hurt, love?'

'No, just scraped and bumped about and getting bad-tempered. You were right, Bill, we're here for the night.'

The Fury seemed to have given up its efforts at the door. Maybe they did get sleepy after dark. I went up and turned the key in the lock anyway, then we piled boxes on the steps. Not much of a barrier, but we had nothing else to use. We tried to find somewhere to make ourselves comfortable.

That wasn't easy. The broken main was still pumping water into our hideout; it was three or four inches deep already on the lowest part of the floor. In one of the walls was a round-topped alcove three feet or so across and raised eighteen inches from the ground. We climbed into it; at least it would keep our feet dry. I'd found some more stubs of candle; I took them with me. Sek looked at us quizzically then got up herself, turned round somehow, and lay in front of us facing out into the dark. I was glad of that; there wasn't much room with the three of us there, but I thought that was all to the good. Before morning it was going to get plenty chilly.

Jane sat and brooded, smutty chin in her hands. Her hair had come partly undone; it was hanging over her cheek. I said, 'Don't worry, it probably won't be long before someone comes and digs us out anyway.'

She shook her head. 'They won't. Not for a long time.'

'Course they will, when they see the house. They don't just leave things like that. There'll be rescue teams.'

She said tightly, 'They'll all be too busy to bother. Their houses will have fallen down too.'

It was rather like a punch in the stomach. I realized she was right; I'd been thinking of the disaster in purely local terms. We had no means of telling how far the damage spread; it could be and probably was countrywide. I felt in sudden need of a smoke. By chance I'd had a packet of cigarettes in my jacket. I found it and took one out. It was battered but usable. I lit it from the candle and Jane stirred slightly. She said, 'Could you spare one of those?'

I was startled. 'You don't smoke, do you?'

She shook her head. 'Not usually. But I want one now.'

I said, 'Here . . .' I gave her a light. She blew smoke; then she leaned her head back against the wall and closed her eyes. Suddenly she looked unutterably weary. She said, 'I've got it all worked out. There won't be anybody. Not for a long, long time.'

We finished the cigarettes in silence; then we tried to get some rest. I think up to then that was the most uncomfortable night I'd ever spent. As the water in the cellar got deeper it began to gurgle and splash; I sat up a score of times convinced I'd heard the tapping of a clawed foot. The Furies were sup-

30

posed to have been destroyed; that was pretty small comfort right at the minute. I wondered how many of them there were, and why they hunted humans so viciously. Was it for food? I tried to remember what wasps ate. I had an idea they liked meat ... When I did doze I dreamed of a black-and-yellow mask that floated towards me, jaws clicking steadily. The third or fourth time it happened I woke up. The candle had gone out; the darkness was absolute. I felt about cautiously, found another stub and lit it. Small as it was, the flame was comforting. In the dark, anything could happen ... I looked at my watch. It still read nine-fifteen. I undid the strap and laid the thing down beside me. If there's anything I hate it's a watch that doesn't go. I'd rather be without it.

Jane sighed and I saw her eyes were open. I said, 'What's the matter, love, can't sleep?'

'No.' She shuddered. 'I'm cold ...'

I tried to wrap my jacket round her. It was the best I could do. I got a cigarette out, reached down, and held the tip over the candle flame. I said, 'Do you want to smoke again?'

'No ...' A pause. Then, 'Is it nearly light?'

'I don't know. I think it must be.'

Miles beneath us, the earth groaned. It was a thick noise; somehow it sounded full of pain. I felt her tense. She said, 'Oh, no ... Please don't let it start again ...'

'It won't. These are after-shocks. It won't happen again.' I hoped I was right.

She rubbed her face tiredly. She said, 'There was something about that noise. I made a fool of myself. I'm not normally like that.'

'You didn't.'

She said, 'I did, I was yelling my silly head off.'

'It didn't matter. So was I.'

She wriggled slightly. She said, 'I'm glad you were there, Bill, I'd have gone mad on my own.'

I could have said the same. I was praying we weren't in for another quake. The noise came again, like the baffled grumbling of an animal. The candle flame trembled; then the sound died away. I said, 'In bulls does the Earthshaker delight.'

'Who?'

'Poseidon, I think. Homer.'

31

She made an effort to change the subject. 'Do you know much poetry?'

'A bit.'

She said, 'I love it. I was going to do Eng Lit at college if I could. Shakespeare and all that.'

'You still can.'

She didn't answer. I started softly on what I could remember of the Dream. She picked me up after a while and we worked through Shakespeare to Keats and Tennyson. It made the time pass quicker at least. I was in the middle of a fairly spirited rendering of the *Morte d'Arthur* when I felt her head go heavy against my shoulder. A short time later I slept myself.

When I woke again I could dimly see the things in the cellar. A thin beam of sunlight was coming through one of the cracks in the floor above and touching the wall. The angle of it told me two things: that it wasn't long after daybreak, and that the house had no east wall. I listened intently but there were no sounds. Just a sort of breathing quiet. There should have been a dawn chorus. A line of poetry was still running through my mind. 'And no birds sing...' I shivered, and woke Jane. We set about fighting our way out.

CHAPTER 3

I HAD A stubble of beard and I ached as if I'd tried to sleep on a bed of nails. I felt personally ready to face any number of Furies rather than spend any more time in that damned cellar. We sloshed through a foot of icy water to get to the steps; I opened the door the original amount and Jane peered out. Nothing moved. She said, 'I think it's all right, I'll go and have a look.'

I caught her wrist. 'No you don't. Come back for a minute.'

'Somebody's got to go first.'

'Yes, but it's not going to be you. Here, Sek.'

She walked up the steps and stood looking at me. I patted the edge of the door. 'Up, girl.' She hesitated then squeezed through. There were sounds of scrambling, and a shower of rubble came down. We waited for barking or the noise of a fight. Everything stayed quiet. After a couple of minutes I nodded to Jane. 'All right, it must be OK. Let me out before you do anything else.'

She wriggled through and started removing the rest of the bricks that were wedging the door. When she'd freed it enough I forced it back and climbed out.

I don't know what I expected to see but I know I got a shock. I stood up in a bomb-site. The house was roofless, two walls had completely gone and a third was only half its former height. Odd things stuck out of the chaos, incongruous against a background of trees and fields; my drawing-board, a hatstand with a coat still on one of the hooks, the taps that had fed the kitchen sink. The air was sweet and still, and the early morning sun lay across the grass, touching everything with gold.

I said, 'Well, it was a good house while it lasted.' I sat on a heap of rubble and lit a cigarette. Jane came and put her hand on my shoulder, stood looking down and frowning. For once she seemed at a loss for words. I smoked the fag through and stamped it out. I wanted to just stay where I was but that was no good. We had to shift about, decide what to do. I tried to remember we had in fact been lucky; without a doubt, the earthquake had saved our lives.

We discussed things quietly. The silence was total and ominous; no cars, no planes. It looked as if the country round about had been pretty badly hit. Also it was harbouring an indefinite number of Furies, all of which could be expected to kill on sight. Jane said if we could get across to Brockledean we could hole up for days, the place was well stocked with food and there were cellars that could be made virtually impregnable. We decided our best bet was to stay around for a time at least and see what, if anything, happened; if things stayed quiet we could risk a dash across the fields later on. Jane kept a lookout while I excavated the remains of the larder. I unearthed a loaf of bread and a couple of tins of luncheon meat, the sort that have openers already fixed to them. I unzipped them and gave one to Sek while we shared the other, washing it down with beer. Not an ideal breakfast but it was the best we could do. Afterwards we went round to the Jag. Any hopes I might have had of making a getaway were promptly crushed. Her windscreen was smashed, and there wasn't much doubt about how it had happened. The Furies evidently employed their battering-ram tactics against cars as well as buildings; any normal form of transport would be little better than a mobile death-trap.

We were still standing in the drive when we heard a droning in the distance. We beat it for the partial safety of the cellar. Three Furies came into sight but they weren't interested in us. They were diving at something running beneath them; as they got closer I saw their quarry was a pair of terrified sheep. They brought them down a couple of hundred yards away, in the field at the back of the house. We watched cautiously; Jane lay with her fists clenched until the sheep stopped kicking. The wasps moved over the carcasses for some time, tapping with their antennae. Then they began to butcher the animals. They worked fast and efficiently; after a while four more brutes arrived, grabbed red lumps of flesh in their claws, and winged off heavily to the west. Half an hour later they'd all gone and nothing remained but the fleeces, stacked neatly on the grass. I swallowed; at least what I'd seen settled any doubts I might have had about their food requirements. I'd had some idea of skulking as far as the village, I put it right out of my mind.

For the time being there was nothing to do but wait. Furies were seldom out of earshot; they sounded like cars on a distant racing circuit. There were no more earth tremors. At midday we raided the ruins again; the stove was still functioning and we boiled water for coffee though we daren't risk cooking. Some time in the afternoon a squadron of a dozen or more insects flew directly over the house; we got ready to run but they kept on course and were soon out of sight. From time to time I tried the radio; I picked up a babble of French, and what sounded like German, but nothing in English. The BBC wavelengths were quiet.

Once we heard firing, automatic weapons of some sort. The noise came to us flat and muted by heat. It was a hopeful sign; it was good to think somebody somewhere was taking the offensive. We listened for a long while after the guns had stopped but there were no other sounds.

I think it was probably about four o'clock when Jane turned her head sharply and raised her hand. Sek got up and came to us, stood looking fixedly in the direction of the lane. We stayed where we were for a moment, staring at each other and wondering, then I got up and ran to the gate. I saw the most welcome sight of my life.

An armoured car was moving down the lane. It was coming carefully, not making above ten or fifteen miles an hour. I could see the thick muzzle of the quick-firer, the commander and gunner sitting in the turret. Both men were carrying weapons that at first sight I took to be sub-machine guns, then I realized they were flame-throwers. I'd never handled one but there was no mistaking the shoulder packs, the squat tubes with triggers and handgrips. It looked as if the Army was moving in prepared to meet trouble much more than halfway.

Jane whooped and ran past me with Sek at her heels. The car stopped opposite the gate, nearly filling the lane. The commander looked very young; he was hatless, with straight fair hair that hung across his forehead. He shouted over the noise of the engine. 'Many of you here?'

'Just the two of us.'

'Been here long?'

'Since the quake. This is my house. Or was.'

He said curtly, 'Very bad luck. Seen any wasps?'

'A few. They haven't come too near.'

He spoke into the intercom and the engine stopped. He swung out on to the armour and dropped down to the road. He said, 'Keep that lookout going will you, don't want any more surprise parties.'

'Sir.'

He wiped his face with his hand, reached into his pocket, and produced a hammered-looking pack of cigarettes. He said, 'Got any water, sir? We need water and petrol pretty urgently.'

I said, 'We've got a cellarful of water, you can help your-selves. Nearest garage is a couple of miles away, in Brockle-dean. I'm Bill Sampson by the way, this is Miss Beddoes-Smythe.'

Jane said formally, 'Nice to see you, Lieutenant. Thank Heaven the Army's here.'

He looked at her for a moment. Then he said, 'Connor. Neil Connor. Glad to know you.' He turned back to the car. 'Alan, get down here with a couple of cans will you? We'll see to the water first.' The driver climbed through the hatch. 'Like to show us where it is, sir?'

Jane said quickly, 'It's in the cellar. It's hard to get in because the door's blocked. Shall I take him?'

I nodded. 'Carry on, love.' She said to the driver, 'This way please,' exactly as if she was conducting a guest at some high-class garden party. They trotted off down the drive and round the corner of the house.

I said, 'Lieutenant, can you give me any idea of what's going on?'

He said, 'Wish I could, old boy. To be frank, I'd like to know myself. You're the first people we've seen today. Alive at least.'

I had a horrible thought. 'You're not on your own, are you?'

He said, 'Cigarette?'

'Thanks . . .'

We lit up. He said, 'Sorry to disappoint you, there's only us. And we're damned lucky to be operational.'

'Where have you come from?'

He was evasive. 'We were on manoeuvres. A couple of Saladins, half a dozen APC's, and some light stuff.' He hesitated. 'We were on the Plain about ten miles from here when the quake started. There was a bit of a flap. Before we could sort ourselves out the wasps were down. They did rather well. Couldn't fight them, they were everywhere at once.'

My throat felt dry. I said, 'So what happened?'

He paused again but it seemed once started he couldn't stop. 'My car was the only one that made it. We managed to get her going and went for the bloody things. Not a scrap of good; they were all over the place, with our people tangled up among them. We got out and left them to it. The brutes have been on the rampage, I tell you. There isn't a village intact for ten miles. Luckily we've got flame. The only thing that stops them. They couldn't resist us for a time. Like moths round an outsize candle. We grounded scores, then they sheered off. Haven't been able to raise our base since last night, God knows what's happening there.'

I felt my back start to go cold. The arrival of the Army had seemed like the end of all our worries, but we were no better off than we had been before. Jane and the driver came back while we were still talking. She said brightly, 'Would your people like some tea, Lieutenant? I thought you might be glad of a break.'

He looked at his watch and shrugged. 'Won't make any difference now, we shan't get to Swyreford before dark. OK by you, sir?'

I nodded. 'Glad to be of help.'

We talked in the remains of the kitchen. I squatted on a pile of rubble with Sek at my feet, Neil sat on the remains of the dresser, the driver leaned against what was left of the wall. The gunner stood guard just outside, the tube of the flame-thrower in his hands. I said, 'The damage is pretty widespread then?'

Neil lit his second cigarette. 'We've taken most of the day coming ten miles. Bloody great crevasses everywhere, of all things. No crossing 'em without bridging gear, we just had to backtrack each time, find a way round. The wasps held us up for a while of course. We did quite well at first with the flame-throwers but they swamped us, we had to shut down. We were stuck then, brutes so thick on us we couldn't use the scopes. Couldn't drive. If they hadn't lifted off we'd still be there.'

'Why did they leave?'

'Don't ask me, I don't know what goes on in their rotten little minds. One minute they were banging and tapping all over us, the next they were up and away. The whole crowd of them, as if they'd got a recall signal from somewhere. They left one of their little people on top of course, ready for us when we popped up. Rather clever. Unfortunately for him we heard him trotting about, we came out pretty smartly and warmed him up before he could do very much. The flame-throwers rather stop the brutes in their tracks, they don't seem to care for them at all.'

Underlining his words came a thudding growl. The house shook; somewhere something slipped and crashed down. The ground quivered; my scalp prickled and Sek rolled her lips back from her teeth. I put my hand on her collar; the tremor died away.

I swallowed. I said, 'And you're headed back to Swyre-ford?'

'Yes. Only thing possible. We're virtually helpless as it is.'

Jane turned round sharply. 'Good Lord. We thought we were in a bad way. But you've got armour.'

He smiled crookedly. 'How about you, sir, what do you intend to do?'

I was still trying to fight down a hollow feeling of panic. It was impossible to adjust rapidly enough, I was only just beginning to realize the scale of the disaster. I said, 'I don't know, Lieutenant. I frankly don't know what to do for the best.'

Jane looked up with a cup in her hand. 'Could you take us with you?'

He laughed. 'There strictly isn't room for passengers. Sorry.'

She looked at me keenly, then back to him. 'Aren't there any more of you? No more cars?'

He hesitated and I said, 'It's all right, she isn't under any illusions. No, Jane, there aren't any more. The wasps got to them last night. The Lieutenant is trying to get back to his base.'

She said, 'Where are all the others then?'

'Scattered round the Plain. There aren't any driv—' An idea hit me and I faltered. 'There aren't any drivers.'

She beat me to it. She said, 'You can take Bill there, he'll drive one. He drove tanks in the Army, didn't you, Bill?'

Neil looked at me sharply. 'That true, sir?'

I said, 'Well, yes. On my National Service.'

He said, 'You wouldn't really want to see me shot would you?' He stubbed the cigarette carefully. 'We've broken enough Queen's Regs as it is. Stocked up with grub at a little village shop this morning. Nobody to stop us but God knows it was still looting. Couldn't get near our own stores, still crawling with insect life. There'll be the very devil to pay if this lot ever gets sorted out. Thanks, m'dear.' That to Jane as she passed him a cup of tea.

She stood back and pushed at her dark hair. She said, 'I'm sorry there isn't a handle but we've got almost no crockery left. If you leave us here we shall be killed.'

I was beginning to see a way out to somewhere, Heaven knew where. I said, 'That's enough, Jane.'

She said startlingly, 'I don't care, it's bloody well true.' Her voice was firm but she was trembling slightly.

I said, 'Finish the tea, will you, love? We shall be all right.' She swung away angrily. I looked back at Neil. 'Where the hell are the brutes all coming from? I thought they'd been wiped out.'

He had been staring at Jane. He turned looking vaguely surprised. 'I don't know. All this lot blew up yesterday, we'd only just moved in when they hit us.'

I said, 'If you could find the nests, lob a bit of HE down on top. If they're exposed, use flame . . .'

He shook his head. 'If there are any brass left at Swyreford they'll want to know what's going on. Do more good down there than starting private wars in Wiltshire.'

I walked back with him to the Saladin. He turned as he was about to climb aboard. He said, 'Who's the girl?'

'She comes from the big house just this side of the village. Only the housekeeper and her husband there. From what I've heard I'd rather keep her with me.'

'What about her parents?'

'They're abroad.'

He said, 'Hmm. Hell of a responsibility. Still it might be best in the long run. Nice kid, look after her.'

'We'll make out.'

He bit his lip thoughtfully. 'Look, I hate to slide off like this but I haven't got much choice. You'd best stay under cover as far as possible; if you see any of the brutes keep very quiet. If there's a chance at all I'll send somebody back to you. Don't count on a thing though. Impossible to say what'll happen now this lot's started.'

I nodded at the *flammenwerfer*. 'It wasn't a manoeuvre, was it?'

He frowned. 'I think you should know the situation as far as possible. Obviously we didn't have these things with us to boil the dixies. We were sent down in a hell of a hurry as soon as the flap started. Unfortunately we were pretty badly beaten up; if the other units didn't get on any better we're in the worst sort of trouble. We know there are at least a score of nests operating on the Plain and there are sightings from the New Forest and some more in Somerset. The Forest is nearly stripped of ponies. In the west there aren't any sheep. And yesterday there were reports of three empty villages.' He spread his hands. 'Just deserted. Cleaned out. Last I heard, our people were occupying them. We were told to keep things quiet but under the circumstances that seems a little pointless. Only fair you should have the facts; if you make any decisions, at least you'll have something to go on. Sorry I can't paint a nicer picture.' He held his hand out. 'Goodbye, and good luck.' A few moments later the Saladin revved thunderously and moved off towards Brockledean.

I watched it out of sight, then I turned back to the house. I was sweating a little; there wasn't much doubt in my mind as to what had happened to the animals. There was still a pile of fleeces out there where we'd watched the Furies working. I had a nagging fear the same fate had overtaken the missing people. What I'd been told made it more important than ever to get away. We were right in the middle of something very, very nasty and I was going to get Jane and myself out of it if it was humanly possible. I'd been sitting around long enough.

She came to meet me. She said, 'What was he saying before he left? He looked terribly serious.'

I said, 'He was terribly serious. Come inside for a minute, I want to talk to you.'

She said, 'I thought it was all over. When I saw the car coming . . .'

I said, 'Yes, so did I. But I think we can do something to help ourselves now.' I told her, quickly, what Neil had said to me. She listened tight-lipped. Then she said soberly, 'I think our only chance is to get out for the time being at least. But I shall have to go to Brockledean first because of the Carters.'

I nodded. 'We'll do that. But not just yet. First of all I'm going to whip one of those bloody cars he was talking about, if I can find his camp.'

She looked at me sharply. 'I thought you might, that's why I shut up. But there'll be a terrible row if you're caught. That's Government property after all. He said you could be shot, he probably wasn't joking.'

I shrugged. 'We'll worry about that later. Now I want you to stay here. As soon as I get back——'

She said quickly, 'I'm coming with you.'

'You're not. Sorry, love. No point two of us risking our necks.'

'But—'

I said, 'No buts. That's definite. Don't make things harder, Jane.' She started to argue again and I shut her up. This was one time she was going to listen. I said, 'I think I shall be OK, I'll tell you why. The wasps aren't interested in this part of the country any more. They've beaten up all the villages and given the Army a terrible hiding, they'll be far too busy right now to keep flying around just to see if there's anybody left. You know we haven't heard any for hours. Now what I'm going to do is drive the Jag to Brockledean and find out just what's happened. It may not be too bad over there anyway, in which case I'll come straight back. If it is bad, I'll get some petrol and go and look for that camp he was talking about. It can't be too hard to find. I'll get one of the cars and come back here. Then we can go and see about your people.'

She opened her mouth then shut it again. She said, 'All right, Bill.' She swallowed. 'What do you want me to do if you don't come back?'

'I shall come back. But if I'm held up, wait till night and try to get home by yourself, if you're not here I'll come to Brockledean for you. Whatever else you do, don't move till it gets dark. Leave it till about eleven. OK?'

She nodded dumbly.

One of the things I didn't want to do was run straight into the Saladin again. I let about forty minutes pass; after that my nerves wouldn't stand any more waiting. I'd decided to leave Sek at the house; if I was attacked in the car her presence wouldn't make much difference one way or the other. I'd found her leash; I put her on it and gave the loop to Jane. She looked dubious but I knew the dog would stay with her. I went out to the Jag, started up, and backed into the lane. Jane came round to the driving window. It looked like she wasn't far from crying. I put my hand out and she gripped it hard. She said, 'Try to come back.' Then she ran for the house, towing Sek behind her. I let in the clutch and moved away wondering if I would see her again.

It was queer to be driving once more. The broken screen gave me a horribly unprotected feeling; at first I kept peering up in the sky and out of the side windows, trying to spot possible attackers. I forced myself to stop it. It was literally pointless, if there was anything out there I would know about it soon enough.

I reached the line of trees at the end of the lane and drove underneath them, turned on to the main road and speeded up a little. Brockledean came into sight in the distance. At first the houses looked undamaged but most of them were little more than shells. The Jag bumped heavily over a crack in the road; I saw by the remains of a fence that there had been a lateral displacement of five feet or more. The land had crept and crawled, wrenching foundations apart.

There was an eerie quality about the damage, a sort of mad playfulness that made my back creep. One cottage had lost its end wall; I saw a bedstead hanging out supported by a mess of beams. Farther on a dressing table, its mirror intact, stood upright in a flower-bed. The *Royal Oak*, halfway down the street on the right, had completely collapsed. The tallest thing in the ruins was a piano. The keys were splintered and across them was a great splash of something that looked like dry blood. It was as if the thing had been kicked in the mouth.

As I got nearer the village centre I began to see bodies. They were sprawled everywhere, legs and arms pushed up stiffly to the sky. There was one man I'd known very well from the pub. He was sitting against the wall of a house with his hands locked round his throat. I can still remember his face, staring horrified over a dark red bib.

The garage was a pretty, low-fronted little place. Virginia creeper trailed round the nameboard and the one stilt-legged pump. I pulled up outside, stopped the engine, and got out. Nothing moved; flies droned in the stillness. I saw the pump cover had been forced and the filler nozzle still trailed on the ground. There was a broad wet patch where petrol had drained from it. In the middle of the road lay a dead Fury, badly scorched. The tarmac round it was blackened and there was a smell of oil. It looked as if the Saladin had been attacked but had got clear. That was something at least.

Across the street the Post Office had given out an avalanche of thatch, stationery, and bottled preserves. There were more corpses; I walked over and stood looking down at one. Oddly enough I felt no anger or disgust, only a sort of numbness. I just wanted to see everything, take it all in.

There was something odd about the body, I tried to think what it was. I shook my head slowly. I was no expert but there seemed to be bullet wounds . . .

I crossed the square again to the pump, put the filler nozzle into the Jag's tank, and started to work the handle forward and back. A few yards away a Land-Rover was parked, drawn up off the road. I'd half filled my car before it dawned on me I was wasting my time. The Rover would be much handier for what I had in mind. I went over to it quietly. Subconsciously I was afraid the slightest extra noise would bring a Fury down on me from the clear sky.

Her keys were in the dash and the tank was nearly full. I started the engine; the bark of the exhaust sounded uncomfortably loud. I left my motor with the pump nozzle still in her tank and drove off. I felt a sudden need to be clear of the place; I put my foot down, swerving round the obstructions that half filled the road.

I drove back the way I'd come, waving to Jane as I passed the house. I didn't stop. A mile farther on I got to the first of the crevasses. It was a weird sight in an English lane; it looked to be ten or twelve feet wide and the edges were clear-cut where the macadam had been split. The Saladin had turned on to the road here, I could see where it had smashed through the hedge. The armoured car had blazed a trail easy enough to follow; I kept up a good speed, using the field gears once or twice on the rougher stretches. I was glad I'd collared the Rover; my car would never have gone over the dirt like that.

I crossed another lane and there was the Plain ahead of me, empty and wide. I pulled in automatically and stopped. I don't think I'd ever felt so alone or so hopeless. Even back in Brockledean there had been some illusion of shelter but if I was attacked out there I wouldn't have any place to hide. And I had no idea where the camp lay. There were marks in the grass ahead of me that looked to have been made by tracked vehicles of some sort but they might easily be a week or more old. It seemed futile to start searching but I had to try. I let in the clutch and moved off, wishing my mouth wasn't so dry. I drove due west, into the levelling sun.

I found the camp. Or a camp. It was sheer blind chance. I'd been driving for half an hour and I was more or less lost when I topped a low rise and saw a huddle of vehicles in the distance, the paler oblongs of tents. The sunlight gleamed on dark green armour.

I stopped the Rover half a mile away and studied the place. I wished I had a good pair of field-glasses. I stayed where I was for twenty minutes or so then I started the engine again and crept forward a few yards at a time. When I got closer I killed the ignition and let the Rover coast down, tyres whispering on the grass. My heart started to bang against my ribs. I was a couple of hundred yards from safety and I badly wanted to make it. It would be lousy to come all this way and then run into trouble but if any wasps were still in possession I was through.

I saw there had been another massacre. The bodies lay about, most of them swollen till at a distance they looked like brown and white balloons. The vehicles were on the far side of the tents; another Saladin parked facing away from me, half a dozen Saracen APC's drawn up in a line. I stopped the Rover and force of habit made me set the brake. I got out and started to walk towards the armour, moving silently, ready to bolt the rest of the way if anything got airborne. There was a steady wind blowing; there's always a wind on the Plain. Ahead of me the torn fabric of a tent flapped slowly. Everything else was still.

I rounded the front of the Saladin a foot at a time, then stopped and stared. The driver was still jammed halfway through the trap; the body had swollen so much it had wedged itself. One hand gripped the coaming, the eyes in the puffy face seemed to be looking for something in the distance. It was like a grotesque idol staring out across the Plain.

That got me. I turned away and was sick. Nothing I could do about it. I went down on my hands and knees and gasped. When the spasm was over I walked away without looking back.

I got to the Saracens. Six great cars standing there quietly, waiting. I walked round the first in line; her emergency hatch stood open, the rest were dogged down. I edged up to the port remembering what Neil had said about rearguards. I was ready for surprises.

44

It was just as well. As I touched the handle the car came alive with a hollow booming. I slammed the trap on a heart-shaped black and yellow mask. I collapsed against the armour, heard scraping noises from inside. It sounded as if the thing was trying to gouge its way out. I wished it luck.

The second car was clean. Her rear doors stood open, I could see right through her. Three or four rifles and flame-throwers were heaped in the back. She'd do; I wasn't taking any more chances. I closed her up, went round to the driver's flap, got in, and shut the lid. I lay back just savouring the feeling of safety. For twenty-four hours now I'd been living with the fear that something was at my back and it had worn me down. I didn't stay there long, I was too anxious to get back to Jane. I sat up, switched on, and pressed the starter.

The engine bellowed then settled to a throb. The APC wasn't as noisy inside as I'd imagined. I had a look at the controls. They seemed straightforward enough; conventional wheel, throttle, footbrake and clutch, handbrake down there on the left, preselector quadrant ... I could drive her. The tank gauge was reading a quarter full, that gave her fuel for Brockledean and beyond ... I opened the flap again, worked myself into the safety harness, and selected first. I tapped the clutch, let off the brake, and moved away.

She handled well for all her size; once I got used to the twin-axle steering I began to enjoy driving her. I opened her out across the Plain. The engine rumbled steadily; the sun was low now, dropping towards the horizon, and the car's long shadow raced ahead. I kept moving as fast as I could, following the tracks again.

CHAPTER 4

THE LIGHT was fading when I stopped outside my house. Jane was jumping up and down by the gate; I levered myself out of the car and she cannoned into me and hugged me. She said happily, 'He kept telling me you'd be all right. I knew you would really but I was still scared.'

I saw she wasn't alone. A soldier had come down the path behind her, a burly man with a sergeant's stripes on his shoulders and the insignia of an infantry regiment. He was carrying a service rifle. Jane said, 'This is Ted – I mean Sergeant Willis. He's had an awful time. He's been walking all day, he walked right from Yatley.' That was a little market town about ten miles off.

I said, 'Bill Sampson. Glad to know you.' I was feeling caught on the wrong foot; the Saracen was sitting there behind me like ten tons of guilt. I put my hand out and the soldier gripped it briefly. He was red-faced, with bright, direct blue eyes. His voice had a west-country burr. He said, 'Pleased to meet you, sir. What was it like at camp?'

I said, 'Pretty bloody awful. I'll tell you later. You're coming along with us, aren't you?'

'If you don't mind.'

I said, 'That's a damned silly crack to start with. Glad to have you.' I thought privately that with one regular aboard the thing might look a bit more legal at least.

He said, 'Where are we makin' for?'

Jane was still hanging on to my arm. I looked at her. 'Brockledean first. After that . . .' I shrugged. 'I suppose I shall have to find somewhere to turn this ruddy thing in. Can't just plough about the country. I'm a pirate.'

He smiled briefly. 'Reckon that'll sort itself out. They got more to worry about just at the minute.'

I went round and opened the back doors. Jane and Sek climbed inside. She said, 'It isn't like the other car. There's a lot of room in this one.' The sergeant whistled when he saw the flame-throwers. I said, 'Can you use one of those nasty things, Ted?'

He nodded. 'Just about, I reckon.'

'Good, might need them before we've finished. Like to go up to the turret? There's radio gear there, we might try to contact something if there's anything moving.'

He started to work his way forward. I closed the doors, walked round, and had a last look at the house, then I strapped myself into the driving seat again. Abruptly, we had become mechanized refugees.

I started up and moved away.

46

Ted came through on the intercom almost at once. 'How far's this place at Brockledean then?'

'Mile or so. Did Jane tell you the story?'

'Said she'd got some folk there.'

I said, 'We shall have to take a look. Don't think it'll be any good.'

'Pretty bad up that way then?'

'Wiped out. Flattened. Everybody killed.'

He whistled again. He didn't speak any more.

I steered on to the main road and built up speed. I slowed by the drive to Brockledean House and turned into it. The carriageway was none too wide for the Saracen; she ploughed along, bushes bending and cracking on either side.

The house was a lot bigger than I'd realized, a rambling eighteenth-century place set round with flower-beds and lawns. From the outside it didn't look to be badly damaged, most of the roof was intact and it still had some at least of its windows. Others had lost both glass and frames. I'd seen damage like that before. I stopped the car and switched off. Jane called from the back. 'Are we there?'

'Yes.' I heard a scraping and realized she was trying to unclip the doors. I said sharply, 'Stay in the car, love. I'll go and have a look. Coming along, Ted?'

He was scrambling about behind me. 'Got any rounds for these rifles?'

'I didn't think to look. Any in the lockers?'

A grunt. Then, 'That's all right,' I said. 'Pass me one through, will you?'

He hesitated a moment, then he did what I asked. He said curtly, 'Ready when you are.'

We climbed down and dropped the hatches after us. We walked across to the house, loading as we went. I felt a lot better with a gun in my hands. The main door stood slightly ajar; Ted put his toe against it and swung it inwards. The hallway beyond was dark. He walked in, stepping quietly. I followed him.

It had been a lovely place; now it was a wreck. Ceilings had fallen, crockery and furniture had smashed. We worked our way through it from room to room, calling as we went, but there was nobody there.

47

At the back of the house was a glass-roofed loggia half covered by an ornamental vine. Tables and little chairs were set about. We stepped on to it through open french windows and Ted pointed silently with the muzzle of the rifle. There were dark patches of dried blood, marks where something had been dragged along. Across the lawn was the half dismembered carcass of an animal. I remembered Jane saying she'd owned a pony.

It wasn't much use standing around. It was almost full night now, if we were attacked we wouldn't see the brutes until they were on top of us. We went back to the Saracen and I opened the rear doors. Jane peered down. She said anxiously, 'Did you find them?'

I shook my head, feeling singularly helpless. 'There isn't anybody there, Jane. Nobody at all.'

'They might be still hiding...'

I said, 'No, they're not.'

She said in a tight little voice, 'Did you see Brandy? He wouldn't have run away.'

I said, 'I'm sorry, Jane, I told you. There isn't anything there.'

She was quiet for a moment. Then, 'I see...' She swallowed. 'I suppose in a way I was expecting it ... Can I go inside, Bill? I've just got to get some fresh things...'

The sergeant shook his head slightly. I said, 'You wouldn't like it, love. And it's getting dark. We'd better go.'

She climbed back into the APC without another word. I started up and edged away down the drive. Ted spoke on the intercom. 'Where are we headed then?'

I was glad to hear his voice. I said, 'Christ only knows. Got any ideas?'

'No use goin' back Yatley way, I can tell ee that.'

I tried to think. 'Reckon our best bet is to go on down towards the coast and hope they've got things sorted out a bit before we get there.'

He agreed with me. 'My base were Colton Forum, reckon that'd be the best way fer me too.' I turned on to the main road and drove towards Brockledean. I said, 'Try that radio, will you? There must be something about.'

'I'll have a go...' He didn't sound too optimistic.

He made a contact within minutes, probably by sheer chance. I pulled in while he talked. I was glad Neil had put some distance between us; he'd probably reached camp by now.

The next words broke apart what little composure I'd got. The sergeant said, 'I'm talking to a Saladin. Holed up about a mile t'other side of Brockledean. Commander wants to know if the civvy vehicle contains a man and a girl and a bloody gert dog. Sorry, but he says his name's Connor. Reckons you knows him...'

I said involuntarily, 'Oh my God...' I wiped my face. 'You know about this car don't you, Ted?'

'Reckon Jane told me most of it.'

I said, 'Right then, what do we do?'

He said promptly, 'What he says. Haven't got a sight o' choice, have us?' The intercom was quiet for a while. Then, 'We're to make contact. Take the first left turn through the village, a few hundred yards on there's a wrecked lorry across the road. Turn right there and keep on over the Plain again. He says there's a sort of hill with a copse o' trees on top, we takes a bearin' on that and there's another copse dead in line. He's in there somewhere. He says to watch it, the ground's cut up bad. That's why he's stopped. Too risky movin' at night with these gert cracks all about.'

I sighed. 'Tell him we're on our way will you? I expect we shall hear the rest when we get there...'

I worked the car through Brockledean. At night it wasn't so bad; I couldn't see the bodies, just a confusion of shadows. I turned left as ordered and picked out the lorry within a minute or two; beside it was one of those inimitable holes in the hedge. I steered through and found myself in open ground again. The moon was rising, throwing the long shadow of the car out to one side; the hill showed up against the sky-line, a dark whaleback topped with an irregular clump of trees. I headed towards it. I felt the car lurch almost at once and swung away from the danger. The ground was criss-crossed with ridges and among them were crevasses. The resultant of headlights and moonlight was confusing; I slowed right down, picking my route. The sergeant helped, conning me from the turret. When I'd come about half a mile a light flashed from ahead and a little to the left. I corrected towards it and flicked my headlamps. It came on steadily.

I made out the bulk of a group of trees; the lamp shone from among them, a calm yellow eye. Someone hailed us; I saw the outline of the Saladin, closed up to within a couple of lengths, stopped, and switched off lights and engine. The night was warm, my shirt damp with sweat. I got out of the car feeling I could use a smoke.

Neil met me. He was a darker shadow in the night. A torch flickered briefly on my face; he said, 'Well then, sir, what's the game?'

I said, 'I ... drove to the village. After what I'd seen I had to get Jane out somehow or another.'

He kept his voice low but he was plenty mad. He said, 'And now I suppose you want a bloody medal. What do you think you've got there, a mechanized Noah's Ark?'

Behind me I heard Ted's boots scrape on steel. There was the clang of the back doors opening and the tinkle of Sek's lead. I said, 'Under the circumstances—'

He raised his voice. 'Sergeant, will you come down here please?'

'Sir.'

He stamped away half a dozen paces, then came back. He said, 'As I haven't a spare driver I'm leaving Mr Sampson with the vehicle. We shall be pulling out for Swyreford at first light. I can probably expect to pick up a number of stragglers. When and if I do the girl stays but the dog goes out. I'll leave it to you to see the animal's shot.'

I said, 'Just a minute, that's hardly fair—'

He rounded on me. 'As far as I'm concerned you're under orders so don't start any barrack-room lawsuits there's a good chap. In case you need reminding this is a state of emergency, that carrier is Government property and this is the Army, not the bloody Canine Defence League. Got it?'

I said, 'Yes.' There wasn't much else I could say.

He said, 'Very well then, you'd better see about a brew-up. After that you can get some sleep. Work out a watch system with the sergeant here, we don't want any of our little pets creeping up on us. I'll be over in a few minutes anyway. Want to hear some more about this little jaunt of yours.' Unexpectedly, he banged my shoulder. 'Under normal circumstances I'd say you put up a fairly good show. As it is I'll just recommend you for hanging as soon as convenient. Nothing personal of course.'

I said, 'Well, thanks a lot.'

He walked away. 'Right then, carry on.'

About midnight we got Jane settled down as best we could and climbed back up to the turret. I said I'd take the first watch; I opened the trap and sat out on top of the armour. The moon was high now, a silver ball riding at the focus of a milky haze of light. The trees were still; there was no sign of life from the Saladin and the shadows round her wheels were inky black. The night was utterly silent, not even the cry of a hunting bird. I had the feeling of being at some node of quietness, like the fabled eye at the centre of a hurricane.

Half an hour went by, then an hour. There was a flare of light beside me as the sergeant struck a match. I said quietly, 'Not asleep then, Ted?'

'No. Want a cigarette?'

I slid back inside the turret and lit up. I said, 'This is a funny set-up, no mistake.'

'Is the kiddy asleep?'

I called back quietly. 'Jane?' There was silence. I said, 'I think so. Why?'

He said. 'This lot stinks, it bloody do. Them wasps are cruel damn things, I never seen their like.'

I said, 'Well, we could be worse off right at the minute.'

He snorted. 'And we could be a hell of a sight better. Sittin' here in a bloody gert tin box waitin' to be picked off. Get farther on foot. These things attract the wasps. Hang round 'em like flies round jam they do. They'll be back down I tell ee. And when they do the beggars'll have us.'

I had to grin to myself. There spoke the footslogger; things hadn't changed in the year or two since I'd been in the mob. I said, 'I don't see why we can't keep going indefinitely.'

He said, 'The old story ... armour's all right till you has to get out of it. Which sooner or later you has to do. They devils know what they're doin'. They're fighting armour to armour right now, but they don't have to get out o' theirs. They can afford to wait.' He flicked ash irritably from his cigarette.

'How fast do the things breed, can ee tell us that?'

I said, 'I don't know anything about them, never studied wasps all that closely. If they are wasps ... All I know is they're a bit like bees but not so highly organized.'

He said, 'They're organized enough, they know what they're doing.'

He seemed to have a fixation about intelligence. I said, 'I don't altogether see that, Ted. They're vicious, and God knows they're dangerous, but I don't think they're doing anything more than forage. They'll need a hell of a lot of food to keep their nests going, they must be colossal.'

He said, 'What about his camp then, didn't they work that out?'

I was quiet for a moment. Then I said, 'It didn't look like an accident I'll admit. But it could have been.'

He said bitterly, 'Then there were twenty accidents just alike. I tell ee this area were thick with Army stuff, they were trucking civvies out by the score. Where's all the blokes now, I want to know? Wiped up, I reckons. Same as his lot.

'We got one nest, the armour went in and burned it up. Only the things were too smart to have it happen twice. They laid for us, made a clean sweep.'

I didn't want to be convinced but he was managing it.

He said, 'They had scouts out, too high up to touch 'em with anything. We banged away for a bit but it were a waste o' rounds; unless you hits the bloody things square a rifle bullet just bounces off. They was watching us all day, working out the disposition o' the troops, where the various units was lyin' like. And us fools lettin' 'em get on with it. Then after dark, wham. The orders go out. "All right, blokes, go down and get 'em. All units press home attacks".' He laughed. 'Christ, listen to me. The wasp High Command. Silly, isn't it? Makes me wonder if—'

He broke off. There was a booming. And a rattling, a clattering. Like no other noise I'd ever heard, except the noise of an earthquake. It seemed to be coming towards us, whipping across the Plain. We waited, gripping the coamings. Impossible not to believe some huge thing was charging us in the moonlight. We stared round but there was nothing to see, just the silver grass and the trees. The noise reached a peak and there was a jar as the shock wave passed under the wheels. The sound began to die away; down below, Jane screamed.

I started to swing out of the turret. I said, 'It's all right, darling, it's over. It won't hurt.' There was silence.

'Jane?'

The sergeant said slowly, 'She's asleep. Cried out in her sleep. Let her bide.'

I sat back. I said, 'There was a fight in Brockledean. I think some of your folks got through to the village before the wasps went for them. I'm still trying to get over it.' I told him what I'd seen. He was quiet till I'd finished then he let out one of those long, slow whistles of his. He said softly, 'Christ, that must have bin a do.'

I changed the subject. 'How did you manage to get away, after the quake?'

'Well, I were over in Yatley when it started, in a pub. It didn't do a sight o' damage, not at first, but the civvies started to panic. There were half a dozen of the boys in the other bar, I went through an' put me head in. "Come on lads," I says to 'em, "better shift a leg, we're goin' to be needed." Then *they* come. Christ.' I sensed him shudder at the memory. He said, 'The winders bust in, see? There were a gert crash. I thought 'twas the quake again but it were them things. The wasps. Two on 'em come straight through the glass, frames an' all. One lands on the mat, t'other up on the bar counter. An' there they were, sittin' lookin' at us, and their faces like puppy-dogs, twistin' about to see. Then the lights went out. Christ . . .'

'How did you get out?'

'Danged if I can remember, not rightly. It were a bit of a scuttle. But we landed up outside. There were fires burnin' already, and torches flashing about an' people running. And them damn things comin' down on their backs . . . There was an MP with a jeep. We piled on, as many of us as could. A mile out on the road one o' the things come down at us, straight in the screen. We turned over in the ditch and the next thing I remembers is wakin' up, and there were the boys. They done a good job on 'em, half took their bloody heads off . . . Reckon they'd have got me an' all only they thought I were dead like. Well, I laid up under a bush till I felt a bit smarter, then I started walkin'. I was wonderin' how long it'd be afore they got me. Walked most o' the day, here and there. Then I saw your place. Reckoned I'd do a quiet recce. I needed water bad, an' a bite to eat. Next thing I knows I'm on me back and the rifle's away out o' me hands and the dog's standin' there on top o' me sort of darin' me to move. Not that I would've ... You knows the rest.'

I said, 'If only we could get to the nests. Go for 'em, burn 'em up before they breed any more. We could knock them out, smash them.' I banged the handle of one of the smoke discharges. 'Even with these. We could lay a screen, they'd never see us in that.'

He wagged his thumb in the direction of the Saladin. 'They tried that this morning. His gunner told me, reckoned after the camp got beat up Connor nearly done his tank. They lobbed all the stuff they'd got on 'em all round by Yatley. Said they didn't do a sight o' good. Things are down deep, he said, wi' little burrows where they comes through. Nothin' to see. Reckoned when they opened up the wasps come up like confetti, smothered 'em. Took 'em a couple of hours to fight back out. Since then they bin on the run. We're all on the run. God knows when we'll stop.'

I said quickly, 'I think Neil knows what he's doing.'

He nodded. 'He's a cool bastard, that. Like ruddy ice. Knows just what he wants, he do. Had time to think now, work it all out. There's a type o' bloke like that, I come across 'em afore. He don't care about you or me, nor hisself. Mebbe not even the kiddy. He wants the Army to win, just for the book. He don't care how. You were damn lucky, I tell ee that. He's got it all weighed out, he's fightin' a guerrilla war already same as we shall all be doin' afore long if we don't look smart. Did he tell you he used that Browning on some civvies this morning?'

I said, 'Good God, surely not. Shot at them?'

He laughed. 'Not *at* 'em. Close over their heads. Damn close.'

'How do you know, Ted?'

' 'Cause I seen 'em. That were up by Yatley, first thing. I were still a bit dazed like, walkin' along the side o' the road. I seed this gang o' blokes, about twenty on 'em. I didn't go much on their looks. They were wild, what wi' the quakes and

54

everything. I got out o' the way a bit, see, then down the road he come. I reckon he was tourin' about lookin' for them damn nests. The civvies gets in his way an' he shouts at 'em to move over, let him through. Well, they starts hollerin' an' I were just goin' to stand up an' flag him, then one of 'em waves a rifle at him. Service rifle, God knows where he got that. But that were it. He let fly.'

He paused reflectively. 'The civvies went in all directions. Made for the ditches mainly, or just went down flat on their faces. I moved a bit smartish meself. Had to, in a manner o' speakin'. By the time I'd got straightened out again he were past and away, then the wasps come down. The civvies got off one shot, that were all. I hung about. I couldn't move out o' cover and anyways I wanted to get hold o' that rifle. I seen what they done. All on it. Christ, the bastards . . . I reckon that must have bin a huntin' party . . .'

I shivered. 'Did you tell Connor you knew about that?'

'No I didn't. What the eye don't see . . .' He left the rest unsaid.

I said, 'He's got the nerve all right, there'll be trouble over that.'

The sergeant said shortly, 'Not off them civvies there won't. And not from the flippin' Army. The way things are goin' he won't have to worry none.'

'What do you mean, Ted?'

'Do ee know a sight about earthquakes?'

'Not much. Why?'

'I was wonderin' how far this muck-up stretches. Could it cover the whole country? Could there be a quake as big as that?'

I said, 'It isn't impossible. There was a monstrous shake-up in Assam fifty or sixty years ago, the devastated area was twice the size of Britain. But that was exceptionally bad. Stones flew in the air, it was that violent. And Assam was in an earthquake belt. Britain isn't.'

He said, 'Britain didn't use to be. And stones flew last night. Straight up in the air, I seen 'em.'

'Surely not . . .'

He said, 'I wish I were jokin' . . .'

I was quiet for a minute. Just how bad were things anyway?

55

I had no means of telling. I'd been concentrating on getting out of the disturbed area into a comparatively safe region. What if there was no refuge? But that was a ridiculous thought. There's always somewhere to run, it just depends on finding it and moving fast enough when you're getting there. No place to run? Then we'd be living a nightmare. The sort of nightmare from which you can't wake up ...

The sergeant said, 'I reckon ye'd better get some rest. No point both on us sittin' it out. I'll take over for a spell.'

I yawned. 'Thanks, I suppose I could try.' I felt dopey and heavy-eyed but I was sure sleep was a long way off. I settled down into the turret. Surprisingly, I managed to doze. I woke at first light to a distant throbbing. I sat up thinking of earth-quakes again, but it was the Furies. Scores of them, very high and moving fast. I could see them through the tree cover above us, greyish dots against the pallor of the sky. Ted was sitting rigid watching them, one hand on the trap ready to shut down if they dived. But the squadrons pushed on, either not noticing the armour or ignoring it. They passed steadily out of sight to the west.

We got under way soon after six. Before we moved off Neil came over and showed me the route he intended to take. We were to move in a wide sweep, heading west at first and then swinging round to the south. That way we might avoid the worst of the broken ground ahead. Eight or ten miles on, our route should cross the M15 where it arrowed over the Plain running roughly parallel to the old A30. If the motorway was usable we'd turn west on it and carry on to Summerton. From there we were to head south-west again into Dorset, with Swyreford distant about forty miles. I nodded over the map; it seemed straightforward enough. I said, 'Can I ask a question?'

'If you like. Make it snappy.'

I said, 'What happens if your base has been beaten up? Could be we'll find it like Brockledean and Yatley. What do you aim to do then?'

He narrowed his eyes for a moment. 'Working on the premise that the rest of the country is as badly hit as the south, I should make for the coast. I think most of the stuff in this area will do the same. The sea would certainly be the best bet, we could regroup down there and there'd be a chance of liaising with the Navy. They can't have been hit too hard as yet. I've got a theory about these damned insects; only an idea so far but I don't think you'll find I'm far wrong. They haven't got much of a flight duration. A few miles at the outside. Couldn't expect much else from the size of them anyway; I suppose later on the boffins will manage to prove they were aerodynamic impossibilities, like bumblebees. Now if the worst happens I say we can expect the top brass to work from islands or floating bases beyond the range of the enemy. I shouldn't think they'd mount much of an attack outside the three-mile limit.'

I stood for a moment trying to take in the implication of what he'd said. He went on briskly, 'That's the pessimistic view of course and I'm certainly looking too far ahead. Impossible to do much long-range planning at the moment. I don't care for this radio silence and we haven't seen a single plane for twenty-four hours but I don't think we can draw any sweeping conclusions from what hasn't happened. Could be our people are all tied up in some other sector, the brutes seem to have made a pretty clean sweep of this one. Anyway, as far as the present jaunt is concerned, if and when we're attacked keep yourselves shut down. Stay close but not too close. Make sure you give the flame-throwers a clear arc of fire; that means somewhere about thirty yards at least. And wait for orders. Apart from that it'll be up to you to keep your noses clean. You'll have to do some rather pretty driving; from here on in the ground's like the arse-end of the moon. If you do get into trouble you can't get out of I shall probably push on to base on my own. Lost enough time as it is. OK?'

Ted had a couple of queries for him. It was decided the sergeant would come with us as far as Swyreford and try to contact his own people at Colton Forum. After Neil had hurried back to the Saladin I leaned on the front of the APC and smoked a cigarette. It was going to be another fine day; somewhere a lark was spiralling up and there was a clean fresh early-morning smell to the air. Ted saw to the stowing of the kit then he hauled one of the flame-throwers out of the back of the truck, strapped the pressure pack on his back, and climbed up to the turret. I followed him aboard, settled myself into the driving seat. Two engines revved, breaking the quiet. We edged out after the platoon leader, keeping about fifty yards in the rear. In about a mile we reached the first of the crevasses; Neil swung ninety degrees right and began to forge west alongside it.

Our course brought the sun astern. Ahead the sky lost its steely colour. A faint blue wash spread up it, deepening towards the zenith. We travelled for half an hour and the downs round Summerton ceased to be vague grey outlines and took on form and depth. I picked out the high point of Brad Beacon, a smooth swell of land, its outline unbroken either by hedges or trees. I'd climbed it once, soon after I moved to Brockledean, counted twelve of the eighteen spires you were supposed to be able to make out from the top, seen the hills of Somerset way off on the horizon floating like a cloud. All that seemed a long time ago now.

The barrier still stretched away to our left and now the downs were almost due south of us. It was obvious we were going to have to find a way through the mess, we were fast overshooting our objective. Neil evidently had the same thought; he stood up in the turret and signalled me to turn on to the rough. I swung left, following him, and saw the Saladin start to lurch as it reached the broken ground.

CHAPTER 5

WE WERE in trouble right from the start. The crevasses opening on all sides made the land look like nothing more than a gigantic crazy paving. Ahead the ground was even rougher; in places compression forces had levered up slabs that looked like dusty ice-floes, their edges a yard or more thick. Driving was a nerve-racking business. Some of the cracks were rubble-filled to within a foot or so of the surface; we crossed the narrowest of them, skirting the wider ones. We daren't risk the great weight of the cars on insecure footings. The crevasses were awe-inspiring; some of them were fifteen or twenty feet wide and there was no telling their depth. We ran alongside one of the biggest of them for some distance. I could see down the raw earth sides for twenty feet or more and there was no sign of narrowing. Ted had a better view from the turret; he remarked tersely over the intercom that 'the bloody thing seemed to go down for miles'.

Time after time the cars ran on to peninsulas of firm ground that proved to be bounded by the fissures, and there was nothing to do but turn back or reverse. In two hours' driving I don't think we could have got more than a mile southwards. As the sun got higher the temperature in the APC began to rise. At speed the open traps would have given a certain amount of ventilation but at our pace there was little or none. Jane complained once about the heat. She wanted to open the rear doors but I wouldn't have it. I'd seen the speed with which the Furies dived, it just wasn't worth the risk.

By nine AM I was beginning to get worried about my petrol. I was on the point of asking Ted to report the fuel situation when the Saladin found a lead of firm ground. Neil accelerated and I followed, keeping about ten or twelve lengths astern. A couple of miles of clear running, a bit more weaving and backing and we were through. Ted expressed his relief gustily. 'Best bloody tank trap I ever seen...' Then after a pause, 'I still reckon we'd have come through quicker on foot...'

The Furies attacked when we were within a few hundred yards of the motorway. I saw Neil wave and point back behind us, there was an exclamation from the intercom and a burst of swearing. Simultaneously the sky became full of insects, glinting like guineas in the sunlight. This time there was no doubt we were the objective. The Saladin stopped abruptly and I turned in a half circle, swinging back to face it some thirty or forty yards away. I shut the trap and clamped it. I said, 'Better close down, Ted.' He swore again. 'The hell wi' that...' There was a whickering, a cloud of smoke rolled across the field of the periscopes. I didn't see the effects of the shot but within a few seconds the flame-thrower hissed again and that time I saw the tip of the burning fuel as it licked at a diving Fury. The insect turned over and fell out of sight.

The periscopes gave me an unreal, panoramic view of the fighting round the Saladin. The car was broadside to me, square in the centre glass. Round it the Furies circled in a cloud, jinking and feinting, keeping just out of range of the flame-throwers. From time to time half a dozen insects would swing out of the cloud, mass a hundred yards or so away then dive back through the cordon in formation. Their aim seemed to be to carry through the barrage of flame by sheer weight. The tactic was unsuccessful; one or other of the guns would catch the wasps, the heavy bodies would drop, cannon into the armour, and roll down to lie twitching beside the wheels. A drift of scorched insects began to gather round the Saladin; it was a bizarre business.

The primary attack lasted some quarter of an hour. At the end of that time the grass was burning in a dozen places and a veil of smoke was making the oncoming Furies harder to see. They changed their methods; one moment they were roaring round as thickly as ever, the next they'd gone, soaring away into the haze. I thought they'd given up; then something glittered beside the wheels of the Saladin and I saw the grass was alive with uninjured wasps, crawling and humping towards Neil's car. I saw one of them get a grip on the rear tyre and swing itself up over the tread, then the vision through the scopes was cut off. There was a distorted glimpse of a dark body, a huge clawed foot. We were being boarded as well.

I had a bad moment. I yelled at Ted, there was a clatter on the plating over my head and the clang of the top hatch being shut. He came down in a heap, encumbered by the flame-thrower. Rasping and scraping sounded from a dozen points on the armour as Furies hauled themselves aboard. Sek started to bark deafeningly and I shouted at her to be quiet. The thing that had been blocking my periscopes moved clear; the view was almost immediately obscured by another Fury crawling up from the ground. Ted was saying something about 'coming scuttling like bloody rats'. The insects had achieved their primary object; they'd got to close quarters, and there wasn't a thing we could do about it.

I called back to Jane. 'You all right, love?'

'Ye-es.' She sounded uncertain.

'Don't be scared. They can't get in.'

She said, 'It isn't that. I'm cooking . . .'

There was nothing we could do about the heat. The ventilation hadn't been designed to cope with this sort of emergency. The sun was high now, beating on the armour. My face began to run with sweat; I mopped my forehead and listened to Ted cursing. 'Stuck here in a bloody tin oven bakin' ourselves . . . Armour never were no bloody answer, never will be. Blanking armour . . .' He was trying to get at the radios, still in trouble with the junk he'd got on his back. I asked him to tell Neil about our petrol. The reply was blistering.

Driving was out of the question now, we were harbouring so many Furies I could only get odd glimpses of the outside world and those usually through the side scopes. We settled down grimly to a siege.

It seemed odd to me that they hadn't used their infiltration technique earlier. The frontal attacks had cost them dear. After what I'd seen it was hard not to credit them with a high degree of intelligence; it occurred to me they might still be learning about us. I tried to imagine how their minds were working but it was impossible of course. I knew very little about insects but I remembered from scraps of reading that their nervous system was very different from ours. There was a brain of sorts but it was a minor affair, most of the actions were governed by motor centres and ganglia scattered about the body. The volume of nerve fibre in those huge things probably equalled that of a human brain; did that mean they were potentially as smart as us? I tried to remember what I'd picked up about that sort of thing. Was there a direct relationship between brain weight and intelligence? I seemed to recall something like that. I knew the brain of a dolphin was larger than that of a man. And people had been trying to teach dolphins to talk . . .

I thought back on what Neil had said. He'd envisaged an alarming situation where a few thousand oversized insects had kicked us right off the mainland. It seemed absurd until I remembered Brockledean and Yatley. Things like that could have been happening all over the country. We had no means of knowing, the brutes seemed to have cut all communications pretty effectively.

That brought me back to the idea of intelligence. After all, they'd even turned the earthquakes to advantage. Perhaps they'd known they were going to happen; maybe as well as

61

intelligence they had a whole range of instincts we knew nothing about. The sort of prescience that makes storm-flies dance before rain ... I wondered whether the gigantism had spread from a few individuals or if it was a sort of galloping mutation that was affecting all wasps everywhere. It seemed crazy but if it was true there didn't look to be much hope for us. There were wasps of one sort or another in nearly every country of the world.

My ideas got wilder. I think it was then I first started wondering just how the arrival of the Furies linked up with the big bombs. Was it only coincidence? Something told me that was impossible, as impossible as the notion that somehow, somewhere, a wasp had suddenly expanded, *plink,* increased its body volume maybe a hundred thousand times. I was no biologist but I knew that was out of any sort of question; I could imagine a mutation doubling the size of an insect, trebling it possibly, but that was all. So these ... beings weren't wasps. They looked like them sure, they acted like them, but that was all. So what, in hell or out of it, were they?

The bombs. The massive releases of energy. Energy can't be lost, it can only change its state or dissipate as heat. What if the creatures, whatever they were, had been waiting for just such an energy splash as we'd provided to complete their metamorphosis into our world? I knew on a global scale the biggest bomb we could let off might be puny, I'd read somewhere about one big storm generating more energy than all the explosives dropped in World War Two. But this energy had been concentrated in a pair of massive instantaneous gusts. I'd seen a weird story once about an H-bomb that shot down an angel. Was it something like that that had happened? Instinct told me I was right; only we'd done worse. We'd brought demons, not angels, thudding down into our fields. I listened to the noise of the claws on the armour over my head. Basically, it was pointless to speculate; maybe I never would know for sure. Maybe the wasps didn't know themselves ...

The stalemate lasted two hours; then, unbelievably, the attackers left. I was lying back in the seat with my eyes shut trying not to think about the temperature inside the car when there was a slithering overhead and a bump, and light shone suddenly through the periscopes. I sat up hastily and was in time to see the Furies leave the Saladin. One minute they were clustering so thickly over the car they obscured its outlines, made it look like some bright unholy cake set there on the Plain, the next they were off and away, zooming over the grass in all directions as they gained height. I shouted with relief. 'They're going . . .!' Ted started to winch the turret round, following them through the command periscopes. He reported them bunching together at a couple of hundred feet and moving off, again to the west. He lost sight of them within minutes.

We resisted the temptation to open up. We re-established contact with the platoon leader and Neil got us to drive round him slowly so that we could check each other. Both cars were clean. I unclamped the hatch, climbed out, and ran round to the back doors of the Saracen. I opened them and Jane practically fell out on top of me. She was pale, and her dress top was wet through. I said anxiously, 'You all right, love?'

She put her face in her hands. 'Gosh . . . There's a little man in my head beating out tunes with a hammer. Oh, those horrible things. Still . . .' She looked up and smiled wanly. 'We beat them, didn't we?'

I said, 'Yes, love, we beat them. No trouble at all.' I reached inside the carrier and patted Sek. She was panting like a steam engine. The interior of the APC was as hot as an oven.

The Saladin came up alongside. Neil shouted from the turret. 'You OK down there?'

'Just about, thanks.'

'Right, back aboard then. Can't stooge around here, isn't healthy.'

Jane shuddered. 'No, please, not for a minute . . .' I hoisted her up and pushed her inside. 'Sorry, Jane, we've got to get going. You'll be all right when we're moving. There'll be a draught then, you'll see.'

The motorway seemed to have escaped major damage. We turned on to it and built up to top speed. As we came over the crest of the down below Brad Beacon I saw smoke ahead; a few minutes later the cars roared into Summerton.

The place was pretty much a shambles. Half a dozen buildings on either side of the the main street were burning fiercely;

a fire engine stood at the kerb and there were hosepipes spread across the road but nobody was making any attempt to fight the flames. We drove past cautiously keeping to the middle of the street. A few hundred yards farther on I had a glimpse of a group of people clustered on the path. They seemed to be looting a shop. They ran when they spotted the cars; I wondered why, whether it was because of what they'd been doing or because we were armoured and liable to attract the Furies. I saw that tanks of some sort had been through the town; their tracks had bitten deeply into the road surfacing.

There was an iron lattice bridge where a railway had crossed the street. It was skewed out of line but it was still supported on the ends of the main girders. We edged underneath slowly; beyond, the road widened and there was an ugly little town hall, all pillars and curlicues. Just before it on the left was a filling station. Neil drew in under the canopy and stopped. I pulled up close behind him. I wouldn't have gone much farther, the tank gauge was reading zero. I switched off and got out of the car.

There was silence except for the rumbling of the flames. The smoke rolled close overhead, veining the sky with black, trailing ginger shadows along the ground and across the fronts of the buildings. I looked up at the town hall. Strings of bunting were hanging listlessly and there was a banner announcing a fête. The tower clock was still keeping time; I wondered how long it would be before it stopped.

We were evidently not the first visitors to the garage. The covers of the pumps had been forced and two of them still had their emergency handles fitted. I hoped the storage tanks hadn't been drained. Neil and the gunner took up positions on each side of the cars while I swung a gantry out across the path and put the filler nozzle into the Saracen's tank. Ted worked the handle and there was a reassuring gurgle of petrol. The mechanism creaked steadily. I watched the dial pointer edging round; the sun felt hot on the back of my neck.

There was a noise of wings. I spun round. Three Furies were heading towards the Saracen in a tight vic, moving fast under the rolling cloud of smoke. They looked absurdly big and somehow Oriental against the background of old stone.

I couldn't let go of the petrol filler, it was as if the thing was stuck to my hand. I tried to crouch against the armour and all the time I was holding the pistol grip and the liquid was sloshing down into the tank. Neil ran forward lifting the tube of the flame-thrower; he was shouting something to the gunner. The Furies changed direction, swooping down at him. For a moment I thought he'd left it too late then there was the familiar whickering, a startling ball of white flame edged with orange where the brightness of the napalm turned to ordinary fire. The wasps landed in the road; two lay twitching, the third was up in a moment and scuttling at him like some great lame dog. Neil jumped to one side; the gunner had moved up in support and the wasp ran straight into the flame from the second weapon. Neil turned back to us with sweat on his face. He said, 'Carry on there.' It was only then I realized the sergeant had never stopped working the handle.

Everything happened at once. The petrol reached the top of the tank and streamed back on to the road, I called out and simultaneously Jane opened the back doors of the APC. She said, 'Bill, what is it, is everything all right?'

I heard Neil shout, 'Get that bloody child inside...' I couldn't move. I was staring open-mouthed at the thing behind Ted.

I wanted to shout but nothing would come. I put my hand up in front of me, stupidly, like somebody trying to ward off an evil spirit. Ted had taken a step forward; he saw my face and stopped. He half turned but he was nowhere quick enough. The Fury launched itself from the opal globe atop the pump, landed on his shoulders. The impact knocked him to his knees.

Whether the insect had been there all along or whether some noise we made had fetched it from a hiding-place, I never knew. There seemed no appreciable time-lag between my catching sight of the black and yellow mask peering down and Ted grovelling at my feet with the thing clipping away at his neck. I saw his head loll forward; his hands pattered on the path. Blood moved away in a swift vee from each side of his head.

Sek came out of the carrier in a bound; Jane had the loop of the lead round her wrist, she measured her length on the road and I fell over her. I clawed for one of the rifles, knowing it was too late already. I turned back and something rolled past my feet. The head of the Fury, jaws clicking. Sek was worrying at the body that still clung to the sergeant, flexing its sting in his back. Jane was screaming and trying to pull the dog clear.

I swung the gun butt and at the third or fourth blow the remains lost their grip and rolled across the forecourt. I followed up, panting. I couldn't stop beating with the rifle. I saw bright body segments splitting, pale flesh welling up. A leg bounced across the path; something splashed my face. I wasn't conscious of putting any effort into the blows; I wanted to smash and smash until there was nothing left of the thing, not one tiny scrap. I can remember Jane getting hold of my arm; that was crazy, she could have been brained. She'd still got Sek, somehow; the dog was plunging and baying. I saw Neil pointing, behind him the gunner running like hell for the Saladin. The redness faded, and the street was full of diving wasps.

My first instinct was to huddle back behind the pumps but that was no good, that was what the brutes wanted. I ran towards the APC, towing Jane. Somewhere on the way I dropped the rifle. I saw Ted's body, blood glittering along the gutter.

The images were meaningless, just so many half-glimpsed snapshots. The back of the car was open; we got in somehow and I slammed the doors. A second later the first of the wasps hit the armour full bore. The crash rocked the Saracen. I was threshing about in the half dark trying to get past Jane to the turret. All I could think of were the two open flaps, one over the commander's position, one above the driving seat.

I got the first one closed, swung my legs down through the turret mechanism, and tried to slide forward. I jammed. Sek was howling; there was another huge blow on the plating. I could see through the flap in front of me. The Saladin was fifty yards away already, moving fast and barraging flame.

I arched my body and thrust as hard as I could. Something gave; there was pain, then I was in the driving seat and the hatch was closed and dogged. I heard the roar as one of the attackers changed course and zoomed up over the turret. Through the scopes I saw the Saladin swing right and vanish. I rammed the starter and took the car away at full throttle. I'd got enough sense left to realize that somehow we had to close up with the platoon leader. Without flame we were helpless, if the Furies got to close quarters again they'd bog us down for hours. I steered right where Neil had turned, saw a wide, clear road, and opened up. Five minutes later we were clear of Summerton and the other car was just visible ahead, a swaying dark-green speck.

We were off the motorway now and the road surface was nowhere near as good. The macadam was cracked and corrugated. I held the APC at top speed. The din inside was terrific; from the back came noises that suggested the contents of half a dozen kitchens had come loose and were banging around. I could only hope Jane had had the sense to get down on the floor where she wouldn't be hurt.

The Saladin was closer; I reckoned I'd closed the gap by half. I rammed my foot on the deck but the car wouldn't take any more throttle, she was flat out already. It went through my mind fleetingly that maybe in the morning the Furies had been confused into thinking the cars were dead. They knew better now; if we let them close again they might camp for a week. Neil had obviously had the same idea; he was trying to outpace the things, tire them and lose contact that way. It was impossible of course, they were five or six times as fast as the armour. They were circling the Saladin as it moved, keeping well out where the flame couldn't touch them. I guessed we were the centre of a similar cloud. Our speed was stopping them from landing but that was all.

I was within six lengths of the Saladin when the way was barred by a crevasse. I saw the leader start to swing and hit my own anchors as hard as I could. The next few moments were bad; ten or twelve tons of APC take a lot of stopping. I saw the danger looming up and yanked the steering. I thought we weren't going to make it; the car heeled her offside wheels in the air, there was the mother and father of all crashes as she came back level then I was bounding across the rough, trying to spot hazards through the restricted vision of the periscopes.

For us, the retreat ended just before three. I suppose it had to happen, it was only a question of time. The Saladin had been drawing away again and I was putting everything into closing the gap when my nearside wheels went into a crevasse.

I swung off as hard as I could, gunning the engine to force the tyres to grip, claw the car back to firm ground. She made it with a leap; I straightened up and saw the second hazard dead ahead. I stamped on the brake but there wasn't a chance. I felt the front of the car drop away, saw the periscope glasses coming at my face. I got my hands up and there was a thud and a burst of light, as sudden and final as the breaking of a cinema film. Then a sensation of falling, a ghastly feeling of sickness ... and nothing, for quite a long time.

I came round slowly and by stages. The first thing I can remember is a sensation of being scraped with a hot, rough towel. I lay still wishing whoever was doing it would go away. It didn't stop and after a moment I sat up slightly and opened my eyes. The movement started a trip-hammer going inside my head. I groaned and the hot towel treatment started over. I put my hands up and touched fur, realized greyly that Sek had worked her way through the turret to me. She was licking my face. I mumbled, 'All right, girl...' I opened my eyes again and tried to orientate myself. I was in near-darkness and there was a pungent, heavy smell that I couldn't place. I touched the steering wheel in front of me, the sloping coaming over my head. The periscopes. How I'd missed splitting my skull on them I couldn't imagine.

My hand was hurting; I seemed to have cut it somehow. I remembered racing the Furies, the Saladin jigging in the scopes, the crazy drive through the crevasses. I sat bolt upright and yelled. 'Jane?'

Silence.

'Jane!'

There was no answer and I moved convulsively, trying to work my way back out of the seat. A few megatons of explosive went off inside my skull and I slid back down and stayed still awhile. When I felt a little better I tried again, more carefully this time. It wasn't easy. The Saracen was tilted at an angle of nearly forty-five degrees, and tipped to one side. I got my body through the turret ring and stuck for a while. My feet scrabbled among a collection of loose objects; a water-bottle, some tins of food, a part of one of the flame-throwers. Instantly it seemed the noise of metal was amplified inside the car. Scrapings and rustlings ran round the turret like eerie echoes. The sound was indescribable, a compound of slitherings, bumpings, rappings, and drummings that made my back crawl. My thinking processes were working better now; I realized we must be covered with Furies. That sharp, cloying stink was the smell of the insects themselves.

For the first time I became conscious of the heat. Even the slight exertion had left me running with sweat. I let the noise die down then I called again, softly. The silence reproached me. I forced myself the rest of the way into the turret. Sek hindered me, bunting with her great head. I shoved her off, groped round till I found a torch. Some light was coming through the command periscopes but the body of the car was black; I shone the torch, saw a hand, a tangle of hair. I got to Jane and turned her over. She had a bruise on her forehead and her nose had bled, spattering the front of her dress. It was hard to see with just the torch but she didn't seem to be hurt anywhere else. She was limp and heavy; I held her awhile, not knowing what the hell to do. Then I laid her down again as gently as I could and hunted round till I found one of the water-bottles. I soaked a handkerchief and bathed her face and throat. It seemed an age before she moved. She put a hand up to her face and moaned, then she tried to sit up. She muttered something that sounded like 'black rabbit...'

I said, 'It's all right, we're all right now, don't worry...' She looked up at me, screwing her eyes as if she was trying to focus. Abruptly, she panicked. I held her wrists. I said, 'It's all right...' She relaxed again and I think she realized where we were. She said, 'Bill...' Then, foggily, 'We fell over...'

She sat up again. I helped her. I said, 'Are you hurt anywhere? Tell me...'

She said vaguely, 'I don't think so, only my head... ow... where's Neil?'

'I don't know, I hadn't even thought. I got knocked out as well.'

She said, 'Got to let him know we're all right. Think we're dead... Bill, it's so hot...'

I said, 'We can't go out, love; there's wasps.'

She looked up. The scraping and rattling had started again. I was wondering if the brutes could hear our voices. She said, 'Oh, no...'

I said, 'Come on, sit still for a bit. You had an awful bang
... what happened, can you remember?'

'I ... no, I can't ... I can remember driving along and
everything was bouncing about ... oh, the wall. It just reached
out and punched me.'

I felt a bit relieved. She must be concussed but if she could
remember that much maybe she wasn't too badly hurt. I said,
'Sit still anyway, rest for a time ...'

'I'm all right.'

'You're not. You were rambling about rabbits a minute or
two ago.'

She said indignantly, 'I couldn't have been ... Bill, what
are you doing?'

'It's all right. I'm going to try to see out.'

The periscopes weren't a great deal of use. The angle of the
turret was acute, all I could see was an expanse of brownish
grass. I started to pull the turret round. As soon as the armour
began to move the noise outside redoubled; I heard picking
and scratching just over my head. I felt a sort of thick rage but
there was nothing I could do.

I saw the horizon, tilted and unreal. Then an expanse of
blue sky, burning with sunlight. Then grass again. For all I
knew Neil might have been standing by. I certainly couldn't
see him if he was.

I turned to the radio gear. I put the head-phones over my
ears and switched on. There was nothing, not even the singing
of a carrier wave. I spent ten minutes clicking controls before I
gave up. The set was probably broken; if it was, there was
nothing I could do about it. Radio had never been my strong
point.

I doubted in any case if the leader would have bothered to
wait. It would hardly have been logical; even if he'd known we
were alive there wouldn't have been a thing he could do. If
he'd succeeded in driving the wasps off without roasting the
pair of us he wouldn't have been able to take us with him.
Much better to push on to base. Maybe he'd try to send somebody back to us; or maybe he'd just wash his hands of a nasty
little moral problem and forget all about us. I swung the turret
again, not wanting to face the fact that we were alone. I
learned nothing fresh.

Jane was peering through at me, supporting herself with one hand against the side of the car. She said anxiously, 'Can you see anything?'

I wiped my face. It seemed I could feel the heat as a physical pressure, squeezing my brain. The pain throbbed slowly, making it hard to think. I said, 'I don't think he's there but we can't be sure.' I was trying to remember the loading drill for a Browning. 'Jane, I'm going to fire the gun up here. If he's anywhere about he'll hear it and know we're all right at least. Better put your fingers in your ears when I tell you, it'll make a devil of a row.'

'A devil of a row' summed it up nicely; I thought my already aching head was going to split. I emptied a magazine before I gave up. I didn't think I was doing any good and I couldn't stand much of that racket. As an afterthought I fired the smoke discharges. The cartridges went off with deafening blasts; it was like being inside a dustbin while somebody clouted the end with a sledge-hammer. We sat with our ears ringing and waited for some noise from outside. Nothing happened. After a few minutes the tip of the smoke cloud came into sight through the scopes, thick and grey-white, curling lazily across the Plain. The wasps on the armour shifted agitatedly for a time then settled down again. It was obvious there was nobody near us. Jane said bitterly, 'It's no good, he's gone. Come in the back again, Bill, you can't do anything else.'

We sat in the half-dark. Above us the clattering and scraping went on spasmodically. I shifted about, trying to find a position where I didn't have to lean on the armour. The sides of the car were baking hot. Sweat trickled steadily down my back; my shirt was drenched.

Jane said tightly, 'He might have tried to find out about us. I thought he would.' Then, in a small voice, 'Do you think he'll come back, Bill?'

'Yes, of course. Or he'll send somebody. We shall be all right.'

I could see the paleness of her dress, her face turned towards me. She said, 'I'm getting sloppy and stupid again I'm afraid. I don't think he will come back. I don't think we shall see him any more, ever.'

71

I reached across and touched her hand. The palm was wet. I said, 'Don't be a clot. Try and rest, and don't worry. We shall be OK.'

The temperature inside the car rose steadily.

CHAPTER 6

ANY MOVEMENT became an effort. The air I was breathing felt as if it was coming straight from a moderate oven; I had no way of telling how high the temperature had actually risen, maybe it was just as well. The morning had been bad but this was far worse. I listened to the scraping and gouging where the wasps were still trying to cut their way in to us. I had a queer thought. Before, their very persistence had been terrifying. Now I didn't see it like that. There was something pitifully inadequate about them; they were dumb machines, throwing themselves hopelessly at things they couldn't understand. I wondered again where in all the hells they were coming from, what they were after. They couldn't wipe us out, beat all our tanks and planes and guns. The human race had had a million years to find out how to wage total war against anything including itself, and it certainly hadn't wasted much of that time.

Or were they so dumb? Just how much did sheer persistence, and sheer numbers, count in the push-button age? I started thinking up all the weapons we could use against them. Guns, bombs, aircraft ... armour had a limited use certainly, so did bombs, but we couldn't just fly about spattering our own country with HE. That would be hacking off our noses to spite our faces; I was pretty sure that for every wasp killed we'd wipe out a hundred humans. England would be in turmoil now, whole city populations on the move, scattered about among the nest sites. We couldn't bomb a mess like that ...

I began to appreciate the sheer difficulty of hitting at a target like the wasps. For the last forty or fifty years our technology had been concentrating more and more on means of mass destruction; we had our A-bombs and H-bombs, but they

72

were useless as strategic weapons. What could you use for instance against an army deployed in the field except the weapons you'd always used against armies? And the Furies were more diffuse than any target in history, their dispersion was effortless and three-dimensional. Throwing nukes at them would make about as much sense as using hand grenades to sweep up confetti ... Their burrows were down deep, the gunner had said. How deep was deep? Could be even if we decided to use low-yield air blasts they wouldn't be knocked out. And ground explosions would foul up the whole country for years ... Abruptly, I stopped feeling sorry for the wasps. It seemed to me they had it pretty good; whichever way we played, we would be the losers.

An hour later I was feeling pretty sorry for myself. The heat was incredible, unbearable. I knew I should have to do something. I tried to think about driving out. I doubted it was possible; the Saracen was tipped over so far it was obvious her back wheels were in the air and it was equally likely the front pair were hanging over a void. She must have buried her nose in the earth on the far side of the crevasse; that left her supported by her middle wheels only. When I started up they'd churn the soil under them and one of two things would happen. Either she'd dig down until she got some sort of a grip with her tail, in which case she stood a chance of clawing back out, or she'd go right in. That would be the end ...

I sat up carefully, trying not to move faster than was absolutely necessary. Jane stirred uneasily. She said, 'Bill, what are you doing?'

I said, 'Stop where you are, love. Don't move more than you have to. I'm going to try to drive out.'

She sat up as well. She said sharply, 'Can you?'

'I don't know. Maybe. I think it's worth trying.'

She said, 'Be careful, Bill, if we slip ...'

'It'll be all right, I'll go slowly. You stay there.' I wrestled my way back through the turret and into the driving seat.

I was afraid the engine wouldn't start but it ran, although it sounded ragged. I selected reverse and revved cautiously. Nothing happened. I throttled harder and the car started to wallow. She levelled slightly then there was a heavy grinding, a crack, a sensation of slipping. I grabbed the wheel, squeezed.

73

The nose tilted down. She was going, going ... She slid a yard, checked, another foot ... and stopped.

I let go of the steering. I found I was gasping for breath; another inch, the slightest movement, and she would be down that hole. I could feel it. I switched off and waited for the shaking to stop. I've always had an inborn fear of falling, that had been a bad few minutes. The car creaked ominously once or twice but it seemed she was still wedged. Unless I did anything to disturb her ... That was a game I couldn't afford to play any more. I worked back into the turret feeling like a dish-rag in need of wringing out. The Saracen had increased her angle of tilt by fifteen degrees or so, she was almost standing on her nose.

My memory of the next few hours is pretty vague. We lay in the back of the carrier feeling the heat pressing down like an unbearable weight. Jane undid her dress and lay flapping it ineffectually; I don't think she was really conscious of what she was doing. Later she fell into a sort of half-doze, turning about from time to time, moaning to herself, shifting her long legs awkwardly in the confined space. I dribbled water on to her face, letting it run down her throat. It didn't do any good but it was all I could think of. The wasps never left the armour.

Had they decided to conduct a war of nerves they could hardly have gone about it better. The scraping and tapping went on almost without a break. Apart from Sek's quick panting it was the only sound there was. I began to distinguish patterns in the noise, and identify them with possible actions. Those sharp raspings and clatterings were undoubtedly their claws as they ran about, and the heavier thumps were the landing impacts of fresh insects come possibly to relieve the guard. The softer, almost inaudible drummings were the tips of their velvet-black antennae as they tapped them nervously on the steel. And the drawn-out, harsh scrapings must be their mandibles as they tried to gouge their way in to us. Gouge and kill, gouge and kill, on and on for ever. They were machines, programmed to destroy us. They would wait like machines. They would wait for ever ...

I started to get hallucinations. I dreamed I was sitting in the bar of the *Basketmaker's Arms*, talking to Tod. I could see it all vividly; the baskets of flowers in the porch just outside the open door, the long counter, the pumps ... On the table in front of me was a pint of beer, cool, straight from the cellar. All I had to do was pick it up and drink, drink ... I did pick it up, a score of times, but it turned into a canteen half full of lukewarm, soupy water, and the pub vanished; we were back in a machine, a crippled, dark thing that stank of the Furies and our sweat.

Another time we were by a brook and the water was gliding deep and green and all we had to do was ease ourselves in and soak up all the coolness; but when we tried Ted came floating up from a void, his neck open at the back and shedding bright blood all round. When that happened I damn nearly screamed ...

I think if it hadn't been for Jane I'd have opened the doors sometime in that afternoon and walked out to the Furies. But somehow she swam through all the dreams and I never completely lost touch. I'd come round and find myself bathing her face or stroking her wet hair, mumbling some stupid thing or another. Once she started to cry. I held her again to make her stop. I asked her what was wrong, what I could do; she shook her head helplessly while the hot tears squeezed out and ran across her face. 'It isn't you, it isn't you, it's Ted ...'

I don't remember noticing any sudden lessening of the misery; all I remember is a time when I could breathe easier, when the heat was not abated but slightly less unbearable. My brains weren't stewing any more, I could start a thought and actually trace it through to its end. It was sometime then that I heard engines.

I waited, listening. The blood was still pounding in my ears and I couldn't be sure of anything. After a time I levered myself back towards the turret. I moved carefully; I'd got an idea the wasps were waiting for sounds from inside the armour. If we could stay quiet long enough they might convince themselves we were dead. I got to the periscope glasses, peered through. The land still shimmered with mirage but I thought I saw shapes moving. Tanks. I rubbed my face and stared again but they had passed out of my field of vision. Shortly after that the sounds faded away.

I heard them again an hour later and that time I was more

certain. I saw them passing, clearer this time, huge things with long guns wearing heavy muzzle brakes. I heard firing, and some of the turrets seemed to be rotating. The things were surrounded by Furies, they looked like great prehistoric creatures tormented by flies. They were soon out of sight and I daren't touch the turret to bring them back into view. I regretted the smoke discharges I'd wasted but there was no way of reloading the tubes without opening up.

I went back to Jane. She was sitting up when I reached her; I said softly, 'Hello, love, how do you feel?'

She put her head in her hands. 'Awful. Bill, can't we—'

'Shhh . . .'

She said, blearily, 'What?'

'Whisper. The wasps are still on top. I was hoping they'd think we were dead. If they hear us they'll know we're not.'

She shuddered. She said pleadingly, 'Can't we get out? Isn't there any way?'

I shook my head. I'd been thinking of how to get at the brutes but the only real answer was a flame-thrower. We had a couple of the things in the car but I'd never handled one and it wasn't a good time to start experimenting. I thought there was a chance I could learn to operate one of them, they looked pretty simple, but I needed something surer than that. If I opened those doors I should have about a second to spare at the outside . . . I said, 'We'll just have to wait, Jane. The worst's over now. They won't stay much longer, you see.' I hoped I was right.

She said miserably, 'I want to spend a penny. I've wanted to for ages.'

I said, 'Oh God . . . Look, if the worst comes to the worst you'll just have to spend it. It's better than being killed.' I shook her shoulder gently. 'You're a big girl now, Jane. I shan't worry if you don't.' She didn't answer, just sat trembling.

The Furies did leave, an hour later. I'd never really expected it. There was a slithering and banging, a huge booming of wings. We looked at each other unbelievingly then I scrambled up to the turret. I was in time to see the whole cloud of them smoking off across the Plain. I raised a cheer that was more of a croak. It was like a reprieve from death.

Jane was already on her feet, trying to edge up to the back doors. I got past her. I said, 'Wait a minute, we've got to be careful. Remember they like to leave one behind.'

'I don't care . . . quick, please, Bill . . .'

I said, 'Don't be daft.' I inched the doors open, ready to slam them again if I heard a buzz of wings. Everything was quiet; cool air blew gloriously against my face. I opened wider. Nothing moved.

I sent Sek out. I didn't like it but there wasn't much choice; if there was a rearguard she stood a better chance of dealing with it than either of us. She gathered herself on the edge of the sloping deck, tensed, and sprang with a clatter of claws. She circled out of sight, nose questing in the grass. I waited a minute; when there were no sounds I swung myself down to the ground. I walked round both sides of the carrier. There were no wasps. I went back to the tail and held my arms up for Jane.

We sprawled on the grass, just drinking in coolness. For a couple of minutes we would have been easy game for any of the huge wasps that happened to fly by, but fortunately none did. Then I sat up and lit a cigarette. I left Jane on her own while I walked round to the front of the carrier to see exactly what had happened.

It was more or less as I'd worked it out. She'd gone nose first into a wide crevasse; she was tipped down at an extreme angle, her front buried in the earth a foot or so below the far lip, the stern and last great pair of wheels high in the air. Her middle wheels had dug into the earth at the edge of the fissure, sinking themselves to their hubs. They still rested on an insecure-looking foundation of rubble. I leaned on the armour and looked down into the pit. I stepped back hastily; there was no bottom visible, the sides stretched away like cliffs till they met in a blackish gloom.

Jane came round to me. She'd caught her hair back with a mysterious piece of ribbon and tidied her dress. She was picking at the fabric disgustedly. It was wet, and smudged with dirt and blood. My own clothes weren't in a much better state. She said, 'I'd give pounds and pounds just to bathe and be able to change. Do you think we can make the car go again?'

'There isn't a chance. If I drive her any more she's going to tip on her nose, see, and go right down. And it's an awful long way to the bottom. It needs something to tow her. If she was pulled backwards she'd be all right but she can't do it on her own.'

Jane looked down the fissure and drew back as I had done. She said determinedly, 'Well we shall have to walk, that's all. We'd better get away because if any more wasps see the car they'll come down and catch us.'

There was a lot of sense in that; the Plain round about was fairly flat, the disabled APC stuck up like a sore thumb. We collected what we thought we could carry; a haversack, some tins of rations, a couple of bottles of water. I hesitated over taking a rifle and decided against it. From what I'd seen it would be virtually useless and it was all extra weight. I took one of the flame-throwers and a spare pack of fuel. Before we moved off I tried the weapon out; as I thought, it was pretty simple. There was a pressure tap on the shoulder pack, and a trigger on the handgrip. Pressing it opened a valve and struck a flint that lit the fuel as it came through. I fired a half-second burst across the Plain and we had to walk round stamping out smouldering grass. After that I felt better. The Furies respected the *flammenwerfer* more than anything else; if we were attacked we might have a chance of holding them off till we reached some sort of shelter. I checked the Saracen again for anything else that could conceivably be of use but there was nothing. I swung down outside, reached up, and slammed the back doors. No point leaving the car open to the weather, somebody else might find her a handy refuge sometime. Jane lifted the haversack. She said quietly, 'Which way?'

I looked at the sun, then down to the south. In that direction lay a range of hills, blue with distance. Behind us was nothing but an empty horizon. A trace of smoke showed where Summerton was still burning. I walked off a few paces then turned back. The carrier looked oddly desolate, perched up there like a little foundered ship. She was covered with wasp droppings; there were grey-white streaks on the armour and wheels where the mess had run down her sides. She'd been my first command; she hadn't lasted very long. I shook my head. I said, 'I don't know which way, Jane. I don't know what's best to do.'

She was at my elbow, waiting patiently. 'What's the matter, Bill?'

I shrugged. 'Somehow it all seems so bloody pointless. Poor old Ted getting killed, and now this. Trust Sampson to balls things up.'

She said angrily, 'You mustn't think like that. Nobody could have done any better. At least we're still alive.'

I put my arm round her shoulders, impulsively. She relaxed against me gently and it was all right. She stayed still for a few moments then she pushed away and giggled. She said, 'You look like a sort of twentieth-century Quixote. You know, terribly serious and all strapped round with guns and things.'

I laughed. I said, 'He didn't have much luck with the windmills. He should have stuck to napalm.'

She twined her fingers in mine. She said, 'Let's go away, Bill. Come on.' We started walking towards the hills.

I'd had some vague hope of picking up the Saladin's tracks but there wasn't a chance of that. The ground was hard, the grass short and dry. Once or twice I thought I saw faint tyre-marks but I couldn't be certain. After a while I gave up looking, concentrated on moving as nearly south-west as I could. I let Sek run free. She kept pretty close to us; after the first few minutes she dropped behind and stayed almost at heel. She knew well enough things were far wrong.

The great crevasse that had wrecked the Saracen curved off to our right and we soon lost sight of it. The land ahead was undamaged. That was the final irony; we'd been almost clear of danger, I'd literally fallen at the last ditch. We pushed on fast until a low swell of ground had hidden the car from us, then we slowed down. There was no point wearing ourselves out, God only knew how far we would have to walk.

The sun set among huge swaths and banners of gold. In the afterglow we came to a road. Near by were tall clumps of bushes; we crawled into the thickest of them and rested long enough for me to smoke a cigarette. We discussed what was the best thing to do. I was hazy about exactly where we were; I wondered if it would be better to keep on across country. Jane wanted to follow the road till we reached houses. We agreed to do that. Basically we both had the same idea; to get

79

ourselves as quickly as possible out of the affected area and back to some sort of sanity.

I don't think I'd ever realized before what a big place England is. Like the rest of us I'd got used to thinking of it as an overcrowded, house-ridden little country full of suburbs and traffic jams, with people standing on each other's heads for room. But now even that one little road seemed endless; we walked for an hour without seeing a light or any sign of another human being. Our world was expanding of course, and we were shrinking in proportion; I was very conscious of the two of us trudging along, the only living specks in all that wilderness of grass and downs. The silence became oppressive. The night was totally still, the only sound the scraping of our shoes as we walked.

Three or four miles farther on we reached a copse. It was just visible against the sky, a dark mass a few hundred yards from the road. Jane put her hand on my arm and stopped. A nightingale was singing. I'd never been over-impressed by them but right then the sound was the loveliest thing I'd heard. The piping was sweet and effortless. Soon the bird was joined by another and another. The wood was alive. It was the first bird-song I'd heard for two days.

We must have stood for a quarter of an hour or more just listening. Somehow at that time I didn't doubt the human race was fighting a battle for existence. I wondered suddenly if we were worth a victory. Taken overall, our species hadn't made much of a fist of things. Maybe it would be better to leave Earth to the nightingales, to a sort of bird-haunted peace.

The mood was past in a few moments. The idea might have been grandiose but you can't hold on to things like that very long. The human race wasn't a statistic, it was people. Folk like Ted and Neil, and Jane. What was I doing, wishing them dead for some cynical abstraction? I didn't want them dead. Very particularly I didn't want Jane dead. I moved closer to her, instinctively. I think she understood just what I was feeling. She linked her arm in mine. She said, 'We'd best get on, Bill. Find a place to sleep.' We moved unwillingly down the road.

The character of the country had changed a lot in the last couple of miles. The land was still rolling but the hills were smaller and more wooded, lacking the miles-long contours of the downs. This was one of the areas where the boundary of the great Plain was fairly well defined. I was glad of it; if we were attacked there was a much better chance of finding cover.

A little farther on we got to a signpost. I'd remembered to pack a torch; by its light we saw that if we turned left down a tree-lined lane we would come to Burton Middlemarsh. The name sounded inviting at least. We followed the direction and reached a straggle of cottages. As far as I could see they were undamaged.

We hung about cautiously for some time. The little village looked deserted but we'd learned not to take chances. Eventually I edged up to the front door of one of the houses and knocked. Nobody came. I tried the latch; the place was locked up. So was the second house, and the third.

Surprisingly, the fourth showed a crack of light. I knocked; there was a long wait then I heard a shuffling inside. A slightly querulous voice said, 'Who is it then?'

Jane answered. 'We're lost. We were trying to get to the coast but our . . . car broke down. Can you help us please?'

I heard bolts being withdrawn. The door opened a few inches, showed an old lady in apron and carpet slippers, cardigan clutched round her shoulders. She said, 'Just the two on yer, is it?'

I'd got Sek to me. I was standing touching her collar lightly with my fingers. I said, 'There's a dog.'

The old woman saw her for the first time and edged back. She said, 'Oh, my word . . .' Jane said quickly, 'We're all right, honestly. I'm Jane Smythe, this is Bill Sampson. We were with some soldiers but they left us. We wanted to get to Swyreford.' The old lady dithered. Then, 'You'd better come in . . .' She opened the door the rest of the way.

I wriggled out of the flame-thrower harness, laid the thing down in the hall, and followed the others into the one lit room. It was a homely little place. An elderly television set stood in one corner and there was a cage with a canary, an old-fashioned open grate. The window curtains were partly drawn; I saw the panes beyond had been blocked with a variety of oddments, newspapers, bits of cloth, a dismantled cardboard carton. In one wall was a door that obviously led to the kitchen. Its panels had been split from top to bottom; there was white wood showing, and long splinters. I looked quickly at Jane. The damage was horribly suggestive.

The old lady said uncertainly, 'Place ain't fit to be seen, not by rights. All this muck an' stuff everywhere . . . Sit ye down, anyhow.' She started hauling chairs about. 'Is that dog safe?'

Sek had investigated the hearthrug briefly with her nose and curled up on it with a grunt. She was watching me, chin on paws. I said, 'She's all right, she won't be any trouble.'

'Got a cat round somewhere,' said the old lady. 'Or at least I *'ad*. 'Aven't seen her since this mornin'. Such comin's an' goin's, I never seen anything like it I'm sure. Look at that . . .' She glared at the blocked window. 'Messed all the paint, using pins an' that tape stuff . . . I wouldn't 'ave bothered only that young feller we 'ad round, he told me I better. Just like the war it's bin all over. I don't know . . .' She changed her tack abruptly. 'Want a cuppa?'

The normality of the question floored me. For a moment I couldn't answer. Jane said, 'We'd just love one if it isn't too much bother. But please don't put yourself about, Mrs . . .'

'Stilwell,' said the old lady. 'And it ain't no trouble.' She stumped for the kitchen. 'We still got gas, but the water 'as ter be *drawn* . . . Lucky we got a well.' I heard a clanking as she worked the old farmhouse-style pump. 'It's all right after it's boiled,' she said. 'It's good an' fresh out o' the well, always 'as bin.' She paused, 'Chalk,' she added, equivocally.

We introduced ourselves a little more fully. She was a widow, she'd been living on her own. A couple of nights before she'd woken to find the whole house swaying and groaning. But the quake had passed without doing any real damage. It was a miracle the village hadn't been destroyed, it stood well inside the Wiltshire meizoseismal area. Old Mrs Stilwell had lain and listened to the shocks tearing past. 'Like express trains,' she said. 'Just like express trains, all night long.' Sometime in the early morning the Army had arrived and set about evacuating the place. 'They had these trucks,' she explained. 'Just like in the war . . . Pilin' everybody in, I never seen nothing like it . . .' A percentage of able-bodied men had elected to stay and guard their property and Mrs Stilwell had likewise refused to budge. 'I told this young bloke,' she said. ' "I'm too old for this sort o' thing," I told him. "I'll bide. Got my son John comin' I have, we'll see what he says. Turnin' out in the middle o' the night," I says. "Never come across anything like this" ...'

The officer had evidently had little time to argue. He'd advised her to stay indoors and show no lights after dark. He'd said a truck would be coming through later in the day to pick up stragglers. But the truck had never arrived, neither had her son. Instead the Furies had come. 'Nasty hairy things,' said the old lady with great distaste. 'Crawlin' all over the place, you should just see the mess upstairs. Had the wardrobes over they did, an' all the stuff pulled out. Acted like they owned the place ...'

I said incredulously, 'The wasps got in here?'

She pointed at the wrecked door. 'What do ee think done that?' she said bitterly. 'Two of 'em there were, great hairy noisy things bigger'n dogs. Not as big as yourn maybe.' She nodded to where Sek was still sprawled on the hearth.

Jane had her eyes on my face. I wanted to ask the old lady why she was still alive but I didn't know how to phrase it. I said, 'What did you do, when the wasps got in?'

Mrs Stilwell compressed her lips at the memory. 'Couldn't *do* much, could I? Big lumpy things, fannin' everything down wi' their wings, rummagin' all over like they owned the place. Stuff all pilin' off the shelves ... I gid en one or two, I tell ee. Laid into en, but it didn't make no difference. Scramblin' about, you should see the mess they made. That were when they done the door, when I were lummockin' at en.'

I said, 'You hit them? What on earth with?'

'Carpet-beater,' said the old woman with a hint of pride. 'First thing that come to 'and ...'

I looked at Jane again and shook my head, baffled. The words conjured a crazy image. The Furies, deadlier than vipers and fast as cats, booming through the house with the indignant old lady puffing behind, swiping at the horrors with a common or garden carpet-beater. It was the first time I'd heard of the wasps not attacking on sight. These hadn't even retaliated. Just searched the place, quickly and destructively, looking for what? Victims? They'd had one treading close behind their armoured tails. The thing was a complete mystery. We tried to suggest less belligerence next time but Mrs Stilwell was firm. 'Not havin'' 'em in my house,' she declared. 'Not while I can do anythin' about it anyways. Not sittin' here lettin'' 'em have the run o' the place. Wouldn't be sense, would it?'

We gave up.

She insisted that we stay the night. We argued about it; we were sure our presence would constitute an added danger. But Mrs Stilwell was adamant; if we were to be killed, it would be in the Lord's good time. She clinched her argument by pointing at Jane's dress. '*Look* at yer,' she said. 'Bin dragged through 'edge back'ards, I shouldn't wonder...' And then, cunningly, 'What you needs, m'dear, is a good bath an' a change o' clothes. Got some things young Ellen left 'ere, my son's daughter; you can use them. Don't know when she'll be back for 'em now ... You'll have ter lump the water up from the kitchen but I reckon that won't 'urt, there's plenty an' enough in the well...'

Jane looked blissful.

We sat down an hour later feeling almost human again. Jane was neatly dressed in blue jeans and a white shirt, her hair was brushed again and glossy and I'd managed to shave. The old lady fed us with canned soup; it was all she had in the house. I hadn't realized until she set the bowl in front of me how hungry I was. While we were eating she elaborated her opinions of recent events. 'Just like the war it's bin,' she said again. 'All the time wonderin' if them Germans were comin'. My hubby were alive then o' course, Home Guard he was. We used ter sit an' hear them planes all the time, throbbin' an' throbbin'. Just like the war it's bin, them things flyin' all about...'

We tried to give her some idea of what had been happening but I don't think she took much of it in. She was more worried about her broken door. 'Have to get John to fix it when 'e comes,' she said. 'I tried, but my fingers ain't no good fer that sort o' thing no more. Time were when I could 'ave done it easy enough ... Only when 'e'll come is more than I can say...' She sniffed suddenly. 'Even the roses,' she said. 'Nice little standards I'd got, had 'em years. They took them orf at the roots, just snipped 'em through. Why they done that I don't know. I'm gettin' too old fer this sort o' thing, I didn't want no more on it...' She went back to the kitchen and we heard her calling her lost cat. Jane shook her head helplessly. It was hard to know what to say; after all there had been death here too, of a sort...

I slept between sheets again that night. Sek came upstairs with me. 'I don't normally take dogs,' said the old lady incongruously, 'more trouble than they're worth. But seein' how things are, it won't matter. Things aren't normal; you couldn't call 'em normal...'

My last conscious thought was of the Furies. I'd left the flame-thrower downstairs; it would be no use to me in the house and anyway if they did crash the windows I'd be dead almost before I'd had time to move. I was too tired to be anything other than fatalistic; I turned over, and was asleep almost at once.

CHAPTER 7

I WOKE AT dawn but somebody was up before me. From downstairs came sounds of hammering. When I got down Jane had fixed the door. She'd made a good job of it too. The old lady was almost absurdly grateful; she refused to take anything for our stay. 'No good havin' money no more,' she said fretfully. 'Went down to the shop yesterday, wasn't nobody there. Could've helped meself for all it mattered...'

We promised to try to get her some food. We left the house about half past six. I had no clear idea of what I intended to do. I carried the flame-thrower; I was beginning to get used to its weight.

Nearly the first thing we saw was a little garage. I went inside carefully. It was dark in there and cool, with that typical smell of petrol and oil and greasy rags. There were several cars in the place; one caught my attention at once. Just inside the doors stood a big stocker, garishly decorated along the sides with not very successful flame painting.

85

I walked round her. From the cab and chassis it looked as if she'd started life as a vee-eight Pilot, though the block that squatted between her non-existent wings had never been made by Ford. She carried no glass of course, and her doors had been welded shut. I saw that someone had reinforced her frame with what looked like lengths of railway line.

There was nobody about. I turned the ignition and touched the starter; the car fired and kept running with a heavy, irregular blatting from her exhaust. I switched off again. She was a temptation; she was the nearest thing to a tank I would be likely to find and she seemed to be in racing trim as well; it looked as if she'd just been overhauled. But it was useless to think of driving; to take any motor out on the road would be the surest and quickest way to the next world, I had no doubt of that.

Jane disagreed. She'd been ferreting round the back of the workshop. In one corner was a pile of mild steel rods; she pulled one out and brought it across. It was nearly an inch in diameter and five or six feet long. Obviously they'd intended using the stuff for further monsters like the one that was sitting glaring at us. Jane said thoughtfully, 'If there was a way to cover her windows, Bill. They aren't very big, and the wasps would never bite through these. We could get to Swyreford in a couple of hours if we could drive again.'

Something of the sort had gone through my mind but I shook my head. 'It'd take hours. And in any case it wouldn't be safe. Remember what they did with the Saracen. If they got on top we'd never keep them out.'

She said, 'But we've got the flame gun, they're scared stiff of those. If we went fast enough they couldn't land anyway, there's nothing for them to hold. If they tried they'd just keep skidding off. And we could go at night. They probably wouldn't even see us.'

She had a point there. I was crazy to think we'd ever get away with it but I was sick-tired of running; in the open we weren't safe from one minute to the next. I said, 'We'll think about it, love. Let's go find some food for the old lady. And we can see if there's anybody about as well.'

We searched the village. It didn't take long; it was only a tiny place, there weren't above a score of houses. One or two of the cottage doors stood open; I remembered the people who'd chosen to stay and went inside expecting horrors, but everywhere was empty. I scratched my head; there was something new here, a factor we hadn't come across before.

The last place we tried was a biggish house set back some distance from the main street. It was deserted too but we found a good stock of tinned food. We'd brought the haversack; I loaded it without too much hesitation. My inhibitions about that sort of thing had already gone by the board.

I found something else too, a rack of guns. I 'borrowed' a twelve-bore and enough cartridges to start a private war. I felt better for that; I'd been worrying about the fuel supply for the flame-thrower. I didn't know how long the shoulder packs lasted but they couldn't have much duration. We were heavily loaded by the time we got down to the road again.

We were very nearly jumped by three Furies. They came through the village low and fast, bunched together in a tight vic. We got under some shrubbery just in time and watched them go. They flew down the main street, swung right, and vanished; a few moments later they were back. They roared away in the direction from which they'd come. I glared after them. They looked just what they were, a patrol quartering captured territory to check for signs of resistance. I started to swear under my breath; in just over two days I'd been converted from a free, comparatively rational human being to something with about the status of a rabbit, a hunted thing that skinned under a hedgerow every time the wind blew. We let the sounds die away then Jane said urgently, 'We'll just never do it on foot, Bill. It's got to be the car.'

I said, 'Yeah, looks like it.' My heart came up into my throat and wedged there at the mere thought, but it seemed she was right. I stood up. 'Come on, let's drop the food off and go have a look at the thing again.'

I don't think I've ever worked so hard or so long as I did over that motor. I made a sort of bridle to fit over the end of the scuttle just in front of the firewall and welded bars at six-inch intervals between it and the roof. I was slow at first; as I got more practised I speeded up a lot. I'd used acetylene gear before, though not for a year or two. I fixed a couple of transverse struts under the first set for general strengthening, then treated the side and rear windows to a pair of bars apiece. I ran out of gas as I was welding the last of them in place. I had to leave the driving window alone; with our windscreen caged that was the only means of entry.

I stood back and studied what I'd done. The car looked more hideous than ever but she was as safe as I could make her. I tested the windscreen bars with my hands; they felt like the Rock of Gibraltar. I guessed the weak point would be the welds where they joined roof and doors. If things went as planned that wouldn't be put to the test; I could only hope we'd get through without attracting half the wasps in the West Country, if they came for us *en masse* we'd be finished.

I checked the time by the wall clock. Twenty to ten; the patrol had last appeared at eight and they'd been coming over at two-hour intervals all day, you could have set a watch by them. If we were going to clear the village before their next tour we'd better get mobile. We climbed aboard; I had a little trouble making Sek understand what I wanted but when she got the message she went through the window easily enough. The flame-thrower and the spare fuel can went between us on the front seat, I loaded the shotgun and propped it beside me with the barrel pointed out between the bars. Not very safe but I had no choice, I knew if we needed it we should need it in a hurry. Then I started up and edged out on to the road.

Our luck was lousy from the start. We ran straight into the patrol; why they'd varied their routine I don't know, they weren't due for another ten minutes at least. They didn't hesitate when they saw us, just dived straight in.

I tried to brake but I was nowhere quick enough. I was still moving very fast when the leader hit us. The tactic was obvious; had we been a normal car the thing would have come straight through the screen, probably decapitating the driver in the process. But of course we were far from being a normal car; the wasp struck the cage-work with a colossal wallop, bounced off, sailed over the roof, and landed somewhere behind us. The impact slewed the Ford across the road but the bars held. The remaining Furies zoomed clear at the last moment; before I'd got the Ford stopped they were heading in to the attack again.

Unexpectedly, I found I had all the time in the world. The

brutes needed a pretty long run-up. I hugged the twelve-bore, waiting for them to close. I'd had a fair bit to do with smooth-bore guns, this was more in my line. Jane was screaming but I let the wasps get nearly on top of the barrels before I fired. I was sitting awkwardly; the recoils nearly broke my shoulder but it was worth it. One of the Furies simply flew apart, came down in a spatter of pinkish flesh and black and yellow sherds. The other was grounded; I saw it crawl out of the ditch and hump painfully towards us. I rammed the car into gear and drove at it. The offside front wheel mounted its thorax but the thing didn't crack. It twisted its face like a puppy, trying to bite the tyre. Jane was shouting, 'Its head, its head ...' I reversed, yanked at the steering. There was a crunch, and that was the end of the fight.

I drove off like a bat from hell. I don't know why I instinctively assumed the things would be telepathic but I'd got no doubt the three we'd killed had been yelling for reinforcements as hard as they could. I watched the sky anxiously, expecting to see more wasps, but nothing happened. We got clear.

A few miles farther on I pulled off the road under the cover of some trees. I lit a cigarette, the last one in the packet. I won't pretend I wasn't feeling good. It was the first positive blow we'd struck and it had been pretty effective, we'd wiped up three of the bastards without any real trouble. Jane was grinning like a monkey. She said, 'It's all right, Bill, it works. We shall make it, they'll leave us alone now.' I looked for some wood to touch. We were still a hell of a way from the coast.

I was better orientated now and it did seem the sea was the best bet. If we could get to the water we'd have three Army camps between us and the wasps, Swyreford inland a few miles, Lulworth, and Colton each side of it. Surely they'd constitute a front line. And we'd be between the great naval bases of Portsmouth and Portland, they couldn't have been knocked out. I expected a lot of people would have had the same idea and that the area would be crawling with refugees but that was something we'd worry about when we got there. I was still assuming of course that the menace was limited; in actual fact the Furies had already extended their sphere of operations far beyond Salisbury Plain, striking north into the industrial Midlands and south and west into Dorset, while their scouts had linked up with the nests re-established in Somerset. Perhaps at the time it was better that I didn't know how hemmed in we were.

I didn't move again until the moon had risen. It was bright, a couple of days off full. That helped a lot as the car had no headlights. We made good time for half an hour or so then the sky clouded over. Simultaneously we came to crevasses again.

I kept going but it soon became obvious we'd travel faster on foot. I knew we couldn't rely on darkness much beyond four AM. It was difficult to know what to do; I didn't want to leave the Ford but it looked as if I was going to be forced to.

Jane gave me the answer. I was edging along, trying not to put my wheels down a yard-wide fissure that was just visible in the stray gleams of moonlight, when she said suddenly, 'If it's any help, I can drive.'

'What?'

She said, 'I thought if you were tired you might like a break . . .'

'I didn't think you were old enough.'

She made a noise like a bad-tempered pony. 'I could drive Daddy's car when I was ten, I used to go tearing round and round the flower-beds when nobody was about.'

'Could you cope with this one?'

'I think so.'

I said, 'Well there's nothing like finding out . . .' I stopped, put the flame-thrower out of the window, and got through myself. Exiting was considerably harder than getting in. I slung the pressure can on my back, went round to the front of the car, and squatted on the fender with a torch. That way I could signal Jane and call to her and we made a bit better time at least. She did very well; there were a couple of initial jerks that threw me back into the open rad core but after that she got the feel of the clutch and settled down. I suppose we made between five and ten miles an hour on the better stretches.

It wasn't enough. By four-thirty the sky was bright enough to make the torch unnecessary and Swyreford was still ten miles away. I took over again. All we needed was a bit of luck; one quick dash and we'd be home and dry.

We were five miles from the camp, with the hills dead ahead, when the way was barred by a great fallen tree. It was a nasty sort of thing to see in the dawn light; there were broken branches and huge black roots that seemed to writhe up miles in the air. Jane shivered, and I backed the car away. There was no chance of going round; the ground to each side was churned and broken, I could see the Ford bogging to her axles if I drove on to it. A hundred yards or so below the obstruction a lane branched off to the right. I took it. Within minutes we were spotted by the Furies.

I'd got my eye on a copse half a mile or so ahead that offered some chance of hiding, I'd been wondering whether to lay up there till the evening again. Some half a dozen insects came into sight ahead; I stopped instantly but they didn't attack. Within minutes I saw the reason way. The sky became full of the brutes, wheeling and circling. It went through my mind that after the incident of the night before they'd decided the car was an armoured vehicle and were proceeding accordingly. They were going to mob us.

I'm not sure what my feelings were at the time. I think after I realized we were as good as dead a sort of numbness set in. I looked at Jane; there were about half a hundred things I wanted to say but there wasn't time for any of them; the Furies were already coming in.

I can remember firing at the first wave of attackers, and the second and third. After that things got really hectic. Some of the wasps had already managed to land; we couldn't watch all directions at once and anyway I could only shoot forward. Two Furies were chipping at the back window and Sek was snarling and trying to get her head through the bars to reach them with her teeth. It was only a question of minutes before one of the insects got to the driving door, it was a wonder they hadn't found it already. The cab was full of fumes and my eyes were starting to smart. I yelled to Jane and grabbed for the flame-thrower. The gun was awkward to handle inside the car; she lifted the pressure container, I stuffed the nozzle as far through the windscreen bars as I could and pressed the trigger. The effect was startling. The wasps sheered off in all directions; I could hardly believe my eyes.

I pulled the starter, shoved the Ford in gear, and wound her up in first. The Furies had reverted to plan B; 'land where possible, ride vehicle until occupants emerge'. Only they couldn't ride the Ford; Jane had been right about that at least. We soon lost the little people from the roof and after that each boarder met the same fate. There'd be a bang and a slither, then just another wasp kicking in the road behind us.

I kept up the fastest pace I could and fortunately the driving surface didn't get worse. I managed to keep the things from coming to close quarters again but all the time I was conscious that we were being forced west away from the place we'd been trying to reach. I took three or four left turns, trying to circle back towards Swyreford, but it was no good. I got lost in a maze of back roads. I started to sweat again; the Furies stayed with us, booming overhead in a cloud.

By six AM I was out of the back blocks but the situation was getting desperate. I'd given up the idea of reaching Swyreford; I was wondering if I could get to the coast somewhere near Weymouth. By the look of the tank gauge we'd got petrol for another ten miles or so, after that what would happen was anybody's guess. I tried to tell Jane what I was doing; she leaned across and put her ear close to my face but it was still hard to make her understand. The row inside the Ford was terrific; the engine was practically unsilenced and the tyres were shrieking on the corners as the direct drive skidded us round.

We crabbed out of a final bend and the view widened ahead. Jane shrieked something and started to point. Away to our left the land shelved into a bowl a mile or more across; and for hundreds of yards, as far as I could see, the grass was covered by a weird encrustation. It was as if somebody had let a king-size bowl of porridge boil over and spill down the slope. It was a few seconds before I realized what I was looking at. It was a nest, or a city. The wasps had given up all attempt at concealment and allowed their woodpulp shanties to sprawl across the hill. There were combs and great brood cells all made of the same flimsy stuff; over them by way of protection they'd hauled all the junk imaginable, bolts of cloth and coco-matting, sheets of galvanized iron, chunks of linoleum, sections torn from fences, bits of furniture, even old motor-car tyres and wheels. It was like a mile-wide corporation tip. Above the rubbish the Furies hung in a golden haze; the thousands of wings made a deep rumbling, like the noise of a massive waterfall.

I didn't have any time to stare. As we came in sight of the crazy stronghold the number of wasps round the car doubled or trebled. Their buzzing rose to a fine pitch of rage; they were diving again now, repeatedly, hurling themselves at the windscreen bars. One of the brutes managed to get a grip on the cage; Jane knocked it clear somehow with the barrel of the flame-thrower. It fell forward out of sight, there was a crash, a hail of black and yellow chips. Steam gushed back. The wasp had torn up the fan, damaged the rad honeycomb. I hung on to the steering while the Ford was chucked from one side of the road to the other. I don't know how we avoided turning over. I saw the bars in front of me start to split under the battering; a few more wallops would knock the whole frame clear of the car.

The rain saved us. As I'd been passing the great nest I'd seen black clouds building up ahead; a couple of miles farther on the first spots lashed in through the windscreen opening. Jane spat and coughed and the next second we were driving through a downpour and I could barely see the road. I stamped on the brake, and realized that for the first time in an hour we were free of wasps. If they were still flying, their speed had been cut; they could no longer keep pace with us.

I throttled up again, forcing the car along. She was losing water fast, every minute we could gain was precious now. I squinted, trying to see through the rain. I was soaked already; beside me Jane was holding her arms across her face. I shouted to her and she looked round and yelled something about the engine. I called, 'It's all right . . .' We were climbing now, into the hills that guard most of the Dorset shoreline. Another quarter of an hour, twenty minutes at the outside, and we must reach the coast.

Abruptly the sea came into sight, grey-green and huge, dizzyingly vague, flecked with white where the squall was lashing at the waves. A turn of the road and we'd lost it again, but I knew where I was; just above Barford Regis, some six or eight miles east of Weymouth. I remembered the place from happier days; it was only tiny, a fishing village turned tourist centre, but there had been boats of all kinds there. I prayed to God they hadn't all gone.

We bounced down the hill into Barford with the engine knocking and missing and the fuel pointer banging against its stop. Whatever else happened, the car was through. I turned left then right, still half blinded, straightened up, accelerated, and drove on to the quay. The boats were still there; yachts and cabin cruisers, all sorts of craft. I saw armoured vehicles drawn up, a Saladin that looked very like Neil's, but there was nobody around. The place was another ghost town.

I scrabbled through the window, got up, and pulled Jane clear. I started to run, holding her arm and yelling to Sek to come on. The rain was pelting down harder than ever; I jumped some steps, on to a boat, across it to another ... My foot skidded, I nearly took a header in the sea. Jane grabbed at me; I rocked about, got my balance again, swung down to the deck of a cabin cruiser. She was locked; I turned round, looking for something I could use to break in. Jane was pulling my arm and shouting. 'Over there...'

We went back the way we'd come with Sek staggering along behind. The second boat was big, powerful-looking; for some reason I noticed the name on her bow. *Enchantress* ... The cabin door was slid back; I ducked through it into a little cockpit, saw a dashboard, a neat wheel. Jane collided with me. She said jubilantly, 'I can drive her, we had one just like her last year...' She twisted a switch, pulled something that looked like a starter. I heard the engine wake up; white water boiled under the counter and the boat swung out, snubbing at her ropes, 'Sek ... Jane, where's the dog...'

She looked up and I saw her jaw sag. I ran out of the wheelhouse, stood staring. They were coming; a long line of them, greyish dots in the downpour, water milling away from their wings ...

I heard Sek barking; Jane was yanking at me. She was screaming, 'Come on, oh Bill, come *on* ...'

But it was no good, we'd never race them with the boat. I could see it all clearly; to us it wouldn't matter if their flight range was ten miles or five or three. They'd take us, out on the water. They'd never let us be.

I knew what I had to do, it was just I couldn't make Jane

94

understand. I was trying to shove her off but she wouldn't let go. I bawled at her, 'Get in the cabin, get out of sight. Then head for the Isle of Wight...' I knew they'd follow the car. I could lead them off, lose them in the rain, circle back...

She had her feet braced on the deck, she'd got my wrist, she was pulling that hard it was all I could do to keep hold of the rail. She screamed, 'I can't...'

'Jane, for God's sake...'

'I can't I can't I can't...'

I swore at the top of my voice, twisted and shoved. I saw her fall against the wheelhouse and didn't wait for any more. I vaulted back on to the quay and started to run. I knew I shouldn't make it now, the things were too close, they were diving...

I'd forgotten Sek. She passed me as if I was standing still, racing to head them off. She hit the first wasp full bore; it didn't even check her. The Fury, already rain-sodden, bundled across the quay and fell over the edge. She fetched the second one down somehow, twisted out from under it, and smashed its head in her teeth. I skidded and fell, rolled across the ground, and saw a third insect come down astride her back. She writhed round but the sting was already darting in and out of her flank. She bucked convulsively, started a high jarring scream.

I collided with the car door, sobbing. I couldn't help my dog, she was as good as dead ... I got in somehow, grabbed for the starter. The engine fired roughly. I saw Sek's head bearded with foam, thrust up from a black and yellow ball of wasps; then the shrieking cut off and the whole fight rolled towards the water. I accelerated, a side street jumped at me, I hauled the wheel, there was a crash, a noise of glass, the car wrenched back straight and kept going. I howled through the little town not caring if I rolled the Ford and died. I was expecting the engine to seize. It didn't. Instead, I ran dry of petrol.

I got out. I was about five miles from Barford; the rain had eased, and there was no sign of the Furies. I walked off carrying the flame gun, holed up under the hedge a hundred yards away. I lay waiting, digging my nails in my palms. If they didn't come it would mean they'd stopped and searched, found

Jane ... I started to pray again. Let them come; dear God, let them be after me ...

They did come, a score of the murderers. They windmilled down to the car, crawled all over it, in and out through the glassless screen and driving door. I left them to it, I don't know how long they stayed.

It was dusk before I got back to Barford. The whole of the area was buzzing with insects, I'd had to take cover a score of times while they quartered the ground near by. Towards evening they sheered off and by the time I reached the houses everything was quiet. When I came in sight of the quay I saw *Enchantress* had gone; I ran the rest of the way to where the fight had been. There were no traces left; the rain had washed out any bloodstains and there was no sign of Sek, not a hair of her. I sat for a few moments with my head in my hands then I got up and looked over the water. The sun was setting behind a ragged mass of cloud; to the south-east, low down near the horizon, I could just make out a band of grey. The Isle of Wight. In front of it was a dark speck; I played with the idea that it was *Enchantress*, lying out there waiting for me. But I was being crazy, I knew it was only a buoy. I went looking for a boat of my own.

I settled for a sturdy fourteen-footer with an inboard power unit. At least I could start her, and the engine sounded smooth. There was plenty of petrol in her tank, and a spare gallon can in the stern locker. I didn't waste any time, just laid the flame gun down on the bottom boards, shipped the rudder and tiller, and headed out from the land.

I reached the buoy I'd seen and looked back past it; the coast was just a shadow. Ahead, the Island had vanished. Night was coming fast; I was afloat in a steel-grey void. Half an hour or so later a wind got up from the south-west, bringing with it a cold lashing rain. I turned up my jacket collar and hunched my back; my hand felt frozen to the tiller and I was shivering violently. Soon the boat was rolling and pitching and the waves round me were soaring and tipped with foam. The mainland had gone now, blotted out behind a watery shadow-show. I had no idea where the boat was pointed, and to make things worse she was starting to take water. I kept staring round, wanting to see a light and find it was *Enchantress*, but there was nothing. Just the rain hissing into the sea, and the dark. I started to lose hope. It seemed I'd spent half my life waiting for a light, waiting for a boat. But the boat had never come . . .

Some time that night the engine gave out. I'd managed to turn the dinghy into the wind, nearly swamping her in the process, and for a time she'd ridden easier, but with no way on her she simply corkscrewed about dropping into the trough of wave after wave. I tinkered with the little block, working blind; I dried out round the plug as well as I could and tried to swing her but it was no use. I thought about getting the oars out but I was past making an effort like that. Instead I found a dipper and tried to keep the boat as clear of water as I could. Towards dawn the wind fell and I sprawled down on the bottom boards, thoroughly worn out. I slept a bit; when I woke the sun was up and the sea calm. I looked round dizzily. I was close in to some odd-looking cliffs. They were grey-black and huge and looked to be made of a sort of peat. From beneath them long flat stone ledges thrust out into the sea.

I rowed in. When the boat touched I got out and dragged her up as high as I could. I dried the flame-thrower and tried to fire it. It worked, but the fuel cut out almost instantly. The canister was empty, and I'd left the spare in the Ford. That was it then; I slung the thing back in the boat.

Up close, the cliffs looked menacing. They were fibrous and bulging, sodden with rain. High over my head stone strata jutted like lines of amber teeth. I worked my way round the headland, scrambling over a litter of fallen blocks, and came to a bay. It was nearly circular and mill-pond-still. Beyond was a hillside of dull grass, blotched with patches of gorse and bramble. I saw a line of blackened brick cottages, a jetty stacked with lobster pots. I wondered where the devil I was; there was something mournful and grim about the place that didn't fit with any parts of the Island I remembered. Maybe I'd drifted right round it and come in on the southern side.

I walked a couple of miles before I got to a signpost. I stood and stared at it, then I sat down. I didn't know whether to laugh or cry. Dorchester nine, Poole sixteen. I was back on the mainland again . . .

I'd got to find another boat, start all over, look for Jane. I walked till midday, moving west parallel with the coast. The sun got hotter; on either side of me the heat began to shimmer. Eventually I reached a village. I still don't know its name. Halfway along the High Street was a pub. The front door stood open; I went in and shouted. Nobody answered. I collapsed against a wall, slid down it, and just lay. When I felt better I went behind the counter, knocked up the spile of the first barrel I came to, and poured myself a pint. I laced it with Scotch, raised it to the sky, and drank. It was a funeral party for one, the only ritual Sek ever had.

After that I just don't know what happened. I'd intended to push on, find another boat; but I was soaked through and stiff, my feet were bleeding, and I'd already spent half the night looking for one little girl on an ocean as big as the universe. I remember telling myself I had to rest, I'd just sit and drink another beer, maybe doze awhile, then I'd be away. The second beer tasted great. So did the third.

I think altogether I must have put down about four or five, and after that I couldn't have gone far if I wanted to. I hadn't eaten for a while of course; I suppose my stomach just couldn't take the swilling I'd given it. I tried to reason with myself but it was too late. The drink had hold of me and I knew I'd never done a damn thing right in my life and it was no use trying. I'd killed my girl and I'd killed my dog; I was beat, the wasps were everywhere, and we were through. Well, if I was only fit for getting drunk I'd try to make a job of it. I managed to edge my way back to the barrels, and poured out another tankard...

Some time in the afternoon Jane walked through the bar. I called her but she wouldn't come. She was smart; she stayed just outside the range of my vision, flitting about like a little wraith. Sek was there somewhere too, but I couldn't get her in. I pleaded with both of them, then lost my temper and damned them all to eternity. Then, mercifully, I passed out like a light.

When I came round it was evening, and very still. Sunlight was slanting across the village street, touching the stone roofs with gold. I sat up; the silence of the place was a reproach. I tried to get to my feet and pain clattered round inside my head. I swore, knuckled my eyes. My gutlessness had lost me a full day but it wasn't too late. It was never too late. I tried to think. Where to find a boat ... Get to the coast, find a boat ... find Jane ...

I heard an engine, and a sound of singing.

I stood in the pub doorway, rocking slightly from the effects of the jug-up. I was still glaring about vaguely when an ancient lorry came round the corner of the street, stopped alongside with a screech of worn linings. I looked up at it, trying to focus. The back was open and it was crammed with people. They were laughing and cheering and every other one seemed to be waving a bottle. I saw a little man in a striped, collarless shirt, three or four beefy farming types, a heap of girls with long untidy hair and leather jerkins, a bearded boy in a fisherknit sweater, guitar slung round his neck. It looked like an artists' colony gone haywire. I reeled round to the tailboard. I said thickly, 'Wha' the hell goes on ...'

Fingers gripped my arms. One of the popsies started to scream with laughter. Somebody said, 'Come on, whack, join the party ...' I landed in the truck and it careered off down the street. A bottle was shoved in my hand. A voice shouted, 'Drink up, th' war's over.'

I tried to take it in. 'What happened? Are the wasps dead?'

Laughter broke like a wave. A blonde lurched across the lorry, tried to grab the bottle, and fell over my knees. She jerked her thumb at the top of the cab, giggling. I looked up and for the first time saw the Fury, straddling the metal with its wide-spread legs and staring disinterestedly down at its human load.

CHAPTER 8

I DON'T THINK there's anything more sobering than being pushed into the company of a group of people who are all a few shades drunker than you are yourself. Within minutes of the lorry moving off, my head had cleared and I was able to realize, icily, just what sort of a fool I'd been. I sat huddled in a corner of the truck, steadying myself as well as I could against the jolting and swaying; round me the merriment went on unchecked. Bottles were drained and bowled lustily over the sides of the lorry while a dozen voices bellowed the praises of the seemingly endless herd of zoological freaks to be found at the Wild West Show. I tried to talk to one of the girls again; she got out a couple of more or less coherent sentences then her eyes glazed interestingly and she slumped back against the fellow next to her, who promptly started trying to force-feed her something from a hip flask. A few minutes later I saw her being sick over the side of the truck. It didn't seem to bother anybody unduly. I moved forward on hands and knees, working my way over a litter of crown corks, got to the little man in the collarless shirt, and yelled, 'What the hell's got into them, they all crazy?'

He was watching the wasp on the cab top, grinning and blinking nervously at it. He muttered, 'Not just now, later. Eh, mate? Not just now . . .' I left him and groped back to where I'd been sitting. He said, 'Not just now,' a few more times, mumbling it like an incantation with his eyes fixed on the Fury.

The lorry ground along, stopping from time to time to collect stragglers drawn to the roadside, as I had been, by the sound of its engine. None of them offered any resistance when they saw the wasp, just got up in a stunned sort of way. We crossed a wide heathland, moving as near as I could judge north-east away from the coast, passed through a couple of villages and one smallish town, all as deserted as Burton Middlemarsh had been. Once I saw an old man standing at a cottage door, blinking at the lorry as it trundled past. It didn't stop, and the insect on the roof showed no interest in him. I realized why Mrs Stilwell had had such a remarkable escape. For reasons of their own, the Furies were fetching in able-bodied survivors only.

The ride seemed endless. The knowledge that I was being dragged farther and farther from the coast and any chance of finding Jane was nearly unbearable. I was nursing some hope of dropping over the side and making a run for it but towards nightfall the idea was scotched by the arrival of a further guard of some dozen wasps. They formed a cordon, circling the lorry a hundred yards or so away. A short time later we pulled into the side of the road and stopped. There was some desultory talk among those who weren't too far gone to care. There was no apparent reason for the halt; we were out on the heath again, it was getting dark and there were no buildings in sight.

One of the airborne Furies came in low, circled, and landed clumsily on the cab top. It nearly pitched over on top of us. The guard faced it for a minute or more there was an industrious tapping of antennae. Then the newcomer took over, straddling its legs as the other had done and staring down at us. The first wasp flew off, heading east. A few minutes later I saw lights on the road behind us and soon another truck came into sight. Our driver started up and moved away and it fell in behind, convoying us a couple of lengths back. I could just see the pale blur of the driver's face. Beside him was something I took at first to be a doll or the head of a dog; then I saw it was a Fury, mask pressed close against the windshield. That cleared up one of the things that had been puzzling me at least; presumably our driver was carrying a mate as well.

A few miles farther on we halted at a filling station. It was a little place, set out in the wilds with no houses near. By that time I was desperate. Maybe I could slip off and get out of sight while the tank was being filled. Our driving door opened and a man swung down on to the apron, a tall, saturnine-looking fellow, bearded and dressed in black tee shirt and jeans. The cordon had drawn off; I could hear the wasps but they were barely visible. It seemed as good a chance as I'd get; I called out, 'Want any help?' and swung my feet over the side of the truck.

Instantly there was a booming. I looked back; the guard on the cab had lifted its body angrily and the mask was staring straight at me. I pulled my legs in sharply and the brute relaxed. They were taking no chances; only the drivers were allowed on the forecourt, the rest of us sat silently till the refuelling was finished. Soon after we moved off another truck joined us, then another, and by the time we'd reached our destination we were leading a column of seven or eight.

I'd been watching the sky-line ahead and for some time I'd been harbouring a nasty thought. My fears were confirmed soon enough; the lorries drove into the outskirts of Swyreford, passing row after row of the oddly bleak terrace houses the

101

Army seems to favour everywhere. They were deserted, their windows dark. Our driver was using his headlights now; I saw some of the flying guards had bunched ahead of the column. They were dipping in and out of the beams as they circled, sending long shadows flicking down the road. We turned in between a pair of white-painted gateposts, drove by a low building that looked like a guardhouse. There were more Furies on its roof. Ahead I saw a scatter of huts, made out the shape of a water tower against the sky. It looked as if after all my efforts I'd finally reached Neil's camp.

The lorry juddered to a halt and the rest of the fleet pulled in behind. Half a dozen of the wasps dropped to the ground in a rough circle round us. It was so obvious what they wanted there was no hesitation. Somebody dropped the tailboard and we got down, half-lifting one or two of the revellers who'd gone beyond the stage of helping themselves. When we were assembled the insects moved forward exactly like dogs herding sheep. We walked off uncertainly, afraid of attack. Nobody spoke. We joined other groups from the rest of the trucks but in the dark it was impossible to tell how many people had been rounded up. I was half-carrying one of the girls; the bearded man who'd been our driver had her other arm. We were crowded towards the nearest of the huts; I found myself jostled up against the door and tried the catch. It was open. I walked in towing the victim of Bacchus. The others pushed after me, hurried by impatient buzzes from behind. When about twenty of us were inside the wasps cut the rest off neatly and jockeyed them towards the next hut in line.

There were no lights; I groped forward, touched the end of a bed, swung round, and deposited my burden on it. Then I sat down on the next one. I was trembling from sheer anticlimax. About the last thing I'd expected was to find myself in an Army barracks again.

And still nobody spoke. There were sighs and grunts as people found beds and settled themselves on to them but that was all; I think we were too dazed and shocked to talk. After a time I swung my feet up and lay back, pillowing my head on the stack of blankets at the top of the bed. I lay till the moon rose and touched the end of the hut with a pale, colourless patch. I heard doors slamming and feet, the booming of

Furies, once the noise of an engine as some late arrival drove past outside. After a while the misty square of light started to advance and recede in front of my face. Then it seemed the brick surface had dissolved and I was looking at the moonlit Channel, the dim shape of the Island on the skyline. Jane was out there somewhere, over the water. That was where I would have been if I hadn't let myself get caught by the wasps.

I dug my nails into my palms. I wanted to get up, yell, run about, anything but just lie there. I felt a thick rage at the creatures that had herded me and shoved me about like an animal. When the fit passed I felt weak and sick. I lay trying to rest.

The moonlight vanished, leaving the hut as dark as the Pit. There were footsteps, penetrating the fabric of a dream. I sat up. It seemed I could hear with clinical sharpness. The noise passed. There was a sort of desperate urgency about it. Then there was a booming, a gasp and a thud, a shriek that rose on a sharp note of terror and cut off dead. For a while after there were indescribable sounds, an unholy slavering and groaning mixed with shufflings and buzzes. Then booming again, and quietness.

Nearer to me, inside the hut, a sobbing started. It went on steadily, dry and racked, the sound of someone at the end of their tether. My head was still spinning, whirling with images of Jane, but I knew somehow I had to stop that row before the panic spread and the whole hutful of us started screaming. I said sharply, 'The girl who's crying. Cut it out, you're not doing any good.'

She ignored me and simultaneously there was a drumming on the door, followed by scrapings and tappings. The sobbing stopped abruptly. I waited until the other noise had died away. Then I said, 'Unless you want the wasps in here with us you'll keep quiet. Now, who are you?'

'W-what?'

'Your name. What's your name?'

The darkness said uncertainly, 'J-Jill Sanders...' Then in a rising shout, 'I want to go home...' She started to whimper again. There was a scuffle, a noise that sounded like a slap. A deep voice said, 'All right then...' And after a pause, 'In the corner there, who are you?'

I said, 'Bill Sampson.' Then a little louder, 'Can't we sort ourselves out a bit, we're lying here like clowns. Who's the truck driver? I know he came with us.'

'Does it matter, mate?' That from the far end of the hut.

The deep voice said instantly, 'Belt up, it matters a lot. Greg Douglas here, from Bristol. Come on the rest of you, sound off. Who's on the bed next to Bill?'

Silence. Then from across the hut, 'Julie McGifford. Only I reckon she's passed out, like.' The man spoke with a north-country flatness. 'Len Dilks here. From Bradford, if it matters. I drove t'truck.'

'Fine,' said Greg. 'Go on, next bed up.'

'Owen Jones, from b-bloody Merioneth. How about g-gettin' out o' this dump?'

Instantly, a hubbub. And the drumming at the door, louder than before. Greg yelled us down. 'They've got sentries each end of the bloody hut, now stow it the lot of you. Nobody's getting out tonight...'

Another voice spoke, from farther down the barrack-room. 'Get on with it, mates. Freddy Mitchell, from Weston.'

'John Castleton, from Dorchester.' Then in a heavy-handed attempt at humour, 'Bricklayer's mate...'

'Harry West, from Bristol.' That voice I could place. The little man who'd been too scared to talk.

'Margaret Ellis. No fixed abode ...'

'Dave Kemp. Block chord guitarist. Mood music supplied, wakes a speciality...'

Once the process had started it gathered pace rapidly. Even the collapsed Julie woke up, demanding blurrily what was going on. And more important, did anyone have a bottle ... When we'd named ourselves Greg and the man called Dilks produced packs of cigarettes, shared them out among those who had none. We lit up cautiously, shielding the glows from the windows, and started swapping stories.

Most of our experiences were similar. Greg was an art teacher from a private school near Sherbourne; he and a friend had been on a walking tour of the Mendips when they'd been overtaken simultaneously by earthquakes and the Furies. The other man had been killed; Grey, an amateur spelaeologist, had used his local knowledge and taken refuge in a cave. He'd

104

holed up there, living on the stuff he'd been carrying with him, until hunger forced him out. Even then he was careful; he saw a lorry in the distance and took cover but he was flushed by a pair of Furies that dived unexpectedly behind him. He'd been in the second truck, the one that had pulled in with us at the filling station. Jill, the girl who'd been crying, was a Midlander who'd been on holiday with her parents. They had been in a cinema in Bristol when the quakes started, she'd been separated from them in the panic and hadn't seen them since.

Most of the first lorryload had in fact been hauled from Bristol; Harry West was a piano tuner who'd survived a wasp attack on one of the suburbs, Freddy Mitchell a scaffolding erector who'd been working on the redecoration of a ballroom. Owen, the Welshman, was a chef from one of the big hotels there. Len Dilks, the two girls Julie and Margaret, Dave the guitarist, and some three or four more were the remnants of a beatnik colony. Together they'd formed a jazz combo that they referred to somewhat diffidently as the Atlantic Eight. They'd been living in a couple of tents and an old bus, earning their food by odd-jobbing and playing nights in three or four dives in Bristol. They had weathered the earthquakes in the cellar of a big pub just off the city centre. When their audience scattered the Eight, showing a sharper instinct for self-preservation, had stayed put, huddled under one of the arches that supported the place. The building had come down on top of them but their only casualty had been the bull fiddle, which was stoved in by a couple of hundred pounds of masonry. Len was still grieving over it; apparently he'd loved the thing like a brother.

They had been trapped for a time before they managed to clear a way out. When they'd seen the chaos round them they'd promptly gone back to ground to wait for rescue teams. They'd existed mainly on the liquid resources of the place, playing bad jazz from time to time to keep up their spirits. Several big fires had started in the city, none at first close to the maimed centre. But by the third morning the flames had spread despite heavy rain until they were threatening the hideout. The colony sallied forth, more than a little pot-valiant, and repossessed their bus, which they'd left parked some quarter of a mile away. Then they'd tried to drive out. They gave a fragmentary but grim description of the burning city; the smashed shops, streets blocked with rubble, the bodies sprawled everywhere. What they had seen had sobered them for a time. They had made the best speed they could, heading south-east in a more or less woolly attempt to reach the wilder country of the Mendip plateau, get away from the big centres that were still being scourged by the Furies. A few miles out of Bristol the bus had broken down irreparably and they'd walked for a time before hi-jacking the lorry. They made good speed with that until they were waylaid by the wasps. Then it was a case of every man for himself. The Eight had scattered, only to be rounded up by the horrors and driven back to the truck. After that they'd picked up one or two walking survivors, Mitchell and Harry West among them.

They had driven most of the day, with stops for meals and refuelling. Seemingly the Furies had been in no great hurry. The Eight, philosophers all at heart, had set themselves to make the best of things, forgetting their troubles with the help of the hooch they'd brought along with them. That explained the circus that had finally caught up with me in Dorset.

The talking had taken my mind off Jane, temporarily at least. I asked Len how the devil the wasps managed to direct the trucks. He laughed shortly. 'Hit and bloody miss, mainly. If they wants yer to turn off like, or stop, they buzzes. If yer gets it wrong they buzzes harder, see? Don't know what'd happen if yer just carried on. Like as not yer'd get yer ruddy head cut off . . .'

Greg said intently, 'They know about the trucks though, Len. They know they need fuel, they stopped you at garages . . .'

He sneered in the dark. 'They don't know a bloody thing. They know cars pause at petrol pumps but they don't ruddy know why.' Apparently the halts had been enforced every twenty miles or so. At the first one the pumps had been dry. In spite of that the Furies had boomed threateningly until Len went through the charade of filling the tank. A few miles farther on he'd run out of juice. 'I thought I were goin' ter be done on't spot,' he said lugubriously. 'But two o' the bastards played footsie for ten minutes or so an' happen they worked out what were up. They let us off with a can anyhow. But I thought for a while I were goin' ter be done...'

I told them part of what had happened to me. I didn't say much about Jane. After I'd finished we tried to make some sense out of the situation. It was obvious the invaders had got a strong grip on the south-west; just how strong we had no means of realizing at the time. They'd played it pretty cleverly all the way along, for creatures struggling with totally alien concepts they'd done remarkably well. Their first strikes, delivered for the most part during the confusion of the quakes, had all been directed at key installations; power houses, telephone exchanges, broadcasting studios, military camps. In Portsmouth for example a score of the brutes attacked the power station, causing total confusion. The Navy moved in under cover of smoke and tear-gas but evicting the wasps from the great masses of machinery was like trying to drive out ghosts. They hid in the shadows and the din, attacking the emergency crews sent in to run the place; despite the guns and grenades it was more than anybody's life was worth to go inside the doors. Then the collier *Pompey Queen* ran aground off Spithead, her crew victims of the first attack the wasps ever mounted over sea, and within forty-eight hours Portsea Island, the great residential areas round Fareham, and most of south Hampshire were without electricity. Portland, Weymouth, and most of the South Coast towns suffered similarly while inland the limits of the captured territory were marked by London, Exmoor, and the Welsh Marches.

Within that huge area the Furies turned their attention to breeding programmes and the organization of what human labour their so-called central command thought would be necessary. Sporadic resistance went on for a time; in Dorset alone, independent units of the Territorial Army knocked out twenty or thirty nests. But as early as the third day the lack of any real communication and supply lines was making itself felt with vehicle after vehicle going out of action through mechanical failure or lack of petrol. By the time we were pushed into the hut at Swyreford organized operations were already, in the south at least, a thing of the past.

I slept towards dawn, woke with a thick head and a sour taste in my mouth. I'd been dreaming of Jane again, reality was nearly too much to take. I muttered and rolled over, realized somebody was shaking my shoulder. I opened my eyes. Sunlight was slanting through the hut windows on to rows of tangled beds, for the most part empty; leaning over me was a blond bearded man, broad-shouldered, and burly without being fat. He said, 'How're you feeling, Bill?' I knew the voice at least. This was Greg Douglas.

I sat trying to get things more into focus. 'Dead and alive ... What's going on?'

'Don't know yet. The wasps let us out anyway. Reckon on going to have a look?'

I stood up uncertainly. I was feeling the strain of the last few days, my legs were wobbly and I had a raging thirst. I followed him into the open air.

There were in fact some half-dozen separate camps at Swyreford. We were penned in one of the smallest. Looking back, I think the wasps must have chosen it because it still had mains water. From where we stood outside the hut we could see a stretch of the perimeter; it was guarded by Furies stationed every fifteen or twenty yards. They were clustered round the lorries too and across at what was evidently the m/t section, where half a dozen Champs and three-tonners stood otherwise unattended. There was no sign of any Army personnel; I realized there had been no uniformed men in the trucks either though there had been enough in the area. Maybe the wasps were killing soldiers on sight.

I felt at a loss. There seemed to be a couple of hundred civilians wandering about aimlessly, watched by Furies perched on the gables of the huts. There had evidently been no attempt at organization. Greg scratched his head. 'Well, somebody's got to start somewhere...' Beside our hut was a pile of empty crates and boxes; he walked over and climbed on to it, started shouting to get people round him. Two Furies took off almost at once from the top of one of the lorries; they howled round his head until it was quite plain the new régime was opposed to anything in the way of public meetings. He got down, shrugging. A few people had turned to stare; they looked away quickly as if scared of reprisals. We moved off in the direction of the cookhouse. 'Somebody's got to feed us,' muttered Greg, hunching his shoulders. 'Even if we're only here as spare meat rations we've got to eat.'

The canteen area was a shambles. Sacks of flour and potatoes had been ripped apart and spilled, vast tins of meat
opened and their contents half eaten. A few people were wandering about, touching this and that in a disconsolate way. In
the middle of the cookhouse, feet apart and a tally in his
hands, stood a small dark man. He was muttering, glancing
out of the windows from time to time as if to assess the
numbers present, licking a pencil and making quick calcula-
tions on the pad. He rolled his eyes when he saw us. 'B-bloody
state to find a place,' he said in a singsong voice. 'Feed 'em for
a week see, with a bit o' c-craft an' guile, but it needs a
workin' party.' This then was Owen Jones. I remembered he'd
claimed he was a chef.

Greg said quickly, 'Could you cope with the catering,
Taffy?'

He flicked a pointed, catty tongue across his lips, smoothed
his already brushed hair. 'If seven years in the C-Caterin'
Corps can't sort this lot out ... But needs a party see? I t-tried
to get things movin' a bit but 'twasn't any go. Can't g-get
bloody through to 'em ...'

Greg took my arm. 'Bill, try to round up that gang of
wandering minstrels or whatever they call themselves, God
knows they're a shower but they could be useful ... See if you
can get 'em along, I'll make a start here ...' He suited action
to words; in one corner of the cookhouse, lying asleep on a pile
of sacking, was what must be a missing member of the Atlantic
Eight. He was breathing stertorously, empty bottle gripped in
his hand. Greg took him by the scruff, and threw him through
the door.

I found the beats sitting in line, backs against the side of
one of the huts. They were amusing themselves by flicking
little pebbles at a grounded Fury that crouched watching them
about twenty feet away. With each missile the wasp clicked its
jaws angrily and raised its wings above its back. I relayed
Greg's message. They took it in stony silence, then Dave
Kemp, enthroned on a box with the guitar slung round his
neck, struck a few chords. 'Want us to go,' he extemporized,
'To cook an' mend ... Want us to go ... To scrape and
sew ...' I turned and walked off. I thought they were going to

stay where they were but they hauled themselves to their feet one by one and ambled after me.

When they put their minds to it they were first-rate workers. Within an hour we'd got the cookhouse more or less in order and two of the stoves were alight. Len Dilks sat on a table, a bucket at his side, peeling potatoes in a melancholy sort of way. He inspected each one he picked up as if it had done him some personal injury. The girls were setting out huge pans and dishes while Owen Jones – Jones Kitchen they called him, and the name stuck – was rushing about with some of the restless energy of an ant. By mid-morning we were cooking and people were starting to drift over to the canteen in a surprised sort of way. Three or four wasps clattered in and took up positions at strategic points but they didn't interfere. Most of our hut were present by then; Mitchell and Castleton, Jill Sanders and Harry West, twitching as ever when the wasps were in sight but outwardly cheerful. 'Gotta make the best o' things,' he said to me. 'Eh, Bill? Make the best o' things.' Sniff. 'Won't be too bad if we make the best o' things . . .' Greg raised his eyebrows and sent him out with Mitchell to scour the place for knives, forks, plates. It seemed few of the prospective diners had had the wit to forage for themselves. When it was finally dished up the meal was surprisingly good; the ex-chef had worked wonders with corned beef, tomatoes, and spuds. I for one was badly in need of food anyway, I hadn't eaten for over forty-eight hours.

The rest of the day we were left to ourselves. The wasps ignored us unless we strayed too near the lorries or the camp perimeter. I stayed on in the cookhouse helping tidy up. The afternoon was hot and completely quiet. Normally there would have been at least a background of traffic noise, now there was nothing. The odd boom of a Fury, the scrape of feet on gravel seemed to echo in the stillness. About four o'clock I saw Len Dilks being chivvied to one of the lorries by a pair of wasps. He came back in the evening bringing another dozen mouths to feed.

At nightfall we were driven indoors again. The guards knew exactly who belonged in each hut; some stray members of the Atlantic Eight tried to dodge in with their pals but the insects cut them out and drove them away. Events repeated themselves on the following day, and again after that. By the fifth day we numbered about two hundred and fifty and the food was running short. Greg brooded over what might happen when the camp stocks were exhausted. By a sort of natural selection he'd become the leader of our hut; in fact nobody on the camp had bothered to question his authority. He talked the situation over with me. In most of their operations the wasps had shown a high degree of intelligence, they must realize whatever their reasons for penning us we still had to eat. Greg thought there might be a chance of communicating with them; but one look at the expressionless masks convinced me at least that the idea was absurd.

Jones Kitchen was more hopeful. 'They're no f-fools,' he said. 'Was one in the cookhouse this mornin', messing about pokin' its b-bloody feelers into everything. I reckon they already know . . .'

He turned out to be right. Later that day Greg, Len Dilks, and myself were rounded up by a pair of Furies and shoved towards one of the lorries. Being hustled by the brutes was still unnerving though by now it was obvious there was no immediate danger. The truck they'd selected was a big, nearly new diesel, a much better job than the one we'd brought in. We climbed into the cab and Len started up and headed for the gates. Mercifully, the brutes decided it wasn't worth getting in with us; one perched on the roof, the other flew ahead circling as if to show us the road to take. We drove through Swyreton; I felt a terrific relief as the camp dropped behind us. Greg said quickly, 'You've been with 'em enough, Len, any chance of shaking the bastards?'

Dilks grinned sardonically and shook his head. 'Not a prayer. If yer tries owt, one in front comes back at yer see?' He gestured upwards with his thumb. 'If yer so much as speeds up, beggar on top starts knockin' ont' ceiling.' He throttled experimentally; almost at once we heard the deep noise of the Fury's wings. The wasp ahead turned and flew at the windscreen. For a moment I thought it was coming through; Len braked sharply and it zoomed clear. It was a pretty straight warning; after that he kept our speed down to thirty.

A few miles on we reached a village. It wasn't much of a place but it boasted a big self-service store halfway along the

111

High Street. Outside it the Fury hung hovering. So they did intend us to scrounge for food. Len brought the lorry to the kerb and stopped. We got down.

One of the street windows had fallen out entirely and another had had a hole smashed through it, presumably by looters. We climbed through. The place was buzzing with flies. The counter fridges had failed, the meat behind their long glass panels writhed with maggots. I tried not to look too closely.

One of the Furies had stayed with the truck, the other was out of sight but we could hear it booming faintly. I guessed it was circling above the place. There was no chance of running, whichever way we bolted we were sure to be spotted. We walked through to the back of the premises, found a storeroom packed nearly to the roof with cartons. We started loading the lorry. Greg did the selecting, I carried the stuff through the shop and passed it out to Len. It would have been handier to bring the truck round to the loading area at the back but we weren't sure we could get the idea across to the wasps and misunderstandings could obviously be fatal. After an hour or so the storeroom was looking decidedly bare and the lorry was piled high, the pavement round it littered with stuff. We pitched in helping Len stow the load. He'd kept a rough tally of the supplies as they came aboard; we checked through it, added one or two forgotten essentials like matches and salt. The guards seemed satisfied; we got in and headed back the way we'd come.

A mile or more up the road three Furies matched speed with us and landed on the load, then another one, then a couple more. By the time we reached camp we were carrying a dozen non-paying passengers. We drove straight to the cookhouse and the wasps organized a fatigue party. That was easily done, they simply cut out a dozen of the people who were strolling about and drove them across to us. We were through unloading by curfew time and walked back to the huts. There was less booming and snapping by the wasps now. It wasn't necessary, we all knew what was expected of us.

After that the lorry went out regularly. Our storerooms started to fill; it looked as though the Furies meant to stock up with as much as possible while it was available. I couldn't help wondering what would happen when current food supplies ran out; it was obvious we couldn't live off the towns indefinitely. Len was always the driver on the provision trips though the wasps never allowed the same people to go with him twice. He told me on a couple of occasions he saw other foraging teams, also directed by Furies, but he was never allowed close enough to talk to them.

About a week after our initial trip the lorry came back later than usual and instead of driving to the canteen it stopped outside our hut. Greg and I were the only two inside, we were lying on our bunks smoking cigarettes Len had smuggled in a day or so before. I didn't pay much attention till I heard raised voices. Dave and Harry West had been seconded for that trip, and they were arguing furiously. I heard Dave say, 'Well do the other bloody thing then, I'm sick and tired hearing you . . .' Then came a kick at the door. I opened it. 'What the hell — Christ, what happened?'

Dave said, '*Squirt* was what I called you, mate, a ruddy little *squirt* . . .' He was encumbered by having a girl in his arms. He was trying to carry the first-aid kit from the lorry as well. West was bouncing about behind him, face screwed up with anxiety. Dave said, 'Give us a hand for God's sake, take that bloody box before I drop it . . .'

The lorry moved away. I was trying to help Dave through the door. He dropped his burden on my bed and turned furiously on Harry West. The little man bolted. Suddenly there was silence. Greg had walked over to the bed and was standing looking down. 'Where the hell d'you find this, Dave?'

He was still breathing hard. 'Westrincham. Little place about ten miles out. Whole family killed. We heard this dog . . . Couldn't leave her like that.'

The casualty was a slim blonde in scruffy blue jeans and check shirt. She was unconscious; her head lolled to one side, long lashes brushing her cheek. Half her face was covered by a crude dressing; that, her hair, and the front of her shirt were caked with dried blood. Greg eased up the bandage, stood for a long moment looking beneath it. Then he said, 'Why'd you bring her here, what the hell do you think we can do?'

Dave collapsed on the end of the bed and glared at him, eyes bright blue and angry over a black stubble of beard. He

113

said, 'God, not you as well. I've had that little bastard yelling in my ear the last hour ... All right, I'll take her back where I found her and chuck her off the truck. OK?'

Greg set his lips and picked up the first-aid box. 'Bill, heat some water up will you? You'll probably have to go to the cookhouse for it. And get some disinfectant, Dettol, anything you can find ...'

When I got back there was a crowd round the bed. He'd coaxed the dressing off. I craned over his shoulder and wished I hadn't. The girl's face had been ripped open in a curve from the left corner of her mouth to the hair. Bone was showing at her temple but that wasn't the worst thing. The wound was flyblown.

Greg spoke without turning round. 'Try to find the girls, Bill. Julie, Maggie. See if they have a needle and thread between them.'

I could feel the sickness welling up in my throat. 'Christ, you can't stitch that—'

He said, 'It can't stay like this either. Go on, do it and don't argue for God's sake ...'

It was dusk before he'd finished. The wasps hadn't let me near the m/o's office, most of the camp admin area was still out of bounds to us. Greg had to make do with what we had to hand. I'd found a little camp stove, we sterilized a darning needle and some lengths of thread over it, boiling them in a saucepan. Most of us with the exception of Harry West gathered round to watch. I don't think anybody wanted to but there was a sort of ghastly fascination about it. By the time Greg had cleaned the wound it was dribbling blood again; Julie sat over the girl tensely, swabbing so he could see what he was doing. Somewhere along the line Jill passed out like a light. I felt I should like to but I couldn't quite manage it. I remember Greg wincing every time he drove the needle, as if the thing was going through his own flesh. Before he tightened each stitch he squeezed in antiseptic cream from the first-aid kit. With the cut closed he smeared the rest of the salve across it and taped a gauze pad lightly over the girl's cheek. When the wound was finally covered Len Dilks walked to his locker, came back with a half of whisky, and handed it to Greg. He took a swig, shuddered; then he said heavily, 'She'll be dead by morning of course.' He walked to his bed and sat looking at the wall.

Margaret and Julie finished the job, cutting the girl's filthy clothes away and washing her. She didn't regain consciousness. Her face was ashen, nearly as pale as the dressing. We left her where she was, I moved up to a spare bed at the other end of the hut. I hadn't much doubt that Greg was right, we'd get up in the morning and find her cold.

But for some reason she didn't die.

CHAPTER 9

DAVE TOLD me next morning what had happened. He was still shaken. Apparently they'd driven out to Westrincham, following the flying wasps as usual, only to find the place a charnel house. There had been no evacuation, either by humans or insects. There had been a wholesale massacre though, the bodies were still piled in the streets. The wasps had forced the crew to go through the usual routine of loading the lorry; fortunately they'd managed to find a relatively unaffected part of the town for that. They'd been on the point of heading back when they heard a dog barking. The Furies had seemed unduly excited by the noise. One of them zoomed off to investigate and Len followed up with the diesel. Dave said they had had some vague idea of bringing the animal back to camp but by the time they reached it they were too late. They swung right following the direction the wasp had taken and saw the dog in the road a hundred yards or so ahead. It was already twitching from a sting wound; the Fury was grounded beside it watching with the usual disinterest. Near by was a small tobacconist's shop. The window was smashed, the door stood ajar. It was possible the dog had run from there. Dave got down from the cab. He saw smudges of dried blood on the door-frame and the path. He went inside. There were several corpses lying around, some of them children. He didn't describe that part too closely. He thought he heard a noise from an inner room. That was how he found the girl.

He said she was conscious when he went in. At first he didn't see her; the place was dark after the sunlight in the street and she was huddled in a corner, crouched in a mess of blood and urine. His eyes hardened again at the memory. 'What a ruddy way to go,' he said bitterly. 'What a state to be in, I couldn't leave her like that. I'm no age,' he added, inconsequentially. 'Never seen anything like that before. I couldn't leave her like that . . .'

Outside in the road the Furies were booming impatiently. He'd tried to talk to the girl but he hadn't been able to make her understand. She was armed with a kitchen knife, he had to take it away from her before he could lift her. He carried her out, hardly knowing what he was doing. On his way back to the truck the wasps dived at him repeatedly, trying to make him drop her. 'I just kept walking,' he said. 'I was sick of the whole bloody business. I didn't expect to make it for a minute. I was hoping when they did me in it'd be quick.' For some reason he'd got away with his defiance. After a time the Furies had seemed to accept the state of affairs and lose interest in it. He carried the girl back in the cab, assailed most of the way by the complaints of Harry West. 'Peaceful coexistence is the motto,' said Dave disgustedly, and spat on the ground. 'Coexistence my arse . . .'

After that he changed his style of music. He used to play endlessly in the evenings, lying on his bed with the guitar; he worked up a thing he called the Fury Blues, a queer wild song about the girl lying in the death house and what the wasps had done to her, and the people, Harry West among them, who wanted to work under the insects for their crusts. Greg took him on one side and told him to pack it up, we'd got enough trouble without starting internal rifts. After that the words were no longer heard but the thing had an odd chord sequence and nothing would stop him playing that, over and over, working it into the fabric of other music until it became a symbol for all the foulness and misery we'd seen.

Julie and Maggie were good to the injured girl. Most times one or both of them would be by her, wiping her face or changing the dressing or just sitting waiting. She was half conscious on the second day and they pronounced her better. Then she relapsed into fever, moaned and tossed most of the night. The

116

crisis lasted through most of the third day but by evening she seemed to be sleeping naturally. The amateur nurses took a break; Julie wandered out somewhere, Maggie just curled up and went to sleep herself. She hadn't had much rest for the past couple of nights. I was sitting by the girl when she came round. I didn't know she was awake until something touched my wrist. She had her arm out, fingers slack. It was a shock to see her eyes open. They were a pale, indefinable greeny-grey, the sort of misty half-colour you see in sunlit water. Her face was delicately shaped, with a square jaw and small chiselled nose, and the eyes were tilted slightly and dark-rimmed. She looked like a sculptured cat.

Julie was still asleep. I called softly but she didn't move. On the floor near the bed was a tray with glasses. I filled one with water and took it back to the girl. She tried to sit up, staring round the hut. I held her shoulders and pushed her back. 'It's all right, keep still. You've been very ill...'

She whispered, 'Where is this place?'

'It's an Army camp. Here...' I raised her head as gently as I could and held the glass to her mouth. She drank half of it in sips then turned her face away. She said, 'You're one of the bastards that brought the wasps...'

'They didn't bring the wasps. They couldn't help it ... They fetched you back here. How do you feel?'

She licked her lips and looked at the cigarette I'd left lodged on the chair. She said, 'Got a fag, mate?'

I suddenly recognized her accent. She was a Cockney. That was about the last thing I'd been expecting. I said, 'I don't think you ought to smoke, you've been very sick.'

She said faintly, 'Gahn...' I picked the cigarette up and held it while she inhaled. She said, 'They got the old dog then. Ole dog...' Her eyes drifted shut. She lay still and when I spoke there was no answer, she was asleep again. I tucked her arm back under the blankets. Julie was sitting up a little vaguely; I said, 'She was awake, just for a minute. I called you but you didn't hear. She was talking.'

She said, 'Christ...' She rose and stood looking down at the bed with a queer half-awed expression on her face. She said, 'We never reckoned on this. You know, her gettin' better...'

By all the rules I suppose their patient should have died.

117

Maybe what Greg said later was right, the maggots in the wound checked the sepsis. I've heard of such things but I'm no doctor, I just can't say. The girl mended rapidly. In time the cut healed. It left a branching scar that quirked up one corner of her mouth in a perpetual little half-smile, and a patch of hair over her temple turned pure white. From what Dave had said it was obvious her family had been wiped out by the Furies but she didn't talk of it and nobody felt like asking her. All she said about herself was that her name was Janette Peterson, but she didn't like it. I got to know her like the rest simply as Pete.

Julie found her an old sweater and skirt from somewhere; the girls got her up and dressed about a week after Dave brought her in. The first thing she did was to go to the door of the hut. Maggie tried to help her but Pete shoved her off. Just outside our billet was a washroom set round with mirrors; she walked into it unsteadily, leaned on one of the sinks, and ripped the dressing off her face. She stared for a time, turning her head so she could see the wound, then she laughed painfully. She said, 'I could allus get a job in a sideshow then. The original scarred lady. Make me bleedin' fortune...' She sagged suddenly and Julie caught her. Pete hung on, let her help her back to the bed.

Maggie said the stitches had to come out by about the tenth day or they'd grow into the wound. Pete wouldn't let anybody do the job but Greg. 'You put 'em in, mate ...' she said pointedly. Julie held her while he was working. Pete made a little noise in her throat as each loop was cut and pulled clear. We were all sweating by the time the thing was finished. After that she left the dressing off and wandered about camp with the rest of us. She didn't mention her torn face again, and didn't talk about the Furies. But she watched them whenever they were near with a terrible intentness, those big eyes grey and cold as the sea. For a time I thought she was scared of the wasps. It would have been understandable. But it wasn't that; it was as if she had to study them, commit every tiny gesture and movement to memory. She couldn't see enough of them, or their ways.

Under the insects each day was like the one before, and the one that followed it. We'd wake up, eat, sleep, wake up again like machines. In the first week after we arrived half a dozen people tried to bolt. None of them reached the boundary fence. After that there were no more escape bids. There wasn't a chance of making it, it was just a picturesque form of suicide.

Our hut retained control of the cooking facilities. Nobody else seemed to care one way or another though as Greg pointed out they'd start to worry fast enough once they ran hungry. He was more sullen than he had been; he'd taken to vanishing for long stretches, I'd find him in odd corners of the camp sitting brooding with his hands clasped round his knees. At least I assumed he was brooding. I couldn't guess the way his mind was working and he didn't take me into his confidence.

The wasps relaxed regulations sufficiently to allow us the use of the workshops. I spent a day with Len coaxing a generator set to work and after that there was power for the machine tools and a limited supply for the huts, one bulb per billet. It seemed hardly worth our bother but at least it was something to do. After that Greg spent a lot of time in the m/t section; he always seemed to be tinkering with one or other of the lorries. He could get away with things that the rest of us couldn't though, if I tried to get near the workshops the wasps invariably drove me off.

If we'd expected any relief we were disappointed. There were no planes, no sounds of the outside world at all. Once we did hear firing. It went on most of an afternoon but nothing came in sight and the wasps stayed quiet, watching us from the hut roofs. That night there was another earthquake; none of the camp buildings were badly damaged but it was nasty while it lasted.

The morning after, Greg came looking for me. He said, 'Got a job on with one of the trucks, Bill, like to give us a hand?' I went along without asking any questions, anything was better than permanent inaction. We walked over to one of the shops and opened the front doors. Outside stood a three-tonner, ornamented as usual by a Fury squatting on the cab top. Greg walked over to it and the insect rose threateningly, ducking its body and booming with its wings. He put his hands on his hips and watched the display ca'mly. Then he said, 'I'm going to service this motor. Get out of the bloody way.'

I watched disbelievingly. For a moment nothing happened.

Then the Fury launched itself from its perch, roared past me, and climbed off into the sky. It settled on one of the hut roofs. Greg turned back and shrugged. 'Sometimes it works and sometimes it doesn't, but it's always worth a try.' He got into the lorry, started up, and drove forward over the pit.

I said, 'Greg, don't tell me they know what you're on about.'

He began to haul a jack across the garage. 'No they don't, but sometimes you can hustle them. As you saw.' He shoved the trolley under the back axle of the truck and started to pump the handle. 'Get a couple of stands, will you? Set 'em under the body then let the jack down a bit.'

I did what he asked. 'What are you doing?'

'Taking the back spring down.'

I frowned, trying to work one of the supports under the side of the chassis. 'There's nothing wrong with it.'

He said conversationally, 'Better get on with it anyhow, we're no longer alone.' I squinted out between the back wheels. A Fury had appeared from somewhere; it was standing just inside the open doors, twisting its head like a puppy to watch us both in turn. Greg said softly, 'Just keep on working and you'll be all right. Don't worry if what you're doing doesn't make sense. The bastards have no mechanical knowledge at all. That in part is why we're being kept alive. It's their one big drawback.'

'Who told you that?'

'Pete. And as it happens, she's right.' He administered a few pointless taps on the wheel-rim with a hammer. 'Get the wheel off then come over to the bench, will you? Take it all nice and slow . . .'

I found a spider and slackened the nuts, pulled the wheel clear, and leaned it against the side of the truck. Then I walked across to him. He had a replacement spring on the bench, he was touching it here and there with an oil-can. He started to talk again; he kept his voice soft, letting long pauses elapse between the sentences as if the words were of no moment. He said, 'I've had about enough of this, Bill. I'm getting out. Want to come along?'

My heart thudded; I tried to speak as casually as he had done. 'Wouldn't mind. How do you aim to go about it?' The

120

Fury clattered forward, sat behind us. I could sense it staring. I picked up a piece of metal from the bench, cramped it in a vice, and started filing it. He said, 'That's the idea, just keep the old façade going. Worries 'em to hell.'

'Night's obviously the best time. I shall want the lorry Len uses for the provision trips. If he can leave some stuff in it so much the better. If he won't drive it will you?'

'Why don't you take it?'

'Don't drive. Never been a thing I've been interested in.'

I said, 'I'll have a go. But I don't think it'll come to that. He's as keen to get out as us. They all are.'

He said, 'Contact him, will you? I shall want it faced towards the gates and not too far from our hut, if he can manage it. Tell him for God's sake to keep it to himself. When the time comes I'll talk to the rest. Till then I don't want it spread. Certainly not through camp.'

I said, 'Do my best.' The wasp on the floor seemed to have lost interest; it certainly wasn't paying us any particular attention. 'What are you going to do about our little friends?'

He got his cigarettes out, lit up, and tossed the packet over to me. 'There's only one guard per hut now. I'm going to shoot the bastard.'

The temptation to blurt out questions was very strong but it had to be resisted. I went back to the lorry and started dismantling the spring shackle. He came over to me in a while carrying the replacement spring and a shaped length of hardwood. He laid the wood along the side of the chassis as if checking its fit. I said, 'What do you shoot it with? There isn't a rifle on the camp. I know, I've looked.'

He said, 'Ever made a crossbow, Bill? They're a nasty tool.'

That time I didn't quite cover my reaction. The thing he was playing with had a roughly worked stock; I saw metal plates and brackets, a milled groove obviously intended to take the quarrel. I realized why he'd been so preoccupied with the workshops. He hadn't been wasting his time. A few minutes later he fetched the stave across. That was a piece of spring steel, drilled at each end to take the string. He fitted it to a mounting on the stock. The Fury assigned to us came across and spent some time tapping the thing with its antennae. I was nervous about it but Greg just laughed. 'They can't extra-

121

polate,' he said quietly. 'They recognize guns, and from what you've said they'd know a flame-thrower. This doesn't look like either; *ergo*, it's a part of the lorry.' He disengaged the weapon from the creature's claws and laid it up alongside the axle. 'Get a pencil will you, and mark this end? I think we're a bit overlong...'

While we were wrestling with the phoney repair job he told me what he intended to do. 'After we've fixed the guard we shall have about half a minute to get the truck moving, maybe less. With any sort of luck we should outrun them; Len says she's pretty fast.'

I said easily, 'What about crevasses?'

'Aren't any. Not the way I'm going. Straight up through Westrincham; Len says it's a good road. After that it'll be anybody's guess. But at least we shall have a start.'

'Where will you head?'

He said, 'Somerset. The Mendips. Used to do a lot of caving over there. I can fix us a bolt-hole the bastards'll never find. OK?'

'Negative. I'm for the coast. Isle of Wight.'

'Why?'

I hesitated. 'They won't get that far. Flight duration.'

He said grimly, 'No, of course not. Wonder how they got to England?'

I was quiet, realizing the hopelessness of the whole thing. The front shackle finally came apart; we moved back and started on the other one. I said, 'That bow of yours finished?'

'Yep. Ironmongery's over on the bench in bits. I've had it together. Looks pretty good.'

I said, 'I'm with you. Until we see what's happening at least.'

He pulled the spring clear and dropped it on the ground. 'Good man. I'll leave Len to you. But nothing to anybody else. I don't want a ruddy exodus.'

I collared Len Dilks in the canteen at lunchtime. It was difficult getting him away from the rest of the gang but I managed it finally. I put the idea to him the same way Greg had put it to me, quietly and casually; there were a lot of wasps present, perched on the roof-ties over our heads. Len didn't stop eating; nor did he answer for a moment. Then he said, 'When do yer want me to fix t'truck?'

'Next time you go out. Today, if they send you.'

He shoved his plate back and wiped his mouth on his sleeve. He said, 'Full tank and facin' hut. It'll be done.' He got up and strolled away.

From time to time through the afternoon Greg passed oddments to me. I slid them into my trouser pockets. There were bolts, washers, cog-wheels from the winding assembly; considering his limited resources he'd certainly done an efficient job. Last piece was the stirrup that fitted on the end of the stock. With that hidden we put the wheel back on the truck. I arranged a little incident, letting the jack down with a rush and staggering about as if I'd smashed my hand; it diverted the guard wasp while Greg shoved the stock down inside his trousers. It gave him a bulky outline but the insect didn't notice. I was just hoping I wouldn't clank. I'd got the bow-stave inside my shirt, and a couple of steel shafts for quarrels. Greg said there had really been no point making more than one. If the first shot missed there wouldn't be time for another.

We drove the lorry back outside and closed the workshop. A thin rain was falling and from the look of the sky there was plenty more to come. I hoped Len had been sent out, it looked as if the night was going to be ideal. When we reached our billet I saw the lorry had in fact gone. The hut was empty; lately most of the camp inmates had got into the habit of congregating in one or other of the main buildings. There were a couple of games rooms and bars, hardly luxurious but better than the barracks. We put the bow together. It was a complex affair. The string itself was a length of brake cable and there was a mechanism that wound it back against a ratchet. The stave could never have been flexed by hand. I primed the bow a couple of times and pulled the trigger. The cable fetched up against the stave with a hard, thudding crack. Greg took the weapon off me. 'Better not play, Bill. It sounds like a ruddy two-two.' He explained the Head of his school had been keen on all forms of archery. They'd made up a crossbow as a curiosity; Greg's lads had done the initial research, the carpentry shop and a local garage-man had weighed in helping build it. He'd been surprised by the deadliness of the weapon; on its first trials it had driven a quarrel through a two-inch oak plank. 'That's how I knew about making one,' he said. 'Otherwise, I wouldn't have known where to start.'

We pulled one of the lockers out from the wall and hid the bow behind it. A short time later the lorry came back, drove across to the cookhouse, and unloaded. I watched tensely as Len got in again and drove towards us. He parked within twenty feet of the hut door.

By nine, when the wasps herded the stragglers into the dormitories, the rain had settled to a steady downpour, roaring on the roof. Greg sat quietly on his bunk for another half-hour. I wished I had his nerves, I smoked half a pack of cigarettes while I was waiting. At nine-thirty he stood up and walked to the centre of the hut. He said softly, 'Bill, go to the door at the washroom end will you? Len, you take the other. The rest of you stay on your beds. I don't want any raised voices, and no arguing. I want you all to listen.' He explained briefly that he intended making a break for it. He said that we were armed and stood a good chance of success. He admitted that the rest of the camp had not been told and asked how many of the present roomful were prepared to go with him.

There was silence after he'd finished speaking. Then Dave, lying on his back with his arms clasped behind his head, said quietly, 'You reckon you're armed, Greg. What with? I haven't seen any guns.'

Greg nodded to me. I went to the locker, took the crossbow out, wound the cord back to the notch, and slipped one of the bolts on to the stock. They were eighteen inches or more long, half an inch thick, and pointed. I held the weapon up for the rest to see then rolled the quarrel off into my hand and laid the bow down again. Pete walked forward and picked it up curiously, hefting it for weight and balance. Then she looked round at us with her striking eyes. She said, 'I'm one, ducky. Any more for the Skylark?'

Julie got up instantly and went to her. She put her arm round her waist and gave her a little hug. She said softly, 'Two...'

'Three...' That from Maggie. She edged down as well towards the washroom end of the hut.

Greg said, 'And myself is four, Bill five ... you coming, Len?'

124

His face was sallow in the lamplight, eyes shadowed under deep brow ridges. He said, 'That's why I parked t'truck outside. I've seen enough o' bastard insects ter last me.'

'Six,' said Greg quietly. 'That the lot?'

Dave, still prone on the bed, stopped rotating his thumbs. 'Just because I'm idle,' he said, 'doesn't mean I'm not thinking . . . I'm seven.'

Greg looked at the others slowly, each in turn. He said, 'Hear the rain. Listen to it beat. The wasps can't fly through that. But it won't keep on for ever, we haven't got long. Owen?'

Jones Kitchen shrugged elaborately. 'I r-reckon I'll have a try, like. Fed up with b-bloody mass caterin' . . .'

Freddy Mitchell said guardedly, 'Now there's a point I've been thinkin' on, Greg. What happens to the camp if we move out? I mean, we're as good as runnin' it from this hut. And there's two hundred people here, over.'

There was a buzz of talk at that. Pete stepped forward stiffly, still fondling the crossbow. Her eyes started to rove from face to face. Greg walked across to a locker and leaned back on it, resting his hands on the metal top. He said, 'I don't think some of you have understood even now what this . . . irruption has meant to us or society at large.' He took a deep breath, eyes on the floor. Then he looked up again. 'I'm not a bloody prophet and I don't like playing God. You all know me, you know what I am . . . But I've had time to think. As you all have. And I think that of the two hundred people here, most will shortly die.

'There are no medical supplies. Soon there'll be no sanitation. No mains water or food. We're eating together, sleeping together. Soon we'll be sickening together. From typhus, from dysentery, from the plague. Bubonic, pneumonic. The good old Black Death, tried and tested. That's the sort of prospect you can look forward to.

'If the wasps all died tomorrow this country has still suffered the biggest disaster in recorded history. To my way of thinking the rest of the world's in the same sort of mess. Even with full resources I doubt we'd check the epidemics that are going to start. Have probably started already, somewhere or another. There'll be a chance, I reckon, for small isolated communities to hang out until the worst of the trouble's passed. That's what I aim to try to do. So answering your question, Freddy, I'm leaving this camp to die. As die it must, whether we go or stay.'

There was an angry chatter, stilled almost at once as he lifted his hand and pointed to the door. 'Out there are aliens. Monsters. Forms inimical to us that have taken us over body and soul for their own purposes. Think on that. I don't know what they are or how they came. I don't care. I can't *afford* to care. Neither can any of you . . .'

John Castleton was frowning, red face puzzled. He said slowly, 'I ain't much of a talker, like. Reckon I needs a bit o' time to think things through. But I says this. It might not be much of a life here. Likely we might take sick an' some of us die. But what you're talkin' about don't come to much neither, do it? Livin' in caves, scroungin' for grub. They blamed things'll hunt you down; you won't know no peace till they have.'

Greg turned swiftly. 'Peace? How much peace do you know here? Or you, or you, any of you? Peace? The cows in the fields know peace, before they're taken out for slaughtering. Is this peace?'

Castleton started to mutter angrily. Greg raised his voice, riding him down. 'What do you think you are, if it's not cattle for killing? Do you think you're the chosen few? Do you think the wasps have suddenly developed a sympathy for humanity?'

There was silence.

He said, 'Right, then. Before you crawl off on your bellies I'll plot out your life for you. Bill told you what he saw down on the coast. How the wasp colonies are expanding. Between now and autumn they'll increase their size a hundred times, a thousand. Next year they'll be bigger, the year after that bigger again. Already the population must be taking a tremendous, sustained effort to feed. They need meat. That they've already got, by the hundred thousand pound. I'll leave you to work that one out for yourselves. But they'll need other things. Sugar for the grubs in the first week of their lives. Maybe fruit in season. Building materials. Don't fool yourselves, they're smart enough to adapt to our techniques to suit

126

them. All that means transport. Transport and labour. People to serve the trucks, help run the nests. People to work the land, process its crops. That's why we're here, I reckon; and that's what you'll be doing, those of you who live through the plagues. You'll work for them. You'll plant and reap and build. They'll use you, once they start. And when you're finished, when you're tired, when you're worn out, when you're no good for work ... they'll still need meat. Meat to feed the racks of big, white, pulsing maggots ...'

Harry West was on his feet, narrow chest heaving, eyes blinking rapidly. He said, 'You're mad. All mad ...' He stared round at a ring of hostile faces. 'I'll tell you what he's tryin' to do. He wants to scare you. Yeah, that's it. Scare you so you'll run off with him. He don't care what happens to you, not him. He's already said so. He wants to run things an' be a b-big bloke. I knows his sort, that's all he wants. He don't care about none of us—'

Castleton said, 'Shut up, you bloody fool. I reckon he's right.'

The little man's face was twitching. He said, 'Well I'm not havin' it, see? Not me. I'm not puttin' up with it—'

Len Dilks spoke from behind him. 'Yer don't have to, whack. Just stop here an' be wet-nursed ...'

'An' what happens to us?' demanded West. 'Eh? You just tell me that. What happens to the ones as stays? What d'you think *they'll* do, them things out there? What's they do to *us*, when you've all run off?'

Greg said wearily, 'Come with us then. You've got your choice.'

He shook his head violently. 'That's where you're wrong. I haven't got no choice. All right for you, all right for you I say. You're young, all on you. You won't hurt, you can lead that sort o' life. I can't. Not no more. It'd kill me ...'

Julie said faintly, 'Oh God, spare us this ...'

Greg was looking haggard. 'There won't be reprisals. They're passionless, they're like machines. Revenge wouldn't be any good to 'em ...'

West said desperately, 'That's fine. That's all very nice. Knows what's goin' to happen behind his back now, he does ...'

Mitchell, the steel erector, moved suddenly. 'Open the bloody door, I'm tired o' this. Miss with that thing o' yours, there's enough here to fix a bloody wasp. Been wanting to pull one of their damned heads off for weeks ...'

Maggie laughed. 'Better sit down, Dad, where you won't get hurt. You can't stop us anyway ...'

There was a general, surging movement towards the door. Harry West's voice rose triumphantly. 'Can't I? Can't I stop you? Can't I do anythin' then, you all too smart ...'

Greg snapped, 'Dave, take him ...'

Dave Kemp moved with startling speed. One moment he was lying on his back, the next he'd launched himself in a sort of rugger tackle. But he wasn't fast enough. The little man eeled away from his outstretched hands. He was already screaming to the wasps outside. Greg was hit in the chest; he fell back, caught off balance. West came down the hut dodging and weaving. I tried for him, Freddy Mitchell had the same idea at the same time. We collided, rolled on the floor. The rest was confused. Voices were yelling desperately; somebody stepped on my hand, I was kicked in the ribs. I had a glimpse of the little man nearly at the door, a sprawl of bodies in his wake. The only person in front of him was Pete. I saw her jaw sag; she jerked the crossbow up, there was a heavy 'chunk' and a thud. I sat up, grunting.

The whole hutful of us were frozen in various attitudes of surprise. On the floor between the last pair of beds was Harry West. Pete was standing over him, her knuckles white where she was gripping the bow. The little man had half turned round, his hands were clenched across his chest. He made a queer noise, like a sort of hoarse giggle, and seemed to gesture to himself as if calling all of us to witness the enormity of what had happened. He grabbed the leg of one of the beds, half raised himself; then his arms and legs twitched together, a ribbon of blood ran from his mouth, he rolled over on his back and lay still. Protruding two inches from his body was the square head of the quarrel.

In the silence, Pete lifted the weapon until she was holding it out to Greg at arm's length. Her face was indescribable but when she spoke her voice held no expression at all. 'It works, mate,' she said.

There was a rapping at the door.

Greg moved fast. He yanked the mattress off his bed; a bayonet slithered across the floor and Freddy Mitchell grabbed it. Greg said, 'Up by the door, quick. If I miss, take him with that. Try and get the neck joint . . .' He snatched the crossbow from Pete, started cranking. 'The rest of you, anybody who wants the lorry, move like hell.' He slapped the spare quarrel on the stock, knelt in front of the door. The noise came again, imperiously. I grabbed the handle and Greg shouted. 'All right, open up . . .' I flung the door back and jumped out of the way.

It was nearly easy. The wasp hesitated when it saw Greg; he held the bow forward a bare yard from its mask and pulled the trigger. The bolt smashed its whole length through the chitin, tore into the thorax. The force of it rolled the insect back against the washroom wall. It lay kicking; Greg yelled again and ran for the lorry. I was hard on his heels. Something boomed at us in the rain, Greg batted it with the crossbow and it plunged away out of sight. The Fury on the cab top seemed half dazed. Freddy Mitchell jumped at it swinging the bayonet. The blade rang on steel; the wasp leaped convulsively, fell past the radiator, and rolled between the wheels.

I grabbed Pete, opened the cab door, and shoved her in. Len was already up on the other side. Greg followed us aboard, there was a bad moment as the starter yammered uselessly then the engine fired and we were careering towards the hut. There seemed to be people everywhere, tumbling over each other to get to us. Len gunned the truck away, looked back, swore, and stamped on the anchors. Dave was silhouetted against the hut door, running desperately, the guitar in one hand. I saw him hauled aboard and we didn't wait for any more. Len opened up heading for the road. The headlights snapped on, showed silvery curtains of rain. The gates swam up ahead, exploded in a white shower of fragments and there was a Fury, zooming to gain height for the windshield. Len swerved, the thing bounced off the door with a crash. The lorry clawed straight, accelerating; when I looked back the camp was lost in the darkness. We were clear.

I shall never forget that drive. Len held the truck flat out wherever he could, we had a long way to go before daybreak.

The rain lashed down, battering the glass between the arcs of the wipers. We hung on as well as we could, steadying ourselves against the swaying and bucking as the lorry leaped ridges in the road. We belted through Westrincham, crossed the Blackmoor Vale heading for Wincanton, Castle Cary. There were maps in the cab, we tried to navigate by the jazzing light of a torch while Len sweated and swore, wrestling with the wheel. Approaching the Mendips things got tougher. We swung off to avoid Shepton Mallet and Wells, then had to detour again to miss crevasses. Towards daybreak the rain eased; dawn found us high on the plateau, crossing a bleak landscape of undulating fields bounded by low drystone walls. Len knocked the lorry out of gear and coasted to a stop; we sat rubbing our eyes, trying to feel glad we were still alive. Then I heard a noise behind us. I wriggled round, stared through the back window. On board we had what seemed to be the entire contents of the hut. They were soaked to the skin and shivering, but they were singing like hell.

CHAPTER 10

THE PLACE Greg was headed for was located in a coombe running south-west away from the main plateau. He directed Len carefully, consulting the map and frowning from time to time. It was full daylight when we reached a crossroads and turned left. The road started to descend almost immediately. I was relieved; being off the table-land gave an illusion of security at least. Soon the big diesel was rumbling along a steep-sided valley, the slopes thickly set with bushes and trees. The lushness was a sharp contrast to the barren area we'd left. Greg stared up anxiously, watching the hillside. A mile or so along he said sharply, 'Pull in, Len, that's it.' He pointed.

At first I couldn't see anything. Then, following the direction of his finger, I made out a recess under an overhanging slab of rock. It was almost completely screened by bushes and grass. I said incredulously, 'That? That's just a crevice.' Greg shook his head. 'That's the mouth of it, Bill. That's Chill Leer . . .'

We got down stiffly. The passengers in the back had suffered from the cold, some of them could barely move. They stood round for a while chafing ankles and wrists and flapping their arms to restore the circulation. Len took the lorry off a quarter of a mile or so down the road; there was no point in advertising our presence by leaving it outside the cave. He hid it as well as he could behind a screen of bushes, draping a tarp over the cab to conceal the brightness of the paint. When he got back we started to climb.

Greg moved ahead, stepping easily across the hillside. I followed with Pete. We made slightly heavier going of it, in places we were both glad of each other's help. The rest of the party trailed along behind. The mouth of the cave was eighty or a hundred feet above the level of the road and the last few yards were almost sheer. The actual entrance was a bare three feet tall at its highest point. I ducked through after Pete and was surprised to find that once inside I could stand upright. The hole gave directly on to a respectable cavern. As my eyes got used to the half dark I saw it was nearly twenty feet long and proportionately wide. The floor sloped slightly into the hill and at the back were the entrances to three or four grim-looking tunnels. Greg told me all but one petered out within yards; the largest of them led to what was called a pitch, a vertical descent impassable without ladders. The shaft opened into a second cave almost directly below the first. That in its turn gave access to the main series deep under the hill.

When we were all inside Greg took charge. 'You're under-ground now,' he said curtly, 'and we shall be going deeper. Anybody done any pot-holing?'

No reply.

He said, 'Right then. Caving's got its own rules. You'll learn some of 'em as you go. The others I'll tell you right here. Don't forget 'em. Never move without at least one light and a spare. We'll fix up the gear later. Don't enter any passages you don't know. *Don't* wander off alone anywhere, for any reason. And, if you're in doubt about anything, anything at all, *do nothing*. Ask. Now then, let's count heads. You're a sorry-looking bunch, I'll say that straight off . . .'

He was right there. Most of the elation had passed; the party sat about mournfully, shivering in their wet clothes. One

131

or two, Jill Sanders among them, were already casting apprehensive glances at the black tunnel-throats behind us. We found we numbered fifteen; all the members of the Atlantic Eight who's been with us in the hut, Freddy Mitchell, John Castleton, Owen Jones, and three or four more who'd decided to risk it at the last moment. The main thing was obviously to dry off before we had three or four pneumonia cases; Greg organized parties to scour the hillside, keeping out of sight as far as possible. They were to look for brushwood, fir cones, anything that would burn. I paired off with Len Dilks; we worked down as far as the lorry, brought back the lids of half a dozen packing crates that had been kicking around in the flatbed. By the time we got back a fire of sorts had been started in the cave and eight or nine people, all more or less naked, were holding out steaming clothes to the warmth. There was something decidedly primitive about the whole scene; Len regarded it sardonically, then turned to look up at the tunnel mouth arching behind him. 'What did he reckon this place were called?'

'Dunno. Chill Leer, I thought he said.'

He sniffed. 'It's a right enough description, any road. But it'd be just the job fer a ruddy jazz club, wouldn't it . . .?'

Greg took us on one side. The truck had been empty, it was imperative we find food and water. There was a spring a few hundred yards down the valley, we could drink from that, but for food we'd have to wait till nightfall. The lorry would have to go foraging again. The hideout was ringed with towns, all within fairly easy reach; Wells to the south, Weston-super-Mare on the coast, Bristol and Bath to the north and northeast. Given a certain amount of luck we wouldn't run hungry. Greg called Jones Kitchen across from the fire. The ex-chef was enthusiastic. 'Got a bit of f-freedom of action, see, boy?' he said. 'Night shuffles, that's the thing now. A couple o' lads, and that shootin'-contraption o' yours, an' we'll see what we can't pick up. Surprisin' what you can do with a nice quick sh-shuffle . . .' He flicked his pointed tongue across his lips and grinned as if he could already taste the results.

I volunteered to take the lorry but Greg shook his head. He said with surprising acuteness, 'You get a whiff of the old salt breeze and I wouldn't trust you, Billy boy. You've got something over the water that's worth more than we are. Good luck to you, but I want the truck back ...' He chose Len instead, with John Castleton for mate. It was arranged they'd go off at nightfall, take the direction they thought best once they got on the road. We left them with Jones Kitchen, working out lists of foodstuffs and utensils; Greg had got another job for me.

Apparently about a mile away was a store where he hoped to find ladders, ropes, and other gear needed for scaling the pitches. He rated the equipment high in the survival stakes. Our main camp was to be located at the foot of the first drop; he maintained that would provide the best possible obstacle should the wasps ever attack in force. The descent was narrow, enclosed by jagged rock walls. The insects would find it nearly impossible to fly down; if they tried, they'd reach the bottom singly and be fairly easy to deal with. Greg wanted me to go along with him to help bring the stuff back; he said he'd take Dave and Freddy Mitchell as well.

We hung around but by mid-afternoon no wasps had come within sight. We'd had a couple of lookouts on the hillside most of the day but it seemed the insects weren't bothering with the area overmuch. The four of us started out, keeping well spaced and ready to dive for cover. The day was cool, with a blustery wind and a low overcast of cloud. As Dave remarked, it was probably bad flying weather.

We reached the store without incident. It was a little place set well back from the road, windowless, and with one heavily padlocked door. It took a while to break in but it was worth it. We headed back half an hour later loaded down with all sorts of junk, lifelines, helmets, torches, and coils of ladder, light-weight stuff with spidery steel rungs and nylon sides. We got back to the cave and piled the stuff in a heap.

Greg announced his immediate intention of going down below, asked if we'd like to team up with him. Mitchell wasn't keen; I looked round and saw Pete sitting by herself in a corner, hands clasped across her knees. She'd hardly spoken since the killing the night before and even Julie and Maggie had been leaving her alone. It was difficult to know what to say ... Most of the others were outside, lounging about within easy bolting distance of the cave mouth; I went across to her and asked if she'd like to come with us. She frowned at me for a moment, then shrugged. 'Ta, mate, might as well. Something to do, ain't it?' She got up and followed me into the tunnel.

Greg moved ahead, his torch beam flashing off the walls. We soon reached the pitch. The hole wasn't sharp-edged; the tunnel floor just steepened into a bulging lip. Beyond it was blackness. Pitons were already driven into the rock; Greg hitched one of the ladders to them and dropped it into the void. There was the briefest of pauses, then the 'thunk' of it striking the bottom. He eased himself over the edge. I followed him.

The worst part was at the beginning, where the rungs lay against the rock. They barely afforded finger and toe holds. Even the vertical descent needed care, the ladder had a nasty habit of twitching away from underneath me. Greg helped, steadying the thing from below. Towards the bottom of the drop the tunnel narrowed until, as I climbed, my back rubbed against rock. I reached ground eventually some thirty feet down, my legs already aching from the unaccustomed exercise. I landed on a slope of loose rubble; while the others were negotiating the pitch I had a look round.

It was obvious at once the second cave was a far better proposition than the first. It was almost as large, and two or three holes connected it with the open air via short passages of rock. The largest of the swallets, just big enough to admit a man, was almost covered on the outside with fern; the light filtering through was a pleasant green. Branching off from the main chamber was a veritable maze of side passages and tunnels. Some of them were shallow, with raised alcoves that would make handy sleeping quarters. Others stretched off into darkness. I listened just inside the largest of them and heard, very faint and far away, the splash and tinkle of water. Air moved against my face. It felt fresh and cold.

Greg came up behind me, shone his torch into the gloom. He said, 'While I'm here I'm going to set up the stuff on the main pitches. Anybody scared?'

No one spoke. He said, 'If you are I'd prefer you to say. Go into a cave series frightened and you've got a good chance of not coming out again.'

Pete laughed. She said in a brittle voice, 'We shan't meet anything worse than ourselves, ducks . . .' He didn't wait any longer, just stepped past us and started walking. I followed; I was uneasy but there was something oddly fascinating about these tunnels widening into the deeps of the earth. I'd barely realized such things existed. On the way, Greg talked. He told us how the series had been discovered a couple of years back by a group of geology students from Bristol. 'Leer' apparently was a variant of lair. It was an old name; there had always been rumours that a cave system opened off the coombe but the site of it had been forgotten for generations. The place was still incompletely mapped; there was a chance it would turn out to be one of the deepest systems in the country, but so far the way had been barred by a water-filled section of tunnel that he said was called a syphon. That was why the dump of equipment had been established; there had been plans for a full-scale expedition later in the year.

We got to the second pitch. It was far more awe-inspiring than the first. For some distance the floor of the tunnel had been shelving more and more steeply and the sides closing in; suddenly the rock fell away and there was space at our feet, like inky black water. Pete leaned out and dropped a stone. The missile raised clashing echoes; the landing impact sounded a mile down. Greg turned on her. 'Right, that's once. Now don't ever do that again.'

She said innocently, 'Sorry, dear heart. Somebody down there then?'

He snorted. 'Next time there might be. Just don't throw stones down pitches.'

Again there were pitons in the rock. He hooked a ladder length to them. A much bigger roll this time. Dave said, 'How deep is it, Greg?'

'About eighty feet. Take it slow, and try to keep relaxed. It's a long climb. Longer on the way back . . .' He swung down and disappeared.

It seemed an age before we heard his reassuring shout from the bottom. I looked over. The torch swam below like a glow-worm. I had a moment of giddiness and fought it back. I think it would have been worse if I'd been able to see what I was doing. I started to climb after him.

We stood at the bottom of the pitch and swung the lamp beams slowly. We were in a wonderland. We'd climbed through the roof of a chamber a hundred feet long and nearly half as wide. All round us stalactite formations hung like monstrous spears, joined roof and floor with brilliant columns a yard or more thick. Above and between them the rock glittered with whorls and bosses, like fan vaulting sketched in glass. Pete broke silence first. Her voice was only a whisper but the strange place heard it, threw back a sibilant husk of echoes. 'Christ,' she said, awed. 'It's like ruddy Westminster Abbey, ain't it?'

We walked across the hall, treading softly; the sensation of being in the nave of a cathedral was uncannily strong. The water noise got louder; we passed through an ante-chamber, reached yet another pitch. Shorter this time, and more enclosed. A few yards away from the bottom of it we caught sight of the stream. It issued from a fissure in the rock wall twenty feet or so above our heads, splashed over a series of ledges to plunge into a deep-looking pool. From there the water moved swiftly out of sight under a rock arch. We followed it, crossing a cavern lower and less impressive than the great hall, with fewer stalactite formations. Its floor was a sloping scree littered with slabs and chunks of stone, some of them a yard or more across. We had to climb over and among them; at the far end of the place the walls narrowed abruptly, the roof bulged down to touch the water. This then was the syphon, the current limit of exploration. We went back by easy stages the way we'd come, and reached the open air.

I spent the rest of the day on the hill, cutting bracken and spreading it to dry. Jones Kitchen and his party left at sunset, taking the crossbow with them; the lorry moved out soon afterwards. For the rest of us there was nothing to do but wait. The night was fine; I sat outside the cave mouth watching the moonrise, dozing from time to time and wondering about Castleton and Len. I badly wanted them to make it back; apart from anything else it was important to all of us that they did. The hunters returned just before dawn, gory but jubilant. They'd shot a sheep, using a battery bolt from the lorry as a quarrel, and Owen had bled the carcass and butchered it on the spot. They were loaded down with chunks of meat; that didn't do us any immediate good, we had no way of cooking it. The fire was out and we'd used all the fuel in the vicinity.

136

There was nothing to be done unless we wanted to eat the flesh raw. Nobody was that keen; we were hungry, but not starving.

By midday there was still no sign of the lorry. I'd given it up for lost when I heard an engine. We sat staring at each other hopefully then Greg got up and ran to the cave entrance. I was standing on the hillside with him when the truck came in sight. Len had started out southwards, he was coming back from the north, the way we'd used the day before. I saw the red cab, the bulky load lashed under a tarpaulin, then Greg jumped at me and knocked me flat. Straddling the roof of the lorry was a Fury, mask staring stolidly ahead ...

We wormed our way back to the cave entrance. I was sweating, Greg was cursing under his breath. All sorts of ideas went through my mind; the main one, the shocking one, was that somehow we'd been sold down the river, they'd brought the insects back to the hideout. The diesel stopped below us and I heard the driving door open and slam. There was a shouting. I peered back cautiously; Len was standing in the road grinning up at us. I saw him reach up and slap the Fury affectionately. The insect didn't budge. I straightened slowly, wiping my face. Greg got up alongside me. Len said, 'You look a right set o' nits, jumpin' about up there. Come an' meet Charlie ...' He yanked the wasp's head off, waved it at us, and put it back on the body. 'He's a right little Saint Christopher in his way ...'

We spilled out down the hill then, crowded round congratulating him. Up close I saw the Fury was little more than a shell; it only had four of its six legs and the thorax was almost completely shot away. The body was held together with wire and battens of wood, and lashed to the cab top so it couldn't slip. It had looked real enough at a distance though and apparently it had fooled the rest of the wasps.

We set to unloading the lorry. It was heavy work; they had everything imaginable on board, crates of food, cooking utensils, camp stoves, fuel for them, even bags of wood and coke. It all had to be humped up the path to the cave; there weren't enough of us to form an efficient chain or the job would have gone quicker. The essentials, the food, fuel, and kitchen gear, were sent up first, and Greg released Owen and a couple of the girls to start fixing a meal. When the truck was off-loaded Len drove it back down the valley. I went with him, filled half a dozen cans at the spring. We carried them back between us. Greg wouldn't let any of us rest until the last of the mountain of junk had been shifted out of sight. It nearly filled the upper cave; we sprawled about among it and on top of it, half cooked by the heat of Jones Kitchen's improvised range. I think the stew he dished up was about the best thing I'd ever tasted; half the mutton had gone into it, and anything and everything else that had come to hand. Nobody said much until the whole lot was finished; then Len handed out canned lager and beer, and pack after pack of cigarettes. He'd certainly done us proud, he'd brought back everything from full-strength Capstan to Balkan Sobranie. While we smoked he told us about the trip.

It had gone badly at the start. Wells had been unapproach-able; some furious activity was going on there, despite the darkness the sky had been booming with wasps. The lorry had circled away towards Bristol but they hadn't entered the city. 'Yer could smell the stink ten miles off,' said Len disgustedly. 'There'll be nowt comin' from there fer a year or two, I'll tell yer that right now...' He'd been forced to use the smaller towns and villages towards the coast. They'd started loading the lorry but it had seemed everywhere they looked they saw fresh necessities. It had taken them till dawn to collect all they needed and rather than spend the day in hiding they'd de-cided, daringly, to travel back in the light. 'I didn't think we'd come up against much,' said Len. 'Whole area were de-serted like.' He'd been wrong there, within minutes of starting they'd collected a Fury that had zoomed in to settle on the cab top. 'We carried t'little chap a mile or two,' said Len, grinning cadaverously, 'then happen he rumbled summat were up. He came down at t'window like, buzzin'...' They'd been armed; a well directed blast from a twelve-bore had shattered the brute before it had a chance to yell for help.

It was then that Len had had his great idea. 'We picked up t'bits and chucked 'em on top o't'load,' he said. 'We carried on a mile or two then pulled off and started buildin' t'dummy. It were a mucky job scrapin' him but I reckon it were worth it.' The dodge had worked perfectly; they joined a column of traffic moving north under the control of the Furies. None of the insects had investigated when they dropped behind and turned off the road. They had snatched a well-deserved couple of hours' sleep, then driven on across the plateau. They had seen a few high-flying Furies but they hadn't troubled them. I wondered what would have happened if any of the brutes had tried to call up their pal. Len shrugged. 'I didn't think too much about it,' he admitted. 'All I know is, it worked. That were good enough for us.'

The trick worked again the following day, and the day after. By that time we'd transferred part of the stores to the lower level and brought in the heather for bedding. I spread my heap in one of the alcoves opening off the main chamber, covered it with a piece of tarpaulin. It might not have been luxurious but I've paid to sleep on worse. Greg fixed a gantry over the cave mouth and lashed a pulley to the end; after that the loads were hauled the last few yards on the end of a rope. It eased things a lot. We rigged a sort of portcullis that could be swung down to close the bottom of the first pitch; it wouldn't stop an all-out attack but it would hold the wasps long enough for us to get a shot at them. Greg didn't think the swallets were too important but all the same we closed the mouths of them with iron bars wedged into the rock. Pete seemed to have got over the killing; she helped a lot with the gate in the pitch. I was working mainly in the upper cave, helping stow the bulk stores; I heard her arguing with the assembly team. 'Well hold the bleedin' thing straight, else how can I fix it . . .?' And again, 'No, dear heart, I don't suppose it will bed down, it's on me ruddy thumb . . .'

We only had one bad incident. That was when we were coaxing Jill Sanders down the pitch into the lower cave. She stopped halfway and began to whimper. I was standing at the bottom of the ladder with Greg; he stuck his head into the shaft and called up. 'What's the matter there?'

An urgent consultation at the top; then Julie's voice said calmly, 'She's claustrophobic . . .'

He was up the ladder instantly. He was very gentle; he talked the girl down all the way, one step at a time. It seemed an age before they reached bottom. They came down the last few rungs with a rush. I caught Jill; her face was chalk-white and running sweat. We got her over to the swallet, where she could see the sky. She was better there, but she never overcame her terror of Chill Leer. After that first experience she slept in the upper cave, close to the entrance. She vanished one night a week or two after we moved in. I often wondered where she went. She'd never been able to come to terms with the life either in the camp or the caves. Maybe she ran back to the wasps; or perhaps she just lost herself on the hills, wandered about, and died some place. Whatever happened, we never saw her again. We missed her; she'd never had much to say for herself and as far as the colony was concerned she was more of a liability than an asset but all the same it was a familiar face gone, the first gap in the ranks.

Apart from that the colony shook down remarkably well. There was surprisingly little bickering; I think from the start we were all too busy to have any time for arguments. Greg insisted that we stock up as much as possible while we had the chance; the lorry didn't stop going out till both the upper cave and twenty or thirty yards of passages were stacked to the roof with food and fuel. Catering for the clan didn't turn out to be as difficult as I had supposed; there was still plenty of live-stock on the hills, sheep and cattle running wild and a seem-ingly endless supply of hares. Jones Kitchen worked wonders. After the first week or so he rigged up a couple of contraptions he called trombone burners; he assured me they always appeared to be on the point of explosion. Some of his culinary feats were memorable and there was no end to his ingenuity; I remember being startled once to find out I'd been eating cooked stinging-nettles. They were very tender too. Without doubt though his best achievement was the acquisition of a dozen river trout. He skulked off with Len one night; they would never say afterwards how far they'd driven, though Len did tell me of a fearsome method employing a torch and a bayonet. He said it was the only time he'd ever felt grateful to the Celts for being thieves bred and born.

Julie and Maggie made a point of spending every other night with one of the men. Julie told me they'd worked out a rota; I've never been sure whether to believe that or not. She said she'd put me on it; there was something undeniably attractive about a night with a raw-boned, enthusiastic blonde but I turned the offer down. I don't exactly know why; I think it was to do with Jane.

I was thinking a lot about her. I knew I should carry on

140

looking for her but I couldn't quite make the break. In the caves I was accepted as part of a unit, a team; if I moved out I would be on my own once more, nobody to back me. I don't know whether I was more afraid of being killed by the wasps or of being shoved into one of their damned camps again. I talked things over with Greg. I told him one night, impulsively, the whole story about Jane and our trip to the coast. He listened carefully till I'd finished, then he shook his head, 'You're your own boss, Bill, you'll do what you want. I'd hate to push you one way or the other on a thing like this. But I say you'd be a fool to leave right now. I don't think you'd make it; there's a lot of country to cross and if what Len says is right most of it's swarming with wasps. In your place I reckon I'd wait a week or two, let the autumn get settled in. We might all be moving out then anyway.'

'Why?'

He said, 'Wasps die at the end of the summer . . .'

Up to then the elementary fact hadn't occurred to me. I sat frowning, turning it over in my mind. 'Do you reckon these brutes will snuff it then? What happens if they live right through the winter?'

He said, 'Wasps never used to.'

'They never used to be three feet long either.'

He shrugged. 'Well anyway, let me know if you decide to risk it. I'll get one of the girls to pack some stuff for you.'

I made my decision. 'I'll stick. For another week or two anyway. But it'll be rough just sitting waiting.'

He looked at me through suddenly narrowed eyes. 'Who'll be sitting waiting? I reckon the nests will die back but like you said it's a long chance. It isn't worth risking. I'm going after the bastards.'

I was startled. 'How the hell are you going to do that?'

He ran his fingers through his long hair. 'Not too sure. I've got one or two ideas and what you've said has given me some more. But I don't want to talk about it yet.' Further than that, he wouldn't commit himself.

He might have been thinking about an offensive but it was Pete who brought things to a head. We were sitting round the cave a couple of evenings later; the meal was finished, the portcullis strapped in place for the night, and I don't think any

141

of the rest of us were considering starting a war. One of our half-dozen Tilly lamps had been lit at the back of the cavern; under it Dave sat with the guitar, strumming softly, singing snatches here and there, some bawdy, others not. Julie was mending a tear in her shirt; she'd taken it off to do it but we were more or less used to that by now. Jones Kitchen sat by the swallets, newspaper spread to catch the last light of the setting sun. The brilliance burned on his wrists and cheekbone, haloed his dark hair. I leaned across to see what he was reading. A six-month-old copy of the *Financial Times*. I started to grin. 'How're the investments going then, Owen?'

He shook his head sorrowfully, unsmiling. 'P-pepper's down a farthin' a ton. I r-reckon I'll sell . . .'

Pete laughed with the rest of us; then she pulled a haversack towards her feet, opened it, and tossed something into the centre of the cave. The head of a Fury, jaws gaping.

Maggie yipped and jumped back out of the way; Dave froze, fingers stifling the guitar strings. Suddenly the atmosphere was totally changed. I saw Jones Kitchen fold the paper quietly and set it down; Julie put her shirt on with consummate dignity and stared at the trophy that lay on the rock. 'Thanks for the present, darling,' she said coldly, 'but it isn't Christmas yet . . .'

Greg spoke angrily. 'Throw that thing out . . . where the hell d'you get it, anyway?'

Pete smiled at us all. 'Found the little dear on the hills this afternoon, cuttin' the guts out of a sheep. He died happy . . .' She picked the head up and started playing with it, opening and closing the mandibles. 'There's still a few of 'em about, actually. Just thought you'd like to know . . .'

Greg swore. 'I said throw the bloody thing out . . .'

'No,' said Pete gaily. 'It's nice . . .' And she put the mask to her face, crooning and rocking it like a baby.

Greg was across the cave in two strides. He slapped at Pete and the mask together; the blow sent the thing spinning across the rock. Pete stayed still, head down, hands spread flat in front of her. She was trembling. Suddenly I wanted to go to her and hold her but you didn't do things like that with Pete, she wasn't exactly the blushing rose type. I think Greg was feeling the same; he said thickly, 'Why do you do this sort of

142

thing to yourself . . .?' Then he turned, faced a dozen pairs of eyes. He said slowly, 'I suppose you all understand what she was getting at?'

No answer.

He took the silence for agreement. 'Unfortunately, she's right.' He reached down and shook Pete's shoulder. 'Come on, you're not hurt.'

She turned a bright face up to him. 'I'm all right, dear heart,' she said lightly. 'What was you about to say . . .?'

He went on dourly. 'Nobody else has done anything about the wasps as far as I can see. It's not enough to sit here and scratch each other's backs. We've got to hit the nests. The brutes have overrun enough of the bloody country already.'

Dave laid the guitar aside. 'I know this is where we came in, but what are you going to hit them *with*, Greg?'

The blond man walked out of the cave into a side passage. He was back in a moment carrying a bottle. It was filled with a colourless liquid and had a rough wick trailing from the neck. He set it down where we could all see it. He said, 'With these, mainly. The prototype contains water. The production jobs will be filled with petrol.'

A sharp intake of breath from somewhere; then Len said tonelessly, 'Molotov cocktails . . .'

Pete edged forward until she could touch a bottle. She handled it curiously, the way she always did with something that interested her. She said, 'Can we get close enough?'

Greg squatted tailor-fashion on the floor of the cave. He felt in his pockets, produced a stick of chalk. 'Anybody that wants out can go. If none of you are interested the scheme's dead. But here it is anyway . . .'

I slept badly that night. For the first time I'd managed to see us in perspective as tiny expendable units caught up in a world-tide of events; for a while Chill Leer had provided the illusion of security but in nightmare even that left me. I seemed to see the rock floor splitting, the whole gang of us, Greg and myself, Pete, Len, Dave, Maggie, and Julie, whirling down through chasms of dark to where the earth finally closed with a monstrous, silent gnashing. I woke up, sat sweating. Grey light was filtering through the rock chambers; it was just after dawn.

I felt I had to get out into the open air. I walked through the main cavern, empty now and dark. I could still see the faces as we'd sat in firelight and lamplight and listened to Greg talk. At the time there'd seemed some point in what he wanted to do. Now there was none.

I climbed the pitch. In the upper cave the light was stronger. I edged past the stacks of crates. Outside, the grass of the hillside was wet with dew. I leaned back against the rock and closed my eyes. There was singing.

I sat up sharply. Below me Pete came along the road, a water can in each hand. I stayed where I was while she climbed up to me, dumped the containers by the cave entrance. She said, 'What's the matter, dearie, had a bad night?'

I nodded. She peered at me then laughed. 'Looks as if you'd took a short course o' death . . .' A pause; then, 'Comin' up the hill?'

'Why?'

She said impatiently, 'Oh come on, it's a ruddy smashin' morning.' She got up and I followed her. We worked our way past the cave mouth, climbed across the slope above to the crest. At the top Pete stood with her hands on her hips, outlined against the sky. There was a slight mist; the sun was struggling with it, breaking through in pearly bursts of light. Somewhere far off a bird was singing; apart from that there was no sound. Just a breathing hush. Pete looked back at me. She said, 'S'funny, ain't it? Like there wasn't no people. Or no wasps. Wasn't ever goin' to be . . . I like it when it's like this.'

I didn't answer. She said quizzically, 'What's up then, don't wanna beat the old nests up?'

I sat down on an outcrop of rock. 'It looks like it's a thing we've got to do. But I reckon it's just a good way to get our throats cut.'

She shook her head impatiently, flicked the short, tawny hair out of her eyes. 'The bastards are as thick as two short planks. We can do 'em in. You just gotta know how to hit 'em right.' She came and squatted at my feet, picked a blade of grass and started to nibble it. Then she looked up. 'We shall be all right,' she said, perkily. 'Be like takin' pennies off a blind man, you'll see.'

'Pete...'

'What?'

I hesitated. Then, 'Where did you get that thing, that head? Did you kill a wasp for it?'

She said shortly, 'It didn't give its bloody self up. I was out on the hill with a rifle, I sort of stalked it a bit. Got it first time. Double top, straight through the nut. Wasn't no trouble.'

I said, 'It was a pretty good shot.'

She looked at her hands. 'Yeah. I'm good at killin' though...'

I swallowed. 'Look, I'm sorry, I didn't mean—'

She cut me off. 'Don't matter. It's done, ain't it? Won't change that. But I think about that little bloke a lot though. The look on his face. Like he couldn't hardly believe it. Poor little bastard...'

'It was an accident, you can't blame yourself...'

She said gently, 'It wasn't no accident, Bill. I aimed the ruddy thing. It was a good shot...' She finished the grass, spat, and picked another blade. She leaned back on her elbow, looked round at the hills emerging from the mist. She said, 'It's funny, y'know. I used to miss the Smoke to start with. But I wouldn't go back to it now. Not if I had the chance.'

I felt around for cigarettes but I'd left the packet down in the caves. 'Had you been out of London long?'

'Couple o' years.' She grinned. 'Hell of a row there were, when the old man told us we were goin'. "I've bought this shop," he says. "We're all gettin' out in the country afore these 'ere bombs gets active. All you kids'll have horses," that's what he told us. "An' we can go an' watch 'em makin' the cows sit on all them little bottles," he says. "Bit of all right, that'll be." That were just like the old man. Never a word to nobody till it were all fixed up, the shop an' all that. He was doin' all right too. Nice little shop that was...'

She stopped speaking suddenly. She'd got on to forbidden ground; her face set, her fingers crept up to touch the scar on her cheek. She sat brooding; then she jerked herself out of the mood. She stretched and yawned. She was very neat and boyish; her breasts pushed softly against the thin material of her shirt, her jean-clad legs were strong and slim. She watched me for a moment with a mask of innocence, then she rolled

145

over and got to her feet. She said, 'Oh well, s'pose we'd better go and give them lazy baskets the wakey-wakey ...'

Three nights later we moved out against the Furies.

CHAPTER 11

GREG'S PLAN was fairly simple. The target chosen lay north-east of us, in a coombe sloping from the hills towards the Bristol Channel some ten miles distant. A road ran up the valley passing close by the nest site; Len was to take the lorry out at nightfall, circle round, and get in position on the road about a mile away from the wasp fortress. Meanwhile an attack party some half-dozen strong would make its way across the hills on foot, edge in over the high ground, and get as close as possible to the nests. That would need caution, Greg said there were sentry insects every few yards. The signal to attack would be given by the truck; Len would drive in flashing his lights, sounding his horn, and generally kicking up as much din as possible. It seemed certain the guards and any other Furies that managed to get airborne would go for the lorry *en masse*. When that happened Len was to drive out like hell, trusting to his speed to take him clear. He'd stand a pretty good chance; the glass had been taken out of the cab and the windows pro-tected by grilles similar to the ones I'd built on the Ford. In addition he would be carrying a couple of passengers with twelve-bores. In the confusion the real attackers would close in the rest of the way, light the wicks on a score of petrol bombs, throw them, and make themselves scarce. We would wait for a wet night; Greg reckoned that hampered by darkness and rain there would be little chance of the wasps catching up with us.

The Furies were by this time in the third stage of their culture. The earliest nests, those from which they had mounted the attacks on Berryton and Yatley, had been built underground in the traditional way though of course on a vast scale. The comb layers and nest wall hung from a central sup-port, usually the root of a tree; as the nest enlarged so the

146

globular space was made bigger and bigger to accommodate it. The construction method had severe limitations; the later huge nests could never have been made like that, the labour of excavation would have been enormous and anyway the structures could never have supported their own weight. The interim period was marked by 'shanty towns' like the one I saw, though as an emergency measure I'm inclined to think they were a failure. I doubt if many grubs reached maturity under those conditions. The nests ringing the Mendips were of a more successful type. Most of them were built round living trees; a comparatively slim sapling was good enough as it rapidly became strengthened and buttressed by the insects' own wood-pulp. The branches were lopped off and the cell tiers slung round the trunk while a domed canopy of pulp layers reached to the ground all the way round. Usually too there was a three- or four-foot excavation inside the finished nest so the lowest, most massive brood-racks were still below ground level and protected from frost and damp. The domes were joined by partially or wholly buried tunnels of wood-pulp; the finished layouts looked like groups of igloos, or the trench systems of the First World War. One odd point was that despite the innovations they made in every other direction the Furies kept the habit of building their brood-cells mouth downwards, opening on the undersides of the combs. Why that configuration, with all its attendant hazards to the grubs, was maintained so stubbornly I couldn't imagine.

On the third morning after Greg announced his intentions I went out with him to have a look at the target. A thin drizzle was falling, interspersed with bouts of heavier rain. We were making a final recce, it looked as if that night was going to be it. When we came in sight of the nest I was startled by the size of the domes. It seemed they'd swollen almost overnight; some of them must have been thirty yards across, and proportionately tall. They clustered thickly along the valley bottom, dark brown with the rain but still showing golden stripes and striations on their sides where the water hadn't soaked the pulp. Scattered among them were half-finished nests; on those the bottom of the supporting trunk was visible under a ragged canopy of wood-pulp. They looked like gigantic surrealist umbrellas. There were tunnels too, in all stages of construction, and despite the weather hundreds of Furies were booming overhead or scuttling between the domes. The noise of the place alone was impulsive; it sounded like the roar of a busy city. Which in effect it was . . .

Our vantage point was above the nests and some half-mile away. We peered through a screen of bushes, inspecting the place with field-glasses. While we lay there Greg stiffened; then he gripped my arm and pointed. I trained my glasses round and saw what had startled him. Visible among the wasps were human figures. We were too far off to make out what they were doing but they were evidently working unmolested by the insects. It was the first evidence we'd seen that Greg's theories were right; these must be labour gangs from some neighbouring camp. Greg swore violently. 'What a ruddy chance they've got. One box of matches and whoomph . . . they could flatten the whole place, save us the bother.'

I wasn't so sure. Most of the slaves were nearly stripped; I said, 'Could be they search 'em. You know they don't take any chances . . .'

He snorted and wriggled back. Out of sight of the wasps he lit a cigarette. He said, 'Well that's it, Bill. How do you rate us?'

I said, 'Pretty good I should think. A few incendiaries among that lot, well spaced, and it'd all go up. Eggs, grubs, breeding queens, everything. But I'm still not happy about getting clear.'

He said curtly, 'We'll make out. They'll be too panicky to know what they're looking for and anyway we shall be gone before they get organized. What few are left. Most of the bastards'll be chasing the lorry, the rest ought to be cooking quietly.' He looked up at the sky. 'Better get back I reckon. If this lot keeps on we're in business.'

The raid went perfectly. I was in the main party with Greg, Dave, Freddy Mitchell, and a couple of others. We closed in as soon as the lorry lights appeared below us. The bombs went down one after another, bursting among the nests. Flames licked up; in the light we saw dozens of Furies milling aimlessly, uncertain whether to attack us or the truck, which was by then moving off at high speed. We didn't stay to let them decide. We separated and made the best speed we could

148

back to Chill Leer. Dave was the only casualty; he went down the pitch too fast, fell the last few feet, and sprained his ankle.

I lost my way in the dark, I was the last one back. We waited anxiously for Len and his mates. It was another hour before they swung down the ladder. There was a lot of cheering and backslapping; Jones Kitchen had heated a vast bowl of soup, everybody sat down to a meal. Len reckoned they must have driven halfway to Cornwall before they managed to shake the wasps. They'd circled then, laid up for half an hour, and joined a column of vehicles northward bound from Yeovil. Apparently the Furies now permitted traffic to move at night. The rogue lorry had driven through Wells then turned off for the caves. Len said to the south were nests by the hundred. The headlights had picked out a sea of roofs.

By three in the morning quite a lively party had started; Greg broke it up at four and we got what sleep we could. We lay up for the following day and the day after that, feeling better than we had for months. We went out again later in the week, hit a nest complex to the east of us. Once more the decoy worked excellently. That time Pete came with the attack team. She stayed by the nests longer than the rest of us; when she got back she described with relish how the roofs had collapsed, disclosing thousands of grubs writhing in a bed of flame. As far as she could see the destruction had been complete. We were jubilant; our efforts might be a drop in the ocean but it was something to be hitting back at all.

We tried the trick again ten days later but we'd overplayed our hand, we were lucky to get away without losses. As soon as the lorry lights appeared the threatened nest erupted into life; but the Furies didn't attack the decoy. They flew in the opposite direction to where our people were lying. I was one of the base party for that trip; Greg told me later it had needed some pretty fast work to get clear. Only one bomb was thrown and that burst on the edge of the nest area and burned out without doing any damage. Len said he had seen wasps hurling themselves on the flames, smothering them with their own bodies. The lorry had driven close enough to fire into the nurseries but the Furies ignored it. It was only on the way back the vehicle had run into concentrations of insects. There had been an

149

anxious few minutes while it fought clear. Apparently by that time the wasps had given up searching for our infantry.

The retaliation was obvious. The following night Greg reversed his technique. The target was a huge nesting area straddling a minor road a few miles from Bath. One man was delegated to light a fire some half-mile away from it. The rest of the group piled into the diesel, and it was the truck that did the real damage. It was a bold scheme, but it worked. When the lorry came in sight of the nests the usual exodus took place; the wasps boomed off in scores searching for the imaginary attackers. While they were keeping busy the truck drove right through the nests showering incendiaries to either side. Despite heavy rain the flames spread like lightning; some of the domes literally exploded as superheated air rushed into them from the linking tunnels. The glow lit the sky for miles.

That night the jug-up did go on till dawn. I'm sure if any Furies had passed within a mile they'd have heard the din. I got pretty merry myself; I didn't intend to, I'd been off drink ever since the Dorset episode, but I think somebody laced my beer. Towards morning things got really hectic; I can remember Maggie, high as a kite, swearing she'd dance the Seven Veils if only Dave could play Ravel's Bolero. The party broke up at six. We'd rigged a trip system halfway down the pitch; a fine wire grid was suspended across the shaft, linked to contacts in such a way that if it was touched it started alarm bells ringing all over the complex. Jones Kitchen, going outside for purposes of his own, accidentally set the thing off; the resulting panic sobered even the worst cases and shortly afterwards we turned in. Greg had been intending to lie low for a time; he said it was a good thing, he doubted whether any of us would be fit for a month.

I woke with a nagging headache sometime in the afternoon. I lay for a while but the caves were quiet as a morgue. Most of the colony were either outside taking the fresh air cure or still sleeping off the jag. I got up and spent an hour clearing the main cavern of the evidences of orgy. Pete turned up when I was almost through and we got rid of the last of the debris together; then I helped her carry bundles of clothes through the corridor to the great pitch. She did most of the washing for the group; usually she humped it down to the water source

150

rather than going outside to the spring. She said it was safer but I don't think that was the real reason. The caves fascinated her, she'd spent hours brooding in the silence under the stacked hills.

I lowered the bundles and followed her down the ladder. We crossed the hall of the stalactites, reached the third pitch and the cataract. Pete kept candles down there, we lit a couple to conserve the torches. She got busy lathering the clothes, rinsing them in the icy water of the pool and heaping them on the rock. Later she'd spread them on the hillside to dry. I helped her; when she'd finished I walked over to one of the rockfalls, climbed on to it, and lit a cigarette. Pete called across to me. 'By the way, dearie, it's bath night. Don't mind, do yer?'

For a moment I didn't realize what she meant, then I saw she'd kicked her shoes off. She stripped quickly; apart from the shoes she was only wearing shirt and jeans. She slid into the pool, swam across, and stood up knee-deep on the other side. She started to lather herself, panting with the cold. She said, 'You still plannin' on leavin'?'

'Don't know. Could be.'

'Still the same place?'

I said, 'Still the same. Isle of Wight.'

She chuckled, then swore as she got soap in her eyes. She flung her short hair back, sending water droplets sparkling in the candlelight. She said, 'You know, I reckon you've got a bit o' spare over there.'

I was startled. 'I wouldn't put it quite like that...'

She laughed again. 'I reckon you're deep, mate. Dead deep ...' She finished scrubbing, ducked under water, and came up spitting. She climbed out of the pool and stood towelling herself; in the uncertain light she looked like a frail sketch of a woman. When she was dressed she climbed up to me. I lit another cigarette and gave it to her. She took it, watching me gravely. 'Penny for 'em, ducks?'

I said a bit dryly, 'You've got a lovely body ...'

She said indifferently, 'Ta ...' She drew on the fag, eyes lowered. 'That were a right little knees-up last night, wadn't it? Proper little do. Poor old Maggie really got goin' ...'

'Did she ever do her Salome act?'

Pete shrugged. 'Dunno. Don't think so, I reckon she passed out . . . It were a proper do though, while it lasted.'

I said, 'I suppose they thought they'd got a lot to celebrate.'

She shook her head, smiling lopsidedly. 'It wasn't that. They're just cashing in afore the old luck runs out.'

'Why should the luck run out? We've done all right so far.'

She looked at me very straight. 'Who're you kiddin', Bill? The bloody wasps'll do us. Bound to. Might be next trip, might be the one after. But they'll get us if we keeps on. Stands to reason, don't it?'

'I thought you reckoned burning nests was a pushover.'

'It were, first time. But it's gettin' dodgy now . . .'

I was silent. She said suddenly, 'Why don't you get out while you've got the chance? You'd get to the coast all right, you did before.'

'What about you?'

She said lightly, 'I'll stick for a bit. It's a laugh, ain't it?'

Suddenly I was sick of the whole business. Killing the wasps was like trying to kill a principle; we weren't achieving anything, she knew that as well as I did. She was just offering her throat to the knife . . . I said abruptly, 'Pete, when did you decide you were tired of living?'

She stood up and flung the half-smoked cigarette into the pool. She said, 'I'm goin' back up. Some of 'em might come round in time for supper, you never can tell. Give us a hand, will you?'

Our luck did run out, a week later. Greg had decided to hit one of the big complexes southwards towards Wells. We recce'd the area as well as we could. The main road ran southwards through a gap in the hills; we decided we'd use our number two approach with the decoy fire. There were odd domes all over the flat country: getting into position to start the blaze was going to be the trickiest job. Greg said he'd fix that; Len would drive the truck as usual, his passengers would be chosen by lots. Pete drew a long twig, so did Owen and Julie; Freddy Mitchell went along, and John Castleton. Greg rode out with the lorry; it was to drop him a mile or so short of the target then wait an hour while he got into position. The truck moved off at sunset. If things went well it should be back soon after midnight. I sat up most of the night playing cards with Maggie and Dave. Waiting was always bad but this time it was worse. I had a hollow feeling of impending disaster. I just couldn't get rid of it.

By dawn there was no sign of the truck and we knew we'd got trouble. We talked it over; it was decided that if nothing had happened by mid-morning Dave and I would go out to try to find what was wrong. By nine o'clock we'd had enough of sitting around. We took a couple of shotguns, some water, and a flask of brandy and edged down the hills, heading south the way the lorry had gone. It was a perfect morning, still and bright. For a time we saw no signs either of wasps or humans.

We met Greg an hour later, by sheer chance. He was as much in the dark as we were. He said the lorry had dropped him as arranged, a mile or so south of where we stood. He'd got into position ready to start his diversion but the truck had never arrived. Instead the whole area began to swarm with wasps. They'd kept him pinned most of the night, he'd only just managed to circle back. His clothes and legs had been ripped by briars and there were dark rings of tiredness under his eyes but he said he was game to go on. We started walking again.

We were still in the hills. About a mile ahead the road swept round to the right, descended through a wide valley to the flatland and the nests. We were a couple of hundred yards away from the bend when Dave gave an abrupt exclamation and pointed. We stopped dead; ahead of us, sharp-edged against the blue sky, a thick cloud of black smoke had appeared. It rose steadily, turned to a column that arched away sullenly towards the south.

I don't know why we all started to run. We could have been heading into any sort of trap but the idea didn't enter our heads. We rounded the corner and pulled up again, horrified. On our right the hill rose in a long curve, its face thickly dotted with clumps of bushes and gorse. The road ran away in front almost straight, bounded by drystone walls. About half a mile ahead the lorry lay on its side, thirty or forty yards off the carriageway. It was burning fiercely.

We reached it gasping for breath. There was nothing near it. The heat was intense; at twenty yards I could feel it wavering on my face. Apart from the crackle of the flames there was

153

no sound. The smoke rose steadily, trailing its thick shadow across the grass.

There was something weird about the whole business. The hillside, the sunlight, the lorry burning itself away in the quiet morning. We walked round the wreck, trying helplessly to see into the bright inferno of the cab. While we were still undecided a voice spoke just behind us. 'Yer can save yer trouble,' it said bitterly. 'There's nobody t'help . . .'

I jumped round. Len Dilks was sitting some twenty feet away beside a clump of bushes. His face was ash-grey, glistening with sweat; it looked more like a skull than ever. He was holding his left arm across his chest. Part of his shirt had been torn away and wrapped roughly round his hand. The dressing was soggy with blood.

We got him away, holed up in the bushes a couple of hundred yards from the wreck. The smoke should have attracted every Fury for miles but none had appeared. Greg poured half the brandy down his throat; it brought him round enough to tell us what had happened. The whole operation had gone wrong; somehow the wasps had known the lorry was coming. They hit it before it was even in sight of the nests, hit it in hundreds. They clung so thickly to the windscreen bars Len had been unable to see or steer. The truck had been moving fast; he'd braked, but not soon enough. The first impact had smashed the door open and he'd jumped. He could remember that but the rest was a blur.

Greg took his shoulders. His face looked haggard. 'Len, try to think . . . How many were killed? *Try . . .*'

He shook his head helplessly, licking his mouth. Then the words came. 'Two . . . in the cab . . .'

'Who, Len? Who?'

He said thickly, 'Castleton. Mitchell . . .'

I said, 'Why'd you burn her, Len? Why'd you set her on fire?'

He looked at me hollowly, eyes half defocused. He said, 'It were better . . .' Then his head sagged. He looked up again a moment later. The flames were dying back now, the smoke pall dispersing. He said, 'That's done then. That's all through . . .'

We laid him in the shade of the bushes and started searching. If he'd got clear there could have been others. We spread out in a line, working our way up the hill, calling their names over and over. We'd forgotten the Furies.

The day wore on and grief turned to weariness. The sun beat fiercely, striking back from the grass in waves of heat. My shirt became soaked with sweat, my head started to throb. When we lost hope we went on looking. There seemed nothing else to do.

I thought the first answer was an echo. I was over the crest of the hill, wading through a waist-high stand of heather and grass. I stopped and shouted. The noise came again. I plunged forward, nearly fell over the lip of an old mine-working of some sort. Nothing left now but a weed-grown trench ten or fifteen feet deep. I threshed my way along the edge to where I'd heard the voice.

There were three of them. Jones Kitchen, Julie, and Pete.

Owen looked up when he saw me and tried to grin. He said faintly, 'Had a bit o' trouble, boy. Reckon I twisted my leg . . .'

Pete was lying across Julie, her arms twined round her. It took two of us to pull her off. I had to hold her down to stop her going back. There was nothing else she could do. Julie was dead.

We lifted Owen. His ankle was swollen alarmingly, it looked broken to me. He couldn't put his foot to the ground; he could only hobble slowly, arm round Greg's shoulders. It was night before we got back to Chill Leer. We took turn and turn about helping the walking wounded. We saw no wasps though we heard them continually droning in the sky. I never want another trip like that.

Or the trip we made later in the night. The burial party.

There were no more raids that season. Len's hand healed and Owen was soon up and about with a stick, messing round his ovens. Our numbers were made up by four farm labourers who came in over the hills, refugees from one of the wasp camps; but things were never the same. The old atmosphere had gone. For the time being we were licked.

Pete brooded worse than anybody. She took to vanishing into the cave complex. Sometimes she'd be gone a day or more. I went down after her a couple of times and so did Greg but we could never find out where she went, she wasn't in the

155

great hall or at the syphon. I found her once sitting out on the hill half a mile or so from Chill Leer. It had been raining for hours, she was soaked through. I spoke to her, tried to get her inside, but it was no good. She didn't seem to hear me, she was in a strictly private hell.

By October it seemed the number of Furies was less, and within a week it began to look as if Greg had been right. The nests were dying off. We stayed in the caves through the shortening days, living on the last of the stored food. Towards the end of the month Greg took off on his own. He came back with a stranger, a Hampshireman called Stokes. They were driving a Land-Rover, we heard them sounding the horn a mile off. By the time they reached the caves we were all outside. Greg said the whole massif was empty of insects. He'd driven south-east, deeper into Somerset; the wasps had gone from there too, their cities were deserted.

I think we all went slightly mad. Len hi-jacked another truck. Dave brought in a second Rover. We got aboard. We took very little with us; most of the stuff we left piled round the caves. I for one never expected to see Chill Leer again.

We had a nasty shock. As a first measure we drove to the nearest of the labour camps, the one from which Stokes had escaped. It was situated a few miles north of Glastonbury; the main quarters were a range of converted farm buildings. I was in the leading car with Greg and Pete. As we got in sight of the place I heard what sounded like a shot. A moment later I was left in no doubt. The settlers opened up with everything they had; and that was quite a lot.

I'd never been under fire before. I didn't find it funny. I stamped on the brakes, heard the lorry tyres squeal behind me, U-turned praying I wouldn't get rammed, and headed back the way I'd come. The rest of the convoy got out somehow. It was a miracle no one was hurt. Once out of range we stopped and tried to think what the hell to do. Greg shook his head helplessly. 'They must be crazy, clean round the bend. But we've got to talk to them somehow, try to make some sense out of this...'

He was right, there was nothing to do but try and parley. They must have the wrong idea about us, maybe they'd taken us for looters. In the end Greg and Dave went forward on foot,

156

carrying of all things a white flag. The rest of us stood round the vehicles and waited. Greg was away half an hour or more; when he came back he was long-faced. There had been no mistake, they knew who we were and where we'd come from. But they wanted nothing to do with us. Apparently each raid we'd made had been followed by reprisals in the camps. Greg had tried to bargain for a safe conduct past the gates but they had refused even that. They promised they would shoot on sight, and to kill.

We had been outsmarted by the insects of course. It was true they were passionless, for them revenge had no meaning, but the killings had not been revenge. With the winter coming and a time of inactivity forced on them, the Furies had deliberately set out to split the human survivors into factions. They certainly succeeded. In all, we visited a dozen camps; the only one that tolerated us was one that had been unable to find guns. But the people wouldn't join us. Even the kids threw stones.

I don't suppose the full story of that period will ever get written. Many parts of the country were virtually reduced to civil war. The Collectives fought the hill people and each other. There was no central authority, no Government. There were massacres, burnings, tiny battles among the winter wheat. Meanwhile the cities died.

That sounds glib; maybe it is glib but it's the only way I can phrase it. Among the crowded urban populations and in many of the wasp camps the epidemics Greg had forecast had broken out and raged most of the summer. Bristol and Bath, Cardiff, Liverpool, Manchester and Birmingham, Portsmouth, Southampton, London, all fell to the ancient twin terrors of plague and fire. Other scourges came in their wake: typhus, typhoid, dysentery, diphtheria; even measles became a killer. Other countries exhibited the same general pattern, with local variations; France saw a resurgence of the deadly dancing manias of the Middle Ages, while in the United States the biggest killer of all turned out to be tularemia, the so-called rabbit disease.

We withdrew to Chill Leer. We weren't the only guerrilla group in the south-west but we had no contact with the others. We started restocking, working as much as possible by night.

We soon learned which of the Collectives had succumbed, avoided the plague-spots in our foraging. With the storage areas full Greg set us another task. He explained the life-cycle of a wasp nest; how the hordes of workers and grubs die off in the autumn, leaving only a handful of hibernating queens capable of restarting colonies. We began an all-out search for the royal insects. We'd burned every wasp stronghold within reach but that wasn't enough. If the hibernators lived through the winter the cities would be as populous as ever within weeks; each queen unearthed meant a potential colony wiped out. Greg got hold of some large-scale maps of the area, marked them off in squares and allocated them to each of half a dozen search teams. At the start I had no real idea of the size of the job. On paper it looked fairly easy but in practice every bush and cranny had to be investigated, every crevasse explored. An army couldn't have combed the massif effectively given a twelvemonth but we did what we could. I knew I should leave, go look for Jane, but somehow I kept putting it off. Just another day, just one more ... I wanted to catch one of the Furies and smash it, then I'd go. Greg said cynically that I was beginning to 'think wasp'.

It took weeks to find the first queen. Pete's group made the capture, on a barren hillside a few miles north of Chill Leer. Greg was away on a provision run and for some reason I'd been generally accepted as second-in-command. Dave brought me the news. He said they'd been smoking a crevasse, pouring petrol down and lighting it. It was a new technique they'd been trying out. The insect had crawled out minus her wings but otherwise unharmed. They'd been using a farmhouse near by as temporary quarters, Pete had had the Fury taken there. She wouldn't let anybody else near; she said she wanted to interrogate the thing.

I swore at that. The idea was to kill wasps, not fool about. I drove back up with Dave. It was middle January, and bitterly cold. The grass was rimed with frost, the sun breaking through chill and red above a pearly-vague horizon. The rest of the party were still working the crevasse; we drove past to the farmhouse. When we reached it the place looked deserted. A thread of smoke was curling from one of the chimneys but when I shouted nobody answered. I asked Dave to watch the jeep, kicked the front door open, and went in. I let the door swing closed behind me, stood chafing my hands. I heard a voice.

The lounge was straight ahead. I walked in, stood staring. A log fire crackled in the grate, near by was a table with glasses and wine bottles. Very festive. Pete was standing in the middle of the room with a bayonet in her hand. She was still wearing her duffel, hood thrown back. Her hair was tangled and she looked flushed. In front of her was the Fury, roped to a heavy length of plank. The great queen was wide awake now, twitching her body in attempts to get free. She was hampered by the fact that she lacked legs. Her mask turned as I walked in. She stopped struggling, watched me incuriously. I looked at Pete, then back to the wasp. I said, 'What in hell do you think you're doing?'

She pushed her hair back, grinning. She said, 'Hello, ducks, come for the p-party?' Her voice was slurred; I realized suddenly she was more than a little drunk. I said, 'Pete, I asked a question. *What are you doing?*'

She said, 'Jus' having a li'l chat. Nice, wadn't it?' She crooned at the Fury, circling with the long blade in her hand. 'Jus' a li'l chat ...' The head rotated, keeping her in sight. She said, 'An' now ole Bill's come to j-join the party ...'

She crossed to me, took my wrist, and pulled me forward unsteadily. 'Come an' see, Bill. Come'n meet my li'l friend. Nice, ain't she?' She reached forward with the bayonet, tried to lift the wasp's mask with the tip of the blade. The queen twisted back, straining to get out of reach. 'Oh, jus' look at that,' said Pete softly. 'Ain't that pretty? Look at the li'l darling. Almost human, they are. But Auntie won't hurt you, sweet. Not jus' yet ...'

'Pete, for God's sake.'

She said conspiratorially, 'Let you inna li'l secret, ole Bill. She's im-important. Real important. An' I'll tell you 'nother. She knows it. She knows all about it ...' Then to the wasp, 'Know what I'm sayin', don't you, dearie? Every word ... You're real important, you are. You're a col'ny. All on your own. Whole col'ny of big hairy black and yellow bloody bastard wasps. All in one li'l body ...'

I said, 'Pete, just kill the damned thing if you're going to.

159

This isn't helping anybody. We're not barbarians.'

She started to laugh.

'And better give me that bayonet. You're three parts cut anyway, how much have you had?'

She spun round, eyes brilliant with hate. 'Why'd you come here, Bill, why di'nt you stop away? What are you goin' to do, preach me a sermon? Is that what you come for, t'be a bloody preacher . . .?' She lunged forward, got my hand again, and pushed it against her cheek. She said, 'Preach on that. What it feels to live behind that morning, noon, and bloody night. That's a little keepsake from these bastards to me. Jus' to remember 'em by. Nice, ain't it? Don't you tell me what I am, just preach on that . . .'

I snatched myself away. 'For God's sake . . .' I tried to grab her but she spun out of reach. She was trembling now, and keeping the blade between me and her. She said, 'Don't get smart, ducky, just don't get smart. I ain't that drunk . . .' She swayed; then, 'You don't know all of it, Bill. Callin' me a b-barbarian. You don't know any of it, you don't even know the start . . .' She swallowed. 'I never told you what happened that day the wasps come, did I? I ain't never told nobody . . .'

I said as steadily as I could, 'Will tormenting this brute bring your family back?'

She ignored me. Her hand was on her face, fingering the scar. She said, 'We were sittin' there. All nice an' cosy. Just 'ad tea. Mum and Dad and the kids. There were this droning, see? Up in the sky. "What's that?" says Dad. I can remember jus' what he said. "Sounds like them bloody insecks they was on about," he says. "You lot better stop 'ere. I'll go an' have a butcher's . . ." An' he goes out inter the shop to see. And all the rest of us after him, crowdin' round the door. "Don't you open up, Harry," says our Mum. "Don't want none o' them things in 'ere . . ." Then they come through the winder. Pop were the first. They had him like a shot. They started on us then.'

She was prowling again, circling the wasp. 'The old lady were next,' she said. 'That's when I got this. When I were tryin' to get the thing orf her. I held it orf, see, when it come at me. It couldn't reach me throat. There it were snappin' and snappin', an' the blood all comin' . . . I couldn't hold it no more, after that. It were too slippery. It were all the blood . . .'

She grinned at me. 'It wadn't nothing like you think, Bill. Nothing. It were quiet, while we were being killed. Dead quiet. I could hear the old man puffin' and our Rita were crying. "Yer face, Jan," she kept saying. "It's cut yer face . . ." "It's all right, Ri," I says. "It'll be all right, I'll do it up in a minute . . ." I could still talk, see, mister? Only I couldn't see her because o' the blood. I couldn't feel nothing . . .'

I said, 'Janice, if you won't stop this for me—'

She screamed, 'Don't call me that . . .' Then she started to laugh again. 'Why not though, it don't make no odds now. Janice, that's a nice name. Yeah . . .'

'Jan . . .'

She said wildly, 'They all knew me, in Westrincham. You ask anybody, did they know Jan Peterson. You'd have got a real laugh. That's the biggest laugh of all. Didn't I ever tell you what I was, Bill, di'n't I say?'

'I'm more interested in what you are now. What you're doing to yourself . . .'

Her voice had developed a thin edge of hysteria. She said, 'I was a whore, Bill. Common muckin' prostitute. Best ride in town . . .' She wiped her forehead with the back of her hand. 'Now look shocked. Now tell me I'm a bleedin' barbarian again . . .'

I didn't speak.

She said, 'I were the old black sheep. That's the laugh. I were the one that wadn't no good. Dad used to tell me. "Never come to no good you won't, my gal," that were what he used to say. "Never come to no good . . ." But when *they* come, they took him orf instead. Him and Mum and the kids. That's the joke, they left me . . .

'I used to work three nights a week at the flicks. Used to get a lot o' trade from that. Rest o' the time I was on the streets. I used to do all right. I'd got this place I went to, this pub. They didn't care. Everybody knew about it. The old man knew. They all knew Jan Peterson. I was at it up in the smoke only Dad di'n't know then. But you couldn't keep things quiet in Westrincham. It wadn't the same . . .'

I said, 'The past is done, Pete. Why the hell rake it up like this?'

She didn't answer. She leaned over the wasp playing with

161

the bayonet. She said, 'These were the ones that sent 'em, Bill. Jus' these few. The rest couldn't think. They were machines. But these could think. "Go out." That's what they said to 'em. "Go out an' kill. Kill all the decent folk. Cut their bloody heads orf. Do it slow. But mind you leave all the rest. Leave the pros and the bags and the gutter scrapings, they're all right, you leave them alone." That's what you told them, isn't it? *Isn't it . . .?*'

The Fury clicked its mandibles.

Pete drew back. She was panting, her knuckles were white-clenched on the bayonet. She said, 'It wants to fight. Look at that, it wants to have a little go. All right then, you've come to the right place, dearie, we'll give you a fight. We'll give you all the fight you want . . .' The blade fizzed down. The stroke was nearly too quick to follow. One of the insect's great compound eyes opened in a leaf-shaped cut. Blood-flecked grey pulp welled up through the wound. The Fury began to tremble, shaking the plank to which it was fastened.

I jumped Pete. There was a bad moment when I thought she was going to use the bayonet on me. I hadn't realized how tough she was. I bent her wrist back, slammed her knuckles across the edge of the table. The blade landed on the floor. She pulled away, ran across the room. She hung on to the mantel over the fireplace, back to me and shaking. She said hoarsely, 'Kill the bleedin' thing, Bill, kill it for Christ's sake . . .'

I towed the plank outside, took Dave's shotgun, put the barrels to the insect's thorax, and fired. Armour rolled across the frozen ground. The shots echoed round the hills, clapped into silence. I went back inside, collected Pete, and took her to the car.

I left her at Chill Leer. We didn't say much to each other. Greg was back, I made my goodbyes to him and Dave. It was as if Pete's flare-up had started a train of reactions outside my control, I couldn't stay around any more. We were all knocking ourselves apart; none of us had any future, there was only death, and blood, and killing Furies until they turned round and killed us right back. I tried to tell Greg but I couldn't get the proper words, it still looked as if I was just running.

We had a collection of cars by that time. I wanted one of the Champs but they couldn't be spared. I took an MG TF somebody had brought in. It wasn't good for what I needed but it was all we had. I started it up and headed south, towards Jane and the sea.

A mile or two from Chill Leer I ran into the army.

I rounded a bend and stared. For a moment I couldn't believe what I was seeing. In front was trouble. A dozen armoured vehicles, Saladins and scout cars, fanned out in a crescent, coming up the road and along to each side over the rough. They were moving fast, swaying over the whitened grass. I hit the brakes. It was just as well. A gun stammered somewhere, the rounds slapped across the road in front of me. They had a loud-hailer, I heard it clearly over the engine. 'The red car, halt ... the red car, halt ...'

I don't know what happened to me. I reckon I'd just been pushed and shoved that little bit too long. I didn't know what they wanted and I didn't care. I was going to the coast, I was going to find Jane, I wasn't going to be pinned by anybody, not any more. I hauled the wheel, the TF screeched, slithered on an ice patch. Then I was round, heading back the way I'd come. I heard the loud-hailer again behind me, the echoes crackling back from the hills. 'The red car ... halt or we shall fire into you ...'

And the hell with that as well, I'd been shot at before. I kept going.

Crock-crock-crock ...

A tiny noise, flat, miles away. Unassociated. Puffs of smoke crossed the road ahead. I started to swerve.

Crock-crock-crock-crock-*spang* ...

The ricochet rang piercing, like a bell. Windscreen starred, fell clear, let in cold air-rush and the noise, louder ...

CROCK-CROCK-CROCK ...

I heard the tyre go, saw rubber flail outwards. The TF rammed her nose down, slewed. The wheel spun, I tried to hold it, it yanked skin off my hands, there was time for fear, I know I screamed. Then grass and bushes rushed me, earth and sky changed places and I fell into brightness then dark and someone's body was being jolted and torn but I wasn't in it, it had nothing to do with me.

There was the darkness. The darkness, and the pain. In the void were sounds. Like the sea. And faces. They floated sickly, vague balloons, hovering, drawing away. They tried to speak to me but the syllables were welded together by the pain, turned into a tangled roaring. When the balloons were close the pain was worse. I tried to fight them, drive them away. I knew I was screaming again but I couldn't hear. The void turned in on itself and I dropped through it spinning, down to total blackness.

The blackness lasted a long time.

CHAPTER 12

THE VOID, the time of not-being, might have gone on a day or a week or a month. As the pain ebbed and flowed the emptiness filled with noise, with jazzing lights, senseless forms, and colours. Fever-images jostled me, melting nightmarishly each into each; Jane and Sek, the Furies, the boat, the burning truck; rocks rained, my house was falling again, smashing my legs, starting lightning-jags of pain. I tried to talk to Jane, but it was no good, her hair had turned blonde or white and her face was scarred, her hands were like cool velvet, but she wouldn't touch me with the velvet, she would only scream kill, kill ... The words, the noise, seemed to shaft into my body to wake the pain up again and I was back in the boat and the sea was rising. I tried to row, but the dinghy turned into a red car that somersaulted, smashing me on to the road. Then the rocks and the house again, over and over ... The dreams ebbed into stillness. Some time, I opened my eyes.

I lay trying to focus them. Above me was a yellow-green texture, vague and meaningless, split with cracks and shadows. The surface seemed to bulge and recede; I put my hand up to steady it but I couldn't reach. I dropped my arm again, felt textures. Roughnesses. A hard edge. I was lying on a ... bed? Yes, bed, camp-bed ... The yellowness came from a lamp. It hung in gloom, glaring and hissing like a dim sun. I tried to sit up and didn't make it. I put my hand to my face. There was sweat.

Abruptly, I remembered. The MG. Meeting the armour ...

164

Something had gone wrong, I'd got to get out. They'd taken me, this was a cell, a jail. Get out before they found I'd come round ... What did they do with guerrillas, shoot them? I rolled over. The bed tipped and my hand was on rock. I tried to lever myself but there was no strength. I heard footsteps and I was fighting somebody, being forced back, back ...

A voice. 'It's all right,' it said. 'All right, all right, it's all right ...'

My vision steadied, multiple images coalesced into solidness. I lay hearing my own hard breathing. I was looking up at Pete. Above her, a rock ceiling. A Tilly lamp hung from a piton wedged in the side wall. This was no cell. This was Chill Leer.

She was wiping my face. I wanted to talk but my mouth was too dry. I caught her hand, gripped it. The fingers were cool. She sat watching me steadily then she turned her head. 'Greg,' she called, 'he's come round.'

His bulk seemed to fill the little chamber. He stood smiling at me, eyes bright and pleased over a thick tangle of beard. 'Well hell, Bill,' he said, 'I didn't think we'd rear you ...'

Pete crossed the chamber and fetched water in a glass. I managed to lift myself till I could drink. She held the tumbler to my lips, grinning. 'It's the roundabouts and the swings, dear heart,' she said lightly. 'Like a ruddy yo-yo, ain't it? First you're up ... then you're down ...'

I said shakily, 'What ... happened?'

She rearranged a pillow under my head then stood back and looked at me professionally, arms folded. 'You filled yourself in, ducky,' she said blithely. 'You made a right job of it too. Didn't he, Greg?'

He nodded. 'They thought you were dead. So did we. We heard the firing. Managed to draw the bastards ...'

'There was a nice little party,' said Pete. 'While they was playin' toy soldiers we nipped down and got you out. Cor, you should ha' seen the old car. Bits everywhere. Pity we didn't take a photo ...'

I began to realize vaguely what they'd done for me. I wanted to talk, get up and hug Pete, but there was no strength for that either. I shut my eyes again, slept naturally this time ...

It was a couple of weeks before I was up, longer than that before I could move without a stick. I was lucky to be alive, I'd been pretty badly cut about the legs where I'd been thrown clear of the MG. Pete said it was lucky I'd landed on my head, not on something delicate. She'd done a great job of nursing. I tried to talk to her about it. There was a lot I wanted to tell her but she brushed it off. 'That's all right, dear heart,' she would say gaily. 'All part o' the Peterson home help service...'

The caves were echoing with new voices, unfamiliar footsteps. We'd had over a dozen people join us in the past week or so. Most of the old guard came in from time to time to chat; Owen Jones brought some fancy concoctions he'd made up, Len Dilks a couple of boxes of cigarettes. When I felt more able to cope I asked Greg what had been going on. He frowned and shook his head. Apparently after the squabbling between the settlers and the various roving bands of fighters had flared up the situation had been complicated by the inthrusts of army units from bridgeheads in the east, in Hampshire and Sussex. One such force I'd met. Information was scanty but it seemed a gang calling themselves the Freedom Fighters had holed up not far from us, at Cheddar. They blocked the gorge road both sides of the caves, proclaimed a People's Republic, and opened fire indiscriminately on anything that came near. The armour had gone in and blown the place apart and since that a state of martial law had existed. So far the regular units had not discovered Chill Leer; Greg said we could thank our luck the place was so little known. The colony was lying low, all operations against hibernating wasps had been suspended.

While I'd been out of the picture Greg hadn't been idle. He'd personally booby-trapped half a dozen of the nesting sites on and around the plateau. He told me with a certain relish that under each one was now a buried cache of petrol drums, blasting charges, and detonators. Wires led back to chosen spots overlooking the nests. He was certain the Furies would be back; when that happened they were bound to use some at least of the old sites. He planned to set the mines off when the nests got well established. He reckoned there was a chance the brutes could be rattled into leaving the area completely.

The wasps did come back. The events of the previous year

166

repeated themselves. By that time I was fit again. I saw part of the withdrawal. The army got out, leaving a scatter of derelict vehicles. Greg hi-jacked a pair of Mark Two Ferrets, hid them under brushwood about a mile down the coombe. He said they'd be handy for the season's activities though I wasn't so sure. I'd seen more than enough of armour.

By mid-April the Furies were winging about in thousands. Greg was baffled. These weren't hibernators and they couldn't possibly have been bred in such a short time. They appeared literally overnight. The Collectives became furiously active again. Many of them had in fact never stopped working; fields had been ploughed, early crops sown. I couldn't find it in me to blame the farmers though Pete hated them bitterly. After all, they had to eat the same as us. It seemed to me it was we who were the parasites. We were still living off the remnants of the old culture. The farmers were trying to stabilize a new ecology, a balance that included men and insects as working partners.

When I was on my feet again I saw less of Pete. She'd withdrawn into herself once more; she'd sit by the hour, remote and untouchable as a china cat. I wondered if she was brooding about what she'd told me the day they caught the queen. I talked about her to Greg one night. We were lounging outside the mouth of the upper cave, watching the sun set over the hills. Greg laughed, leaned his head back against the rock, and let his eyes drift shut. He was quiet for a time; then he said softly, 'Did she ever tell you about herself? What she was, before all this?'

I nodded. 'Once. In a few well-chosen phrases.'

'And what did you think?'

I looked at him sharply. 'I didn't think anything. I told her it was in the past. In any case I don't care. I don't have that sort of moral sense.'

He stayed still, nodding to himself. 'Morality. That's about the key to it, I reckon . . .'

'Key to what?'

He didn't answer directly. 'When I was a bit younger and a bit crazier I used to think a lot about morality. Heaven and hell and all that stuff.' He laughed. 'I reckon I'd have liked to start some sort of new faith. Try a new morality. One that

167

maybe didn't hang on sex. There's more ways to be unmoral than hopping into bed with someone you like. Or someone that'll pay you. Could be I'm crazy but it seems to me a prostitute could have morality. Maybe not the Christian sort. But still morality.'

'What's that got to do with Pete?'

He said, 'Pete has a psychosis this wide.' He held up his hands. Then he opened his eyes, looked at me quizzically. 'Pete thinks she helped bring the Furies. She thinks they *are* Furies. Come to harass mankind for the sins of the damned. She sets herself among the damned...'

I said, 'Christ, that's going off the deep end a bit isn't it?'

He shook his head impatiently. 'I can't argue this, Bill, I'm no psychologist. I'm not trying to say that's a conscious thought process in her mind. But she's a deep little girl, complex. Lives on a lot of levels. Don't let the East End small talk fool you. She should have been punished but she wasn't. So she wants to punish herself, go the way her family went. That's a death wish.'

Phrases went through my mind. 'Kill all the good folk. Do it slow. But leave the pros and the bags and gutter-scrapings. They're all right...' I said slowly, 'So you think she really does want to die?'

He sighed. 'A part of her does. Maybe it's dead already. This is a shell, walking, talking...' He got up suddenly. 'Anyway, what the hell does it matter? We've all got a death wish. Else why are we here ...?' He shoved aside the growing strands of fern over the cave mouth and vanished into the dark.

The colony resumed its attacks on the nests. The first sorties were small-scale affairs; little damage was done on either side. Greg's mines were more successful. Five of the six booby-trapped sites were reoccupied. We destroyed the nests with no trouble. Greg devised a time fuse. The thing was simplicity itself, it relied on a candle burning through a length of string. The string controlled a spring-loaded trigger that closed a contact, fired the buried detonators. To heighten what we hoped would be the unnerving effect we set the charges off in daylight. Some of the blasts were quite spectacular. For hours after each explosion the plateau buzzed with angry wasps.

168

They found nothing of course. The insects must have thought, if they thought at all, that they were fighting ghosts.

Despite Greg's hopes the Mendips were not evacuated. If anything the Fury hordes increased. We soon discovered the reason. To the north, again in a valley sloping down from the massif, the insects had established their biggest nest complex to date. It stretched a mile or more along the coombe; the numbers of domes ran into hundreds and some of them were monstrous affairs, linked to their neighbours and to each other by grotesque tunnel networks that resembled nothing so much as the root systems of giant trees. Greg was sure the place represented the capital of the region. Pete wanted to attack it but the rest of us hung back. Risking our necks was one thing but deliberate suicide was quite another.

By June we had fired the last of the prepared mines and were back to the old business of feinting and raiding. The Ferrets were a big help though we didn't escape without losses. I had some very close calls and so did Greg. Pete seemed to bear a charmed life; maybe it was just because she didn't care.

I remember the time mainly as one of continuous struggle; the struggle to find food, petrol, oil, ammunition, the struggle to stay alive against steadily increasing odds. In July we suffered the first attack against Chill Leer itself. It was surprising the Furies took so long to discover our hideout. I'm inclined to believe they'd known about it for some while, I think if we'd left them alone they wouldn't have troubled us. I don't know how many insects laid siege to the caves but they gave us a fairly hot time. A hundred or more were killed in the first pitch before the rest took the hint and cleared off. After that we were never safe outside without a weapon of some sort. The wasps kept the area under constant surveillance; it made arranging attacks and provision trips a hundred per cent more difficult. The upper part of the cave system was manned on a round-the-clock basis as a safeguard against surprise attacks, and one or other of the scout cars was kept near by in case the Furies made another mass sortie. They never were able to resist armour, the Ferrets drew them like mechanical Pied Pipers.

We moved our attacks farther afield to areas where our

169

activities were not so well known. Even then we had to depend on surprise and on constantly changing our tactics; we soon learned a trick used successfully against one nest could not be safely employed the following night against another fifty miles away. We were beginning to appreciate the intricacies and advantages of the group mind; that old crack of Greg's about 'thinking wasp' was coming more and more true.

We started noticing additions to the range of symbiotic human activities. From our observation posts in the hills we watched gangs of symbos, as we'd come to call the wasp-slaves, stringing heavy wire to posts. One such feeder passed within a few miles of Chill Leer. We blew the line apart on principle a dozen times or so but the workers pushed on. Eventually their intention became clear. They were engaged in supplying electric power to the nest complex to the north. There seemed only one inference to be drawn from lighting and heating in the dooms. The Furies were planning a round-the-year breeding programme. Once that got started we really would be through. A short time later somebody discovered parts of the railway system were running again and after that track sections were surreptitiously loosened every other night. It was a nasty game but we felt we were fighting for our lives.

The tempo of the attacks on Chill Leer was stepped up. It was obvious we had become a major thorn in the side of the Fury culture. I wondered why they didn't mount an all-out drive, besiege the place, and starve us into the open. I realized later their efforts must have been split between various bands similar to our own and bases to which the army was still clinging on the eastern mainland.

Jane was never far from my mind through that hectic summer though the chance of getting out to the coast seemed as remote as a dream. I almost caught myself envying the people in the wasp camps. They at least were free to come and go. Road traffic was continuous now; I played with the idea of taking one of our vehicles and driving out openly towards the sea. But I knew it wouldn't work; if the wasps didn't kill me the first symbos I came across would. I'd had some experience of what they thought of guerrillas.

In August we lost Dave.

It was a rotten business. We'd mounted a small attack on a

group of nests to the south-west, down on the Somerset plain. Both Ferrets were involved, and a handful of people on foot. The thing went off smoothly enough but only one of the cars got back. The other, driven by Dave with Jesse Stokes as gunner, skidded into one of the crevasses that still seamed the countryside. A winter of rain had done little to lessen their depth; on most of them the edges had eroded back a few feet but that was all. As soon as we heard, half a dozen of us loaded some ladder lengths into one of the lorries and headed for the scene of the accident. We reached it after a lot of detouring. The crevasse was massive, looked bottomless. The car was wedged some forty or fifty feet down, both turret and driving hatch rammed into the muck. Greg climbed down to it, spent an hour trying to dig his way in. In the end the thing turned over and plunged another seventy or eighty feet, nearly taking him with it. While we watched, the car fell again, deep into the earth. Rumbling echoed back from the chasm for half a minute or more. Greg climbed slowly back to the surface. He said there'd been no answer to his rappings, the crew were either dead or unconscious. Even if he'd opened the car it would have been an almost impossible job getting them up.

A night or two after that he sent for me. For some time he'd been using one of the side caves in Chill Leer as combined office, workshop, and sleeping quarters. I went down to it. One Tilly lamp was burning; it hung from the arched centre of the roof, hissing softly and throwing a greenish glare beneath it. Greg sat just beyond the light, on the only chair the place boasted. With him were Pete, Len Dilks, Jones Kitchen, and Maggie. Pete was squatting on the rough bench in one corner of the chamber, the rest were disposed round the floor on a variety of boxes and rugs. The Cockney had something in her hands; I didn't recognize it for a moment then I saw it was the crossbow. God only knew where she'd dug that up from.

I stopped when I saw the group. I said, 'What's this, the gathering of the clans?'

Greg nodded. 'Something like that. Find somewhere to put your carcass, Bill, we've got a bit of talking to do.'

I sat down between Maggie and Owen. Greg said without preamble, 'Seems we've got some dissension in the camp, Bill. I called you down because you're the last of the old guard.

We're complete now, what's left of us. I thought you'd want to be in on this.'

I said, 'What's the trouble anyway?' I had a good idea I already knew.

Maggie was toying with the hem of her jersey, frowning and plucking at the worn wool. She said, 'We want out, Bill, Len an' me and Jonesy. We talked it over, like. After poor old Dave . . . well, we just don't want to stop round no more.'

I shivered. I hadn't been able to shut out the memory of the black plunge of the scout car into the crevasse. The same thing had so nearly happened to me. I said, 'I know what you mean, Maggie. Question is, where do you aim to go?'

She looked uncertain. Len Dilks turned to me, slowly massaging his ruined left hand. His eyes had always been deepset; now they seemed completely vanished, lost in the darkness of the sockets. He said quietly, 'It's like this, whack. Once there were a dozen of us. Fifteen. Now look. I can count us on me fingers. Even me . . .'

'We're not getting anywhere,' said Maggie. 'We can't win. We know that. We always have. It's just waiting and waiting and being killed in the end, it don't matter what we do.'

Pete said bitterly, 'That's what you came here for, ducks. Some people ain't ever satisfied . . .'

'Shut up,' said Greg evenly. 'You can have your say later, Pete. Let's hear Maggie through first.' Pete set her lips, held the crossbow out from her body, and pulled the trigger. The string cracked against the stave. She began sullenly rewinding it.

Maggie said slowly, 'I don't think I've got anything else to say. Except that what Len says is right. Once there were fifteen of us. Now there's six. And we shan't last long now.'

There was silence.

She said tensely, 'If there was a reason for it, Greg. That's all. If . . . well, you know, if there was some sort of point. But we're through. Finished. The army can't beat the wasps so I know we can't. There just don't seem any point.'

'You've said that, ducky . . .'

That from Pete. Greg stared at her. She ignored him.

I said, 'You think the same, Owen?'

172

Jones Kitchen gave his typical shrug. 'S-sort of. Doesn't seem a lot of bloody f-future, do there?'

Maggie smoothed her sweater. She'd grown up a lot in the year; she was heavier now, buxom and tough. She said, 'Well, we've had enough. All of us. We want out, Greg. Anything's better than this. We were talking about just nippin' off. But we thought well, you know ... we'd sort of like to tell you. Seemed only right...'

He nodded slowly. The light from the Tilly was making his face look drawn. 'Thanks for the thought, Maggie. But you don't owe anything. All I've done is have most of you killed.'

I said quickly, 'I can't agree there. You got us out of that bloody camp. If we'd stayed we might all be dead by now.'

He smiled. 'No good thinking on what might have happened, Bill. Only on what has...'

The crossbow cracked again.

Jones Kitchen said tentatively, 'We were wonderin' ... well, how would it be for you to sort of c-come along, Greg? We all go together, see? The rest o' the folk here ... well it'd be up to them now, wouldn't it?'

Greg was still smiling. 'The idea had crossed my mind. As Bill said though, the question is where to go?'

I said, 'I think I could put up an idea at least. We go south. To the Isle of Wight or farther out. We know there's organized resistance somewhere. Logically it'll be on islands. Places the Furies can't reach.'

Pete laughed abruptly. 'Good old Bill. Never gives up, does he?'

Greg said, 'He might well be right. I think it's the best alternative.'

Maggie said in a smothered voice, 'There is another ...'

He waited.

'Give in,' she said. 'Go to one of the camps. Or go to the wasps. They need people to work for them. They haven't killed the people in the camps. If they were going to they'd have done it by now ...'

Greg shook his head. 'I told you once, in a camp, what was going to happen. I wasn't far wrong. Now listen again.

'That isn't an alternative, not for me at least. The rest of you will make your own decisions. But I say this. We're still

173

in a transitional phase. We've got a lot of skills the wasps need. We can help keep 'em warm, keep 'em fed. Maybe we're indispensable now. But that won't last. Those horny bastards are learning, all the time. They've proved that. When they've learned enough, when they can do without us, when they can plant our crops, drive our vehicles, then ... ckkkk ...' He drew a finger across his throat. 'End. Finish. They'll kill. They can't afford to keep us round the nests indefinitely. They want us sure, they want our knowledge. But knowledge is a two-edged sword. It always was. Human knowledge gave us the chance to shape our environment, order a safer world. It also gave us the fusion bomb. Without which, don't forget, we wouldn't be in the present bloody mess. The wasps are no fools; they'll realize that, as they learn about us, so we're learning about them. And somewhere people will always be working on ways and means of destroying the brutes. I don't know how. A selective virus maybe; we know enough about germ warfare, we know enough about a lot of nasty things ... No, when the time comes, there'll be a *pogrom*. It might not be this year or next but it'll happen. That's why I came to the hills. Because this is where the survivors will bolt, when the killing starts again. That's why I'm keeping on fighting. Even if we do have a lost cause.'

I said carefully, 'Do we have a lost cause, Greg?'

He shrugged. 'Who can tell? Not me, certainly. All I've said is we're between the devil and the deep. We haven't got a lot of choice.' He looked round at the others. 'Well, do we put this thing to a vote or are we no longer a democratic assembly?'

Maggie said stolidly, 'I want to go. There might be a chance down on the Island. Like Bill said ...'

Len and Owen seconded her. Greg pursed his lips. 'Right, that's four against staying. Pete?'

She grinned. I'd expected an outburst but it didn't come. She said lightly, 'There'll be wasps down there too I s'pose. Might as well go an' give the little dears a treat ...'

Greg stood up. 'Right, then I'll go along with the majority. We move out, the rest can leave or stay. I'll talk to them. But first I've got a proposition. Before we get the hell out I want to do a worthwhile strike. Leave the wasps something to remember us by. A few miles north of here is a ruddy city. I reckon

174

it's so damn big they won't be expecting us to try for it. I want
it flattened. I've thought it through and I think we can get
away with it. There'll be one hell of a rough-house afterwards
but there've been rough-houses before and we lived through
the rest. After the row dies down we'll go. By that time operations on this plateau will have become virtually impossible
anyway so we'll be doing no good by staying. What do you
reckon?'

I looked round the circle of faces and knew nobody was
going to say no. We'd do it all right. Just one more job . . . In
the silence, Pete started rewinding the crossbow again. I
watched her gloomily. The stave flexed, became an arc. There
was a ringing snap. The steel, overstressed, broke across the
centre. The pieces clattered on the floor.

Pete sat with the stock in her lap, staring wide-eyed. Then
she laughed and threw the thing across the cave. She said, 'Oh
well, it was a nice life. Or didn't anybody notice . . .'

I stood on a high point of ground and watched the petrol
tanker labour towards me up the slope. The going here was
tricky, the earth criss-crossed with small cracks and gullies.
Pete and Greg were walking by the lorry's wheels, fetching it
along with quick, tense waves of their hands. I listened uneasily to the din of the engine. I could imagine the panting
clatter carrying for miles. The diesel was noisy, there had been
no way of quietening her. We could only hope the sound
wouldn't reach over the bluff ahead to the wasp city.

We were committed now to the big strike. Behind me,
silhouetted against a sky full of light from a rising moon, stood
three Land-Rovers. Their windscreens had been replaced with
lattices of iron bars. The crews were huddled together on the
grass a few yards away, smoking and talking. Beyond, the
ground sloped abruptly to the coombe that held the great nest.
I stepped forward to where I could see the domes. They were
ringed with catwalks, presumably for the use of the symbos;
service lamps gleamed here and there on the curving walls of
pulp. The place looked like an oil refinery gone haywire. I
checked my watch. Soon – in half an hour, if things went to
schedule – hell would start popping down there.

This was the most complex plan we'd ever tried. Some-

175

where away to the north the one remaining Ferret was waiting with a couple of lorries. Through the coombe a road ran nearly due north between the nests. That was the way the decoys would come. The attack would consist of two parts. The scout car would push forward on its own, try to get as close in among the nests as possible. Then the lorries would start diversionary fires on the northern edge of the site. We hoped the wasps would be fooled into thinking our whole strength was concentrated on the plain; the flames should make it look as if the sortie had gone wrong. While the Furies were busy the tanker would be pumping petrol down the hill, right on top of the domes. How long we'd have before we were detected was anybody's guess. Greg had reckoned three or four minutes at the outside. When we were spotted we were to throw our grenades and get out the best way we could. We would leave a huge conflagration; Greg hoped most of the attackers would die in the flames or be unable to gain enough height to fly over them. So did the rest of us . . .

We'd had a far from easy trip across country. The Rovers had gone through with no bother but there had been times when I'd thought the tanker wasn't going to make it. We'd had to detour widely; behind us, a half-mile away, was one of the biggest crevasses any of us had ever seen. It meandered through the hills, slashing the massif apart for over five miles. We'd recce'd the route in daylight some half dozen times but even so following the great chasm had been tricky work. The moonlight had helped. Greg had chosen a fine night as being essential for moving the vehicles over the rough; he also felt the unlikely weather would catch the Furies off their guard. In that he seemed to have been right, there were no flying sentries anywhere over the city.

The lorry reached the crest of the hill, revved massively as it backed into position. The sound seemed to blast back from the other side of the coombe. If the Furies hadn't heard that they must have gone stone-deaf . . . I peered down the hill again but nothing was moving. The insects had grown complacent in the days of their dominion.

The engine stopped at last. Len got down from the cab and began coupling the delivery pipes to the cocks at the tail of the truck. With everything ready and the pipes laid out down the

176

hill we crouched round under the bonnet of the diesel and lit cigarettes. I felt a regular shaking start deep inside my body. I always had the jitters before a raid. I wondered if the others felt the same.

My watch read twenty minutes to go. Greg leaned back against the fender of the lorry, blew smoke slowly. 'Everybody sure what to do?'

Len nodded. 'Start pumpin' soon as the wasps go fer the decoys. The rest's straightforward. We light up when the wasps come fer us, then get out. It's a ruddy cinch . . .'

Greg chuckled. 'Glad you think so . . . You OK, Bill?'

'I'm fine.'

He laughed again. 'You liar, you're nearly as scared as I am . . .'

There was a thick rumble. The hill stirred almost imperceptibly. The noise came again, louder. That time the shock was heavier, a distinct, sharp jar. The grumbling died away, seemed to recede north in great dim washes of sound. I'd broken out in sweat. The primeval voice of the earthquakes had been silent a good many months now.

Pete stubbed her cigarette viciously. She said, 'That's just what we need, that'll wake the bleeders if nothing else does . . .'

Greg was turning uneasily, listening for movements, the boom of wings. Everything stayed quiet. The diesel ticked as it cooled. Above us the moon, high and serene, washed the sky with light. I remembered the noise of the first quake, the one that had wrecked my house. The cellar, Sek and Jane. But Jane was miles away, across the sea. I stamped the fag out and got up. If I lived through this raid that was where I was going. Out across the sea. Nothing was going to stop me, not any more.

At five minutes to zero we were finally in position, lying staring into the coombe. The scout car appeared almost dead on time. I saw the headlamps far off, swerving and jazzing. They lit the far sides of the great domes, showed the gantries and eerie suspended tunnels in sharp silhouette. There was a distant rattle of gunfire.

The city was slow to react. When it did the effect was indescribable. Insects smoked up in thousands, whirled hundreds of feet in the moonlight, filled the air like the ash

177

pall over a volcano. For long moments the whole mass hung undecided; then the lorry lights appeared and simultaneously fires sprang up along the far side of the nest area.

If there had been any doubt remaining in the group mind of the Furies that resolved it. The whole bellowing canopy of them seemed to fall away from us as they plunged at the attackers. I saw the lights turn back; I could only hope the decoys made it, there was nothing we could do to help them now. The cocks on the tanker were already open, petrol streaming across the hill. I waited, gripping the grass. The flood must have reached the southernmost domes by now. What was happening to the Furies, were they all dazed ... Greg was standing tensely a few feet in front of me, staring down. I saw him look back at the tanker. Still nothing. The moonlight on the domes, the fires beyond nearly smothered now, the huge cloud of wasps milling northwards over the plain ...

Suddenly the air round us was filled with booming. Greg yelled; bombs went down from half a dozen points, burst on the round roofs below. Flames ran over the domes, rivulets of yellow light. Then the petrol caught.

I was half blinded. It seemed the whole hillside had blown up. There was fire everywhere, licking at the sky. I saw Furies turning over in the air, plunging into the inferno. Then I was running for the cars.

Blasts of heat whipped back at me. I dived into the nearest Rover, Pete and Greg bundled in alongside. I accelerated down over a sweep of grass. The car was swaying and bucking, I could hardly hold the wheel. Behind me the night was stained with red.

We'd all realized our mistake before we reached the great crevasse. Rising ahead of us was what looked like an immense, wavering black and yellow curtain, flat, out of scale, lit by the flames. Furies by the thousand, climbing to cut us off. The huge vent must have been packed with nests, deep down where our scouts hadn't spotted them. We were caught in a pincers, we'd never get through.

Pete screamed something, I don't know what. Then the mirror lit white, there was the yelling of a hooter. I yanked the wheel instinctively, felt the Rover heel, crash back straight.

The tanker passed with a bare six feet to spare, heading down the slope flat out with the hoses leaping behind it like demented snakes. I just had time to realize the lorry was never going to miss the crevasse. At that speed it couldn't turn.

It made no attempt to.

On the edge of the gulf it hit a ridge that threw it all eight wheels in the air. For a split second the huge machine hung impossibly, poised on its nose like a kid's toy, then it fell forward. There was a moment of silence and blackness then a thudding roar that shook the ground, punched up through the Rover's wheels. The crevasse lit for hundreds of yards with an orange glare. All the insects still below ground must have been annihilated; the host above were blown sideways, twitched out of the air by the blast.

It was all confused, Len may have jumped. But if he did I didn't see him. I just didn't see him . . .

The Furies were hard behind us by the time we reached Chill Leer. Two of the Rovers came through. I don't know what happened to the third, I never saw it again. We ran up the hillside to the cave. The base party was already outside, blazing away at the diving wasps. We practically fell down the first pitch, rammed the gate in place across the bottom of it. The obstacle didn't stop the insects. They reached the top, folded their wings, and fell like stones. The impact of the bodies on the grating started to split it apart; those Furies that survived the drop began instantly chipping at the bars with their boltcutter jaws. We blew them to pieces as they landed but more came down and more until the gate was bulging, the bottom of the pitch a writhing mass of black and yellow armour. While we were keeping busy the brutes came through the swallets.

They were in among us before we knew what had happened. The gratings hadn't held them, they must have torn them out wholesale. The place became a chaos. The one Tilly lamp was knocked from its hook by the beating of the huge wings. It sailed across the cave, hit the wall, and exploded with a roar. Something snagged my ankle, I stumbled in the dark and a shotgun went off next to my face. Somebody started to scream in agony.

179

The cave was full of smoke, I couldn't breathe. I was trying to fight my way to where I'd last seen Pete. Something cannoned into me. I shoved my hand out, felt the coldness of chitin, twitched away. A torch flashed, showed me heart-shaped masks, a swirl of bodies. Pete was crouched against the rock wall. I grabbed her wrist and ran. Down the passage to the second pitch, a torch ahead now and the noise behind, the booming and the shrieks. Pete was panting, trying to wrench away from me. I found the ladder somehow, shoved her on to it and followed her down moving as fast as I could in blackness. Halfway to the bottom I nearly fell off the rungs. Somebody was climbing after me, they stepped on my fingers. Something brushed past, landed with a crash like a boulder falling. Then booming was loud again overhead. The wasps were following. The attack had finally enraged their patience, this was the time of truth. They were going to take us now, keep on till they did.

I reached bottom and Greg hit the scree beside me a few seconds ahead of the Furies. There were torches stored below the pitch, I grabbed two, shoved one in Pete's hand. In front of us a voice was calling. We ran through the great hall, the torch beams scattered off the crystal pillars of the place. We tackled the third climb with the wasps close behind.

Four of us reached the syphon; Greg, Pete, myself, and Owen Jones. Furies were bellowing in the third pitch. Somehow the little Welshman had carried a shotgun down with him but that was the only weapon we had. We'd never fight the insects with one gun, and hampered by the dark.

There was no argument. There was only one answer and we all knew what it was. We would have to swim for it. If the submerged tunnel section was short we would have interposed a barrier not even the Furies could get through. If it was long . . . well, one death was as good as another.

Pete went first. She swam out to the arched mouth of the trap, kicked her heels up, and dived. Then Owen. I followed; I saw torchlight glinting on the water, heard Greg's shout and the confused noise as the Furies burst into the vault. Then iciness and blackness closed over my head.

I've never been a strong swimmer and the closeness of the rock walls hampered my movements. After the first half-dozen strokes I badly wanted to breathe. I held on, counting. Ten, eleven, twelve. Thirteen, fourteen ... Just two more, another one ... It was useless, the rock still hemmed me in. There was a roaring, I saw bursts of light. I expelled the air and instantly I was drowning. I lashed out in panic, my head struck a projecting sill then I was floating upwards. I broke surface and dog-paddled, coughing from the water in my lungs. I felt my arm caught, I was pulled forward. My hands touched something, I heaved and I was out of the water, lying choking and spitting on a rocky ledge. Round me the darkness was Stygian, the silence that of a tomb.

CHAPTER 13

BY THE TIME I was able to take an interest in things again Greg was through the syphon. Owen had brought a torch with him, rammed in the pocket of his trousers; it wouldn't work at first but after a lot of fumbling he managed to coax a yellow gleam from it. We saw the ledge on which we'd landed was some forty feet long by eight or ten broad. It sloped down towards the water; beside it the stream flowed silently, its level a bare two inches below the lip of rock. The cave roof was invisible except on our right where it dipped to the syphon. It seemed the passage widened farther on into another hall; the feeble light of the torch showed the opposite rock wall curving away, and when we shouted the noise woke a choir of echoes.

The torch soon began to dim; the Welshman switched it off to save the batteries. We huddled together in blackness, listening for splashings from the syphon. None came. We had no means of telling time; Greg was wearing a watch but it had stopped, its cover glass full of water. I wondered how long we would have to stay where we were and how the Furies would react to our disappearance. Would they presume us drowned or would they wait with that cat-patience of theirs till hunger drove us back through the tunnel? We discussed what to do in strained voices. I asked Greg what he thought but he refused to comment. This decision would have to be ours, he was through.

The disaster had hit him hard. He blamed himself bitterly for the destruction of the colony. I tried to remind him of his own arguments; he'd convinced me at least more than once that the way we'd chosen to live had been the only possible one. But he wouldn't hear me out. 'Don't tell me about logic, Bill,' he said thickly. 'It's too late for that ... I guess I'm just a bloody hypocrite anyway, maybe I knew it all along. You were the logical ones. Maggie was right, the only sane thing to do was stay in the camps and take a chance with the rest. I didn't talk logic with you, I chopped it. I'm not a logical man.'

'But when—'

He said savagely, 'Ever read John of Gaunt's speech, son? This royal throne of kings, etcetera ... It's a great bit of jingoism, it'll stir the heart of any schoolboy. I guess you'll find my answer in that. What mattered to me was that this was England, this was happening in England. Maybe there wasn't much of it left to be proud of. Not so many green fields to babble over ... We'd developed it, raped it, built it damn near out of existence. But it was still our own place, it was all we had ...

'I used to have a vision of the whole country covered with nests. From Scotland across the Pennines, across Wales and the Midlands, through the south, through Dorset and Somerset right to the sea. Just nests, a porridge of them, bellowing and booming everywhere, the black and yellow of the wasps. Not a land any more, a scrap tip. A slum. A nursery for the horny bastards to grow fat in. That could still happen and that was what I wanted to stop. It was just emotion, I was trying to keep a bit of the old country clean, that was all ...'

Pete said with surprising gentleness, 'Did you ever ask anybody, Greg, why they was keepin' on? They might have told you just the same. You di'n't have to twist no arms, they knew what they was doing ...'

He made an impatient noise. 'It's no good, Pete, I don't have the image any more. I think I'm blind ...'

I sensed her move against him. Then, 'Turn it up, dear heart,' she said lightly. 'You're giving auntie the jerks ...'

There was silence.

I still dream about that silence. I thought I knew what quietness was. Sit on a Dorset hill on a calm day in autumn and there'll be a silence you can listen to. But it isn't the same. There are still sounds, tiny and far-off; susurrations, breathings from machines and animals and men and the sea. The silence of the caves was total. When I was a kid I used to try to imagine outer space and it was always the silence I thought of first, the dead nothingness of the gulfs beyond the planets. Now I think I know what it would be like. Like the heart of Chill Leer.

I lay listening to the electric singing of the blood in my head. After a time it seemed my ears were microphones, sensitive and incredible like the machines they use to hear the preening of a moth, the sounds a raindrop makes running down glass. The microphones strained but there was nothing to record. My mind began to supply the deficiency; I heard shouts, echoings, ghosts of our own voices maybe, back from some thousand-mile trip to Earth's core. And another noise, steady and thick, a muffled thudding like a drum beating counterpoint to some melody played outside the senses.

But that was for real. It took me minutes to identify it; I was lying with my head against Pete's breast, I could hear the beating of her heart.

Some time, Greg started talking again. He was back in control of himself; he used his voice to fight the silence, break it up before it crept into our bodies as surely as the cold and sent us scatty. He told how the caves had been formed. How the hills had come shouldering up from an old sea, slowly, slow, with the rain working inside them all the time, carving its passages deeper as the rock bulged above the water table. He talked about the stalactites edging and inching to touch the floor, growing through the ages till they seemed not so much products of stone and rain as the glassy fossils of time itself. The hills were for ever, and the caves were as old as the hills. They once underpaved the camps of Rome and they were there before that and before, when the great red deer moved in the mist and there were no men. Here for once we could touch the eternal. Recorded history was nothing to the life of Chill Leer; all civilization, jet planes and longboats, pyramids and comptometers, was a bright flash against the abyss of geologic time, one tick of a clock whose pendulum was the earth, whose face was the sun ...

I slept while he was talking. And woke, dozed, slept again. Time had already lost its meaning for me. I tried to think about the colony, recall faces, but it was nearly impossible. Len and Dave, Julie and Maggie belonged already in some cardboard pageant that had hardly left an impression on the senses. They had had no life so their deaths were meaningless. There was no fear now; the Furies might or might not be waiting but they weren't real either. They were part of the charade I'd watched, painted devils on a backdrop miles away.

Pete was real because I could touch her, feel the movements of her breathing. She edged away once, went to the side of the shelf to drink. It sounded as if she lapped like a cat. I called her until she came back; she put her arm over my shoulders and I took her wrist and pulled myself closer to her again.

We stayed in the caves a thousand years. Intellectually I knew the time was measurable in hours but emotionally, subjectively, I lived through a millennium. Surely nothing would wait that long for us, not even the Furies. If it hadn't been for Pete I think I might have lost all hold on reality, slipped into the water, and drifted down till if there was a hell my body found it. I verbalized the fear once and Greg laughed. He reminded me of what was so hard to believe, the fact that we were still above sea level. Far from sinking to Hades I'd probably be flushed unromantically into the Bristol Channel by the next heavy rain. I was grateful to him for that, it helped me stay on the rails.

We held out as long as we could but the time came when we all knew we were reaching our limit. We were suffering from hunger and we were nearly too stiff to move. We spent some while stamping up and down the rock shelf beating our arms to get the blood flowing again, then Owen sat the torch down near the syphon so that the beam slanted across the water. The light was even dimmer than before, and fading as we watched it.

We couldn't afford to hang about.

Greg insisted on going first. He told us to wait for some sign from him; if there were still Furies in the outer cave he'd dive again and swim back, if the wasps had gone he would try to float a rope through to us. Pete called across as he slid into the water. 'Good luck, mate . . .' He grinned at her, raised his arm; then he was gone, stroking powerfully under the arch of rock and out of sight. We put the torch off and sat waiting again in darkness. Nothing happened; the stream flowed quietly, invisible at our feet, the rock walls echoed back our unsteady breathing.

It seemed like an hour. Probably it was only a quarter of that. Then I couldn't stand it any more. I said, 'OK, Owen, he must have got some trouble. Shine the lamp, I'll go take a look.'

They argued with me but I'd made my mind up, if I didn't try to swim out soon I'd never find the guts to do it at all. If there had been Furies Greg would have been back by now, he must be having difficulty fixing the rope. I eased myself into the water, shuddering again at the coldness of it, edged across to the tunnel mouth, and dived.

The second time was worse than the first. I thought I knew roughly the number of strokes it would take to get through but as soon as I entered the submerged section I could feel the current pushing me back. It wasn't strong but I had a sudden fear I was making no headway, just threshing round in the same spot. I struck out harder, grazed my knuckles on rock. I opened my eyes but there was nothing ahead, no light. Half-way through I was fighting the idea that I was trapped in a huge, cold womb.

I surfaced at the other end of the syphon. I'm still not sure how I did it. I hung on to the side, blearily surprised at the torch that was shining in my face. I spoke a couple of times before I realized Greg wasn't holding the light. It was propped on a rock, nobody was near it.

I hauled myself out of the water, lay for a moment panting. The cave was silent. I walked across and picked the torch up. I called questioningly and started swinging the beam.

I can't remember feeling any emotion when I saw Greg. Just a blankness. It didn't make sense, it was as if I'd been given an equation with only one answer and that crazy. He was lying on his back a few feet from the water. On top of him, gripping with its legs, was a Fury. He'd torn the creature's huge eyes apart, his fingers were still bedded in the pulp behind the lenses. The front of his shirt was bloody, and he was dead.

I can guess what happened. When he got through the trap he found the place was quiet. He climbed out of the stream, lit the torch to guide the rest of us. The Fury made no sound, didn't warn him with the booming of its wings. It just fell on him from some cranny in the roof, fell silently like a stone . . .

Maybe Greg did send some people to their deaths. It isn't up to me to judge him, I only know this. His own end was harder, and lonelier, than all the rest. Nobody to help him. Just the darkness round about, the torchlight, the silent cave; his breath rattling, his boots scraping rock. And the machine-thing on top of him, snapping and nibbling at his chest . . .

I was still kneeling staring when the others came through the syphon. Nobody said much, we were too shocked. We just stood in a group and looked at Greg. Then we pulled the dead Fury aside and started, silently, to build a cairn of stones over his body. When we'd finished and the mound was four feet tall, I stood back. I still felt dazed, as though I was acting in some vast dim tragedy I barely understood. I said slowly, 'He . . . had great feeling for the caves. You could tell by how he spoke about them. I think he'd prefer to be here of all places . . .'

There was silence. I said, 'Does anybody . . . Is there anything else we can do?'

Jones Kitchen stood with his head down, hands clasped in front of him. When he started speaking his voice barely raised the echoes of the place.

'The L-Lord is my shepherd; I shall not want. He maketh me to lie down in green pastures; he l-leadeth me beside the still waters . . .'

We waited till he'd finished. Then he looked round. ' 'Twasn't maybe appropriate,' he said tonelessly. 'But 'twas all I could r-remember . . .'

Pete gripped his shoulder. 'It was all right, Jonesy,' she said. 'You done it all right. But it was only words, wasn't it? You couldn't help that. It di'n't mean nothing . . .' She looked back at me, eyes bright. 'It's funny y'know. It don't ever seem enough. Just sayin' words. Like somethin' big ought to happen. Some big ceremony . . .'

She got her ceremony.

The noise began as a thick rumble, nearly too low-pitched to hear. I felt it in the rock under my feet. It seemed to rush upwards through the deep passages of the caves; then it burst round us, a bellowing that filled the air solid and shook it. Rocks slipped and crashed down. Pete was staring open-mouthed; I felt my back hair lifting, I couldn't speak. The sound died off, came again, a monstrous black drumming; the fissure by the waterfall split, a bore lashed down the stream to the syphon. Water swirled round our legs, flooded up into the cave.

That broke the spell. I yelled, 'Earthquake . . .' I grabbed Pete's wrist and bolted, Owen Jones alongside me with the torch. Across the cave to the first pitch, scrambling among the stones, round us now a howling as if the cavern was a throat sounding up the rage of the Pit. We got to the top of the ladder and ran across the great hall, stumbling through drifts of fallen calcite. The second ladder was swaying and twitching; the whole place was tearing itself apart. We climbed as fast as we could, Owen, Pete then myself. But it seemed time was slowed, my movements had the underwater sluggishness of nightmare. The torch beam swung crazily, I saw one of the huge pillars shatter and fall. Stone fragments stung my cheek then I was at the top, clawing at vibrating rock, and Pete was yanking my arm. 'Come on . . . Bill, come on . . .'

The Welshman was still in front, the light jigging in the tunnel. The air was thick. The drumming, the shriek of shifting stone, I couldn't think . . . Something blundered against me and Pete screamed. I saw the Fury, jinked and it was behind us but there were others. The high levels were full of them, I could hear the booming now mixed with the noise of the quake.

There was daylight ahead. I was crossing the main cave, not knowing how I'd got there. Bodies were lying about but there was no time to look. The insects were close behind, Owen was already on the last ladder. I shoved Pete ahead of me, tangled with the remains of the grating, wrenched clear and followed her, my face level with her heels. My arms were a burning

187

pain now; the ladder was surging about, I was banged against rock. The hill was shaking, the pitch was choked with dust. I started to cough, looked down and there was a Fury, climbing in the haze, swinging from side to side in the confined space. Others milling below it. I kicked out, driving the insect back down, yelled to hurry but nobody could have heard. Then there was a crack that penetrated even the noise of the quake. I looked up and saw an avalanche coming at my head.

Pete and I were just beneath the overhanging lip of the pitch. That saved us. We clung to the ladder, there was another crash, a tearing yell. Jones Kitchen fell past me, legs and arms flailing. He landed atop the Furies and the whole struggling mass was blotted out by boulders. A stone bounded off my hand, half numbed the arm; I kept my grip of the ladder somehow, edged up until I could hold Pete between the rung and myself. Something hit her in the side; I didn't see it but I heard the thud. She yelped, the ladder swung more violently than ever; then the quake ended as quickly as it had started. The rumbling died to a hoarse groan and there was silence.

I looked down, shaking. The pitch was filled with rubble to within a few feet of the top, there could be nothing alive under it. Pete was holding the ladder and gasping. Her face was half turned to me, her cheek was wet with sweat. I felt a clawing of panic. 'Pete, are you hurt . . . ?'

She nodded, biting her lip.

'Where . . .?'

She tried to rub her side. 'Broke me bleedin' ribs. Christ . . .'

I said urgently, 'You've got to climb. Before there's another shake. We've got to get out . . .'

'Can't . . .'

'Pete, *please* . . .'

She moved painfully then, hand over hand. It was a long time before we got to the top of the pitch. She rolled over on the rock of the upper cave, lay swearing and hugging her middle. I half carried her out to the hill. Once clear of the cave mouth the reaction got me. I sat down on the grass and put my head on my arms. Pete lay on her face for a minute or two then she levered herself up and started trying to be sick. I scrambled across and held her, praying she wouldn't vomit blood. She didn't, there was nearly nothing to come at all. When the spasm was over I looked at her side. Bruises were showing already and she was in a lot of pain. It seemed she was right, she had damaged a rib. But it was vital to get away from the caves. Except for a knife Pete was carrying on her belt we were unarmed, and at any moment the sky could fill with wasps. If that happened we would be through.

I stood up shakily. It was early evening; we'd been in Chill Leer the better part of twenty hours. Below in the road the two Champs were standing where we'd left them. Nothing moved near by; the hillside lay quiet and golden in the sunlight.

I helped Pete down to the cars, trying to cause her as little pain as possible. We reached the nearer of the Champs, she leaned against it panting and trying to wipe her face. I opened the door and eased her inside then turned and looked back. A faint haze of dust still hung above the cave mouth. Somewhere under the hill, deep in blackness and stillness, Greg Douglas was lying in as weird and splendid a tomb as a man could imagine. And Jones Kitchen, and a dozen more. The quiet of the place would never be broken now. Maybe not for another million years . . . I shuddered, got into the Champ, and started up. There was something absurdly reassuring and homely about the bark of the engine. I let the brake off and coasted away, not thinking about wasps. I was just glad to be clear of the caves, and still alive.

The mood didn't last. Common sense came back and I realized I was running a big risk. It was against logic to assume the Furies had deserted the massif after the determination they'd shown the night before. They would be on the lookout for survivors from the colony, any vehicle moving in the area would be liable to be attacked on sight. And we were on a major road, we could run into a patrol any moment. I started watching anxiously for side turnings.

I found one six or eight miles from Chill Leer, swung right into a narrow lane. It proved a good choice; within minutes the main road was out of sight and I was moving over desolate country with no sign either of houses or the domes of the Furies. The road surface soon worsened; Pete gripped the dash, trying to steady herself against jolts. I dropped speed to a crawl, picking my way. It was near sunset when I reached a straggle of cottages. There weren't more than a dozen, not enough to be called a village; it was hard to see why they were there at all, stuck out in the wilds like that. I stopped the car and listened. I was sure the place was deserted, I'd developed a sixth sense for that sort of thing. I had a quick look round but there was nobody about. I helped Pete inside the first house. Getting in was easy enough; the front door had been smashed, it hung drunkenly from one hinge.

The place only boasted a couple of downstairs rooms. In one of them was an old couch. I settled Pete on that and left her while I hid the truck. One of the cottages had a rough lean-to garage built on to it, I drove the Champ inside it out of sight. Then I went foraging. I didn't have much luck; the houses had all been searched destructively, any edibles had been taken. I did find a tin of condensed milk and a half of cheap brandy, shoved out of sight in a sink cupboard. I took them back to Pete, knocked a hole in the tin with a stone, poured a little of the milk into a cup. I topped it up with the spirit and gave it to her; I had no idea whether I was doing right or wrong but it seemed to ease her. She was half asleep, or half unconscious; I felt she would be better upstairs on one of the beds but she didn't want to move. I found some blankets, made her strip her wet shirt and jeans, and wrapped her as well as I could. I managed to get a fire going in the kitchen grate, sat half the night drying Pete's clothes and mine in front of it. Towards dawn I dozed, lying back in an ancient, comfortable chair. I slept fitfully, troubled by a recurrent dream. I saw a Fury, resting on a pile of rocks. It looked a perfect insect but somehow I knew that under the shell it was a machine, a thing of gears and cams and spangled golden oil. In the dream, the Fury heard or saw something that I couldn't detect. It sat up alertly, relays closed and opened, cogs clicked; the puppy face turned, the eyes stared ... That was all, over and over. I woke at first light, bitterly, full of the knowledge that you can't fight machines.

There was a booming. I realized I'd been living in dread of the noise so long my body reacted to it automatically awake or asleep. A dozen wasps passed low overhead but they ignored the house. I thanked God the fire was out and that I'd hidden the truck.

Finding food worried me for a time. There were hares and rabbits round about and a few chickens but they'd gone wild, I couldn't get near them. I searched the cottages again, found something I'd missed before: a couple of yards of thick elastic, the sort that's still used for catapults. I made one. It was crude but it worked. I'd never been much of a shot as a kid but it was a case of having to learn fast. I managed finally to knock over a leveret. It took me another couple of hours to prepare it and stew it. I'd found salt, and there were carrots growing wild in one of the gardens. I stirred them in with the meat and the result wasn't too bad at all. I did the cooking at the far end of the hamlet; I was determined if the Furies smelled it and hunted me out they wouldn't take Pete as well. She was still very sick; I had to coax her to eat, then she only took a couple of mouthfuls. I gave her the rest of the brandy and prepared for the second night, nailing the broken door in place as well as I could. I spent most of the time awake; I heard no Furies but a dog pack was howling somewhere close. I listened uneasily; the animals didn't come into sight, and eventually the noise faded away.

We stayed in hiding five days. By the morning of the sixth Pete said she was well enough to travel. I doubted it but she insisted; if we were going on, the sooner we started the better.

Towards nightfall I brought the Champ down to the house. I'd found Pete an old sweater; I had to help her into it, she couldn't lift her arms higher than her shoulders. Her side was badly discoloured; I thought binding it would help, that was what people used to do with damaged ribs. We tried, using strips torn from a sheet, but the effort caused her so much pain we had to stop. I put her into the truck and drove away hoping to find a road that would take me to the coast.

The next two days were bad. The land to the south of the Mendips was thick with nests and symbo traffic was continuous. It was impossible to use the main roads. I was forced eastwards; I travelled mostly after dark, detouring and backing to avoid crevasses, circling round both nest areas and human towns. By the second night I was miles off course and well into Dorset, but I knew the ground ahead of me. Most of the coastline of the county is guarded by hills. To seaward of them is a string of towns; Bridport in the west, Weymouth,

191

Swanage; and Barford, from where I'd once set out looking for Jane. Inland to the east are tracts of heath, sour and flat. A lot of them used to be Army ground, tank training areas and gunnery ranges. I'd nearly reached the wasteland, and my hopes were starting to rise, when the Champ blew a tyre. And we carried no spare.

I drove on the rim for half a mile but it was useless; I couldn't hold the car straight and the jolting was hurting Pete. We'd be better on foot. We got out, left the car on the side of the road, and started walking. When dawn caught up with us we were out on the heathland, the Purbecks showing ahead of us blue and vague, nothing round about for miles but heather and scrubby grass. We carried on for an hour, moving slowly. By then it was getting hot; there had been no rain for days, and the sun still beat from a cloudless sky. We stopped in the shade of a straggle of bushes. I'd brought a bottle of water from the Champ, we shared it then pushed on again. After another hour the hills seemed no closer and Pete admitted she couldn't go on much longer. We holed up again, finding what cover we could. About midday Pete shook me out of a doze. I sat up and rubbed my face, wished we hadn't finished the water. I said, 'What is it, love?'

She was looking back fixedly the way we'd come. She didn't answer, just raised her hand and pointed. I stared, screwing my eyes up. The horizon was shimmering with heat haze, for a minute I couldn't see a thing. Then I made out bright dots rising and falling, hovering over the grass. Furies. They were strung out in a line right and left, as far as I could see.

Pete licked her mouth and grinned. She said bitterly, 'That's our lot then, Bill, there the little dears are. I thought they was bein' slow . . .'

I was still staring at the wasps. They seemed to be beating, exploring every nook and cranny, but they weren't using their intelligence. If they were really after us, if they knew who we were and that we were on the heath, why the devil didn't they quarter it from the air, they'd flush us easily that way . . . I said, 'Maybe it's nothing to do with us, just some crazy game of their own.'

She shook her head. 'They found the car, we should have hidden it. They're on to us all right, you better get out . . .'

'What the hell do you think you're going to do?'

She took the knife from her belt. 'I can get one of 'em . . . go on, Bill, while you got the chance . . .'

The wasps were closer now. Their progress was slow, but it was inexorable. Odds were they'd spot us as soon as we moved but we couldn't just sit and wait. And I was tired of heroics. I pulled Pete up by the wrist. She started banging at my fingers with the hand that held the knife. 'What're you doin' . . . Bill, damn an' blast you, *let go* . . .'

'Don't be a bloody little fool. And put that thing away before you hurt somebody . . .'

She squirmed, pulling back, leaning her weight against me. '*No* . . .'

I yelled at her, 'Do what you're told . . .' I didn't expect her to obey me but she did. We headed away from the cordon. There was no cover, the Furies must have seen us. But they didn't fly, why wouldn't they fly?

We kept going most of the afternoon, resting when we had to, watching the endless dance of the insects behind us. Whenever we lay down I thought Pete wasn't going to get up again but she always managed to. At times I thought we were gaining on the wasps, at others they would encroach suddenly, close the gap to a quarter of a mile. And then we'd try to hurry. Pete didn't complain, and she had no breath now to argue. Her lips were set, somehow her face looked frozen, a cat-mask that couldn't show feelings. As the day wore on it seemed she found fresh energy. There was no coaxing now; she was moving as fast as I was, faster, pushing her body to its limit of endurance, giving it all the pain it could take before it found a release in death. This was her Way of the Cross. She was deliberately choosing the worst path for herself, jumping gullies, forcing her way through bushes. Once when I stumbled she yanked at me and tried to laugh. I wanted her to slow, stop again, do anything but what she was doing to herself but she wouldn't listen. Not any more.

The heath. It reached away for miles, dry, russet-purple, empty, vibrating with heat, a background to hopelessness. There was no sound except the noise of our breathing, no movements but the dancing of the mirage, the rising and bobbing of the cordon behind us. My tongue started to feel

193

like it was too big for my mouth, my head was pounding. In front the hills were higher, more solid, but the heath still stretched round us, bright, flat, uncaring ... And the Furies were closer now, I could hear their booming dully through the noise of the blood in my ears. I kept moving but it was futile. We'd been anachronisms from the start, outlaws in an alien culture. The only way was to kill us, get us both, just let it happen quickly ...

There was a road. It arrowed away each side of us. Beyond it bushes and scrub; then the heath again, pulsing with sunlight. We crossed the macadam, staggering a little, fell into cover on the far side, lay trying to get our breath. Pete was the first to move. She got to her knees; then she started to laugh. In front of us was another cordon. The wasps were close enough to see the brilliance of their markings, the silver haze of wings. I spun round. The first line was closing fast to cut us off.

Pete stayed where she was, kneeling upright. She'd pulled her shirt open across her breasts, her hair was in her eyes, she was running sweat. She glared from me to the wasps and back. 'Bastards,' she said. '*Bastards* ... They di'n't need to fly, Bill. It was more fun like this, it was slower ...'

I heard the noise of an engine.

The truck rolled towards us out of the endless brilliance. It was old and dilapidated; its cab was square and high, its sides were extended by tall wooden racks that swayed as it moved. It left behind a faint trail of blue fume that hung in the air. The lorry stopped opposite us and its driver climbed down. He was short and ruddy faced, dressed in shabby trousers and sweater. He stood looking round, then he shouted. 'If you'm anywhere about, show yourselves. Where are ye?'

We'd shrunk back behind the bushes. Pete stood up quickly. The knife was in her hand again. She said, 'We're here, mate. What's it to you?'

He ran across to us. 'Come on for Christ's sake, we ain't got but a minute ...'

I followed him dazedly. The wasp lines were very close. He was already dropping the tailboard of the truck; I picked Pete up and swung her aboard, scrambled after her. There were a pile of sacks, a heap of straw, an old tarpaulin. I huddled

194

under it, pulled Pete after me. Before we were out of sight the truck was moving again. Minutes later I realized we'd got clear.

We couldn't tell where we were headed. I sensed once we were climbing a steep gradient, minutes later we coasted down a hill. I crawled to the side of the truck. Pete edged up alongside me. There was a gap in the boards an inch or so wide. I craned my neck. We'd left the heath already, I saw cottages, a rolling hillscape. Pete yanked my elbow and crowed, pointing; I saw miles off between the hills the dazzling shield of the sea.

Some time later the lorry stopped. It was stuffy under the tarp and airless, but we kept still while more sacks were loaded aboard. When we moved off I went back to the peep-hole. We were crossing some sort of compound; in the background were small domes surrounded by catwalks and gantries. We passed a bay where trucks were being piled with produce; the loading area was protected by a roof of the same scaly paper the wasps used for their nests. After we left the camp there were three or four more stops. Each time, sacks were off-loaded. This was the Fury economy in full blast.

A half-mile farther on the road curved abruptly to the right and we lost sight of the sea. The truck slowed; for a moment I thought it was stopping again then the driver turned sharply and the lorry began to bounce across a rough track. I felt Pete grip my arm. A second later I heard the noise that had startled her; a deep, continuous booming, audible above the clatter of the truck's engine. I'd heard that sound before, too often to mistake it. Ahead of us was a wasp city.

Pete started to struggle. I hung on to her. It was too late now to try to bolt; we were surrounded by Furies, I could see bright clouds of them through the chink in the boards. Then the nest area came into sight. It was the biggest I'd ever seen; it covered the top of a high down, spilled across the nearer slope towards us. How far it extended out of sight I could only guess. It was a panorama of gold and blue; the afternoon sun brightened the endless domes, picked out the scales and shingles, the striations that ran through the pulp like primitive patterns. The nearest nests were big but they were dwarfed by those beyond. Topping them all was an edifice that must have

195

been two or three hundred feet high. Round it on level after level fibrous tunnels looped and branched, striped, ganglionated, pierced by soaring lattices of girders. It was like a great animal, it was like a machine, it thundered with the life of more Furies than I had ever seen. The swarm towered hundreds of yards into the sky; inside it, a cosmic maths lesson had gone haywire. I saw shapes, triangles and momentary cubes, rhomboids, circles, and squares that melted into each other and into brightness.

The lorry swayed and bucked. My throat was dry and I could feel sweat running down my face. Pete was still fighting silently to get free but keeping still was our only chance. I was still clinging to the hope that we weren't being taken in to be killed. After all the symbo had hidden us out on the road. I put my arm across Pete's shoulders and gripped the lorry side; she tried to wriggle backwards but I'd got her pinned. She gave up suddenly, lay with her face down panting and swearing. I put my eye to the crack in the boards again.

We were entering the nest complex. The great domes were out of sight now, rearing above my angle of vision. We passed under an overhanging roof of pulp, into a brown twilight.

There were beaten roads inside the nest but they turned and twisted till I lost all sense of direction. There was a confused din; somewhere a hooter was blaring and men by the dozen were scurrying about and yelling. I got glimpses of cars, lorries, whole shanty villages half hidden under sloping planes of wood-pulp. The huts were beehive-shaped and low; round them naked children were playing and dogs were running about. The air was humid and the whole effect tropical and primitive somehow. Tunnels and catwalks overlapped above us; through the rare rifts sunlight lanced down golden and startling as if through the interlaced branches of a jungle. We passed an m/t section, a dim cave lit by service lamps in heavy well-glasses. Then another, open to the pathway, where a dozen men were hauling along something that looked like a huge heating unit. I saw loading bays stacked with sugar and grain, once a workshop where women were assembling lengths of scaffold tube into complex shapes under the green glare of a mercury vapour lamp. The air was full of the scent of the Furies themselves, musky and thick as incense.

196

We pulled in finally beside a loading platform of beaten earth. The driver came round and flicked back the tarpaulin. I sat up quickly, still holding Pete's arm. I opened my mouth to speak but the symbo shut me up abruptly. 'Can't talk yere,' he said gruffly. 'Come on, quick ...' He flung a terse piece of advice over his shoulder. 'Don't pay no heed to the wasps. They woan't touch 'ee now ...'

Pete's face was pale in the gloom and her hand was on the knife at her belt. I steered her after our guide through a winding tunnel of wood-pulp. Twenty yards on, the tube turned to the left and dipped sharply. I edged down an earth slope, ducked through an archway, and straightened up again.

The air was stiflingly hot, and the smell had intensified. It had a heady quality that seemed to work its way into the blood, fuzzing up thought. I realized we were inside one of the great domes; the curved walls distorted and magnified the noise from above till it sounded like a dozen huge organs playing together but playing no tune, just pitches that swayed and shifted round the threshold of audibility.

There was light but it was confused and brown; that and the roaring made it seem as if we were swimming underwater, lost in a sepia ocean. I made out objects, senseless at first and vague. In front of me was what looked like a monstrous tiered wedding cake, or the Campanile at Pisa. It stretched upwards till it vanished in gloom; each layer was four feet or more thick and supported from the next by innumerable squat pillars. The whole thing was laced with steel girders and round the edges of the tiers ran looms of cable, strung haphazardly with glowing electric elements suspended every few feet. The light reflected redly from thousands of roughly-made cells but it was only when I saw the protruding heads of the grubs and I realized I was looking at the side of a monstrous brood comb.

Our guide was waving to us impatiently. I moved forward, feeling Pete quiver. We were on a gallery that ran round inside the nest wall; to our right an excavation like a bomb crater housed the roots of the comb. The place must once have been a whirl of activity but now it was nearly deserted; the nurses had left to join the aerial dance over the city. I saw odd wasps wandering aimlessly, making no attempt to feed their charges.

One turned to stare at us as we stepped past and my back hair rose but we weren't molested. Many of the larvae had lost their grip and fallen from the cells, lay throbbing like yard-long white stacks. I peered over the edge of the hole; below were heaving drifts of grubs.

Halfway round the circumference of the dome a metal stairway rose into darkness. The symbo hurried up it; we followed and found ourselves in one of the tunnel systems.

In places the walls were very thin and some process had rendered the pulp translucent; through it flowed a creamy-brown light. The complex had been designed more for flying traffic than humans; the way was full of twists and swellings, we tripped on brightly-painted girders; there were queer levels and drops and sometimes whole floor sections gave and swayed as we walked on them, bringing me out in sweat. My head was whirling again; there was nothing for the mind or hands to grasp, it seemed as we climbed through those dry arteries we were skewed out of reality into some mad dimension. The booming was below us now as well as above, and mixed with the noise of the wind; it seemed I could feel the whole system giving and surging to its pressure.

A Fury passed us, scuttling like a dog; something unidentifiable trailed from its mouth-parts. We passed another curled up in a side chamber. It was slashing and crunching busily; I saw with no sense of surprise that it was eating itself, tail first. Its abdomen was curved under it, gripped in one of the great pairs of legs; the mandibles rasped, tearing aside sections of chitin, chopping at the pinkish quivering flesh beneath. The mask lifted for a moment and stared; Pete turned away, pressed the back of her hand across her mouth. We moved on; another passage, a steep scrambling climb and the arched doorway of a large chamber showed ahead. The symbo paused and slapped at the pulp bulkhead. A voice spoke quietly; our guide turned back and gestured us forward with a movement of his head.

The chamber was high and airy, filled with the dim roaring of the swarm. Pulp windows, veined and textured like rich stained glass, reached from floor to vaulted roof. In front of them, at a lightweight metal desk, a man was sitting. He was elderly and lined with thinning, wavy silver hair. He wore rope sandals, jeans, and a faded check shirt. He got up as we entered, smiling, slightly. 'Thank you, John,' he said, 'I don't think we need keep you any longer.' Then to us, 'Sit down please, will you?' The smile became a little broader. 'You look as if you could both use a drink...'

CHAPTER 14

I DON'T KNOW what I'd been expecting but for a moment the transition to normality floored me. I sat stupidly, holding a glass and staring at its contents. The symbo waved a hand in a deprecating sort of way. 'Home-brewed, I'm afraid,' he said. 'The best we can offer. It isn't too bad; or maybe one grows used to it.' He steepled his fingers and watched us calmly. I took a sip of the hooch and coughed. I looked round at the incongruous details of the office; I saw a filing cabinet, its top piled with folders and notebooks, and a telephone; in one corner was a purring electric fan and the side wall carried a line of coat-hooks. Hanging from one of them was an old tweed jacket, leather patched at cuffs and elbows.

The symbo produced a cherrywood pipe, lit it, and extinguished the match carefully in a can of water beside his chair. He blew a cloud of rank-smelling smoke, watched me a moment longer through it. 'Well,' he said, 'I suppose I'd better answer the more obvious questions for you. What this place is, who I am, etcetera.'

I nodded and found my voice. 'Yeah,' I said. 'That'll do for a start.'

He was enjoying himself in a rarefied sort of way. He gestured again briefly. 'The complex you saw on the way in is known to us for convenience as Nest 481. In a sense it represents the capital of the region though "capital" is a purely human concept, there are few real points of comparison between Keeper culture and our own. My name is Harmon; I'm Symbiotic Controller for the nest, and incidentally for a large part of the south-west. Rather a high-flown title; unfortunately the position is ... ah ... unsalaried.' He smiled again, fleetingly.

I grasped at a straw. 'What did you say, Keeper? *Keeper* culture?'

He nodded. 'Yes. The ... ah ... creatures you think of I believe as Furies. An interesting description though classically unsound, the original Furies were of course exclusively female...'

Pete was sitting on the edge of her chair. I could feel the tension in her. 'Get to it, mate,' she said coarsely. 'Have we come here for the chop, or haven't we?'

Harmon raised his eyebrows, tamped the bowl of his stage-prop pipe. Then he shook his head. 'No,' he said. 'Oh no ... But your position is ... ah ... delicate. I'm afraid we're entering on a difficult period.'

Suddenly I wanted to lie down and sleep for a week. 'Look,' I said. 'Just tell me what goes on, will you? Keep it simple. You know, for the morons. But don't be funny. I lost my sense of humour.'

His eyes watched me steadily for a moment. 'Yes,' he said. 'A lot of us have.' There was tension; then he relaxed and started to talk. It was from him I first heard the story of the beings that had called themselves the Keepers, and of the colossal hoax they had perpetrated on mankind. How they'd studied our planet, compared its life phylia; how they'd chosen the lot of the social insects, how they had built the first bodies painfully, molecule by molecule, built them from nothingness, from water and air. How they'd sent out the first of their kind tentatively, in twos and threes, till the day of the bombs came, and the great invasion. Three or four men wandered in while Harmon was talking; they were bearded and hard-faced, they lounged about watching us bleakly. A tight feeling started to gather somewhere at the bottom of my throat. We were in worse trouble here than we had been on the heath; one wrong move and we would be for it. I glanced across at Pete. Her nostrils were dilated slightly and her face was white as chalk.

'You've been rather an inconvenience to all of us,' Harmon finished up mildly. 'So much so in fact that when I heard you were out on the heath I decided to have a look at you. Vulgar curiosity, I'm afraid...'

'Harmon,' I said. 'What in hell—'

The phone buzzed. He excused himself and picked up the handset. He listened frowning; then, 'Yes ... Yes, I see ... What? If you possibly can ... yes, any way you can ... Yes hank you, I'll let you know.' He dropped the phone back on he cradle, and turned to one of the men who'd come in. 'Our riends from Dome Eight, Gren,' he said. 'Trying to reach the armoury. The third-level folk have cut another six tunnels ... Get some more people up there will you, and a couple of fire control parties. Just in case ...' The symbo left, quietly.

Harmon looked back at me inquiringly. I said, 'So you're a grade one boy on theory. But the bastards still look like wasps to me. You reckon you know all this, what do they do? Talk to you or something?'

He spread his hands flat on the desk and looked at the inger-nails. When he lifted his head, his face was greyish. Yes,' he said. 'They talk to me. Or something ...'

Right from the start, there had been humans who could link n with the group mind of the wasps. Just a handful, scattered here and there. They didn't have to be anybody special. Harmon spoke like a biology lecturer or a college don; he'd been a soap salesman. He'd walked in a grass field that first wild night and listened to the voices piping from nowhere, threatening and promising. If voices is the proper word, he talked of a goldenness that was not light or sound but a colloidal blending of both ... It was Harmon and men like him who'd made the railways run, built the pylons and the steel-frame nests, started the farms and refineries again. I could have guessed at something like that, extrapolated it from what I'd seen of the interlocking of human and Fury culture. Only I'd been too busy trying to stay alive.

He kept on talking. 'Under normal circumstances, of course, your colony would have been exterminated some time ago; and John certainly wouldn't have been able to bring you here so easily. But the last wasps to be programmed are now nearly as mindless as machines. They're still hunting for you on the heath; the cordons have crossed and recrossed several times now.'

An idea that had been picking at the roots of my brain shaped itself suddenly. The attack on the great nest had been crazy from the start, if the Furies had been normal we wouldn't have got near. And the brainless behaviour of the creatures on the heath, the wild swarming, the self-destruction . . . 'Harmon,' I said. I was nearly shouting. *'What's the matter with the wasps?'*

He had been brooding, chin on linked hands; he turned to me vaguely and I saw his eyes refocus. 'The wasps,' he said. 'The wasps are dying. Racial regression . . .' He spoke as if the thing had no importance.

I opened my mouth, and shut it. The swarm outside sounded faint then roared loud in my skull. The phone buzzed again; one of the symbos answered it. I didn't hear what was said.

'I suppose,' said Harmon, 'you would call it madness. It . . . ah . . . isn't madness. Not as you conceive it at least. It's very interesting . . . very interesting indeed . . .'

The words dropped out expressionlessly, little dry husks of sound; I sat trying to take them in and realize the implication. 'I remember a story once,' said Harmon, 'in which a man was buried alive for . . . ah . . . purposes which I forget. There was as I recollect a tube, which enabled him to breathe. None the less he died. Somewhat ironic; the implication appeared to be, that the only fit occupant for a coffin is a corpse. In a slightly similar way the . . . ah . . . the Keepers misjudged the gross influence of material bodies.' He slumped lower in his chair while his hands, white and thin-fingered, fluttered in front of his face, shaping theorems in the air. Nearly, I thought inconsequently, like the antannae of a wasp . . . 'Consider their problems,' said Harmon. 'And its solution. Their need for an armoured, a perfect, body, a form adapted totally to the environment they had decided to own. Something powerful, nearly indestructible . . . What better, logically, than to take a machine, the shell of an insect, something shaped by countless millions of years of evolution, a thing already perfect in itself, suited to the business of living on this odd little world. To take such a shell and copy it membrane for membrane, joint for joint. This they accomplished, and breathed life into the result. Their life . . . But they didn't realize until far too late what they had done.

'It would seem that irrespective of size a worm or a gnat has little chance of acquiring true intelligence. Too many . . . ah

202

... inbuilt behaviour traits, the body form conditions intelligence as the brain dictates the movements of the shell that houses it. A worm will be a worm, and a man a man, and a wasp a wasp ... Their wasp-brains defeated them, the ancient skills, the racial memories ... they were building their own new minds, had they realized it, as they formed the exoskeletons. Once trapped inside them, they became ... wasps. Chewers of wood, feeders on flesh, and jam...' His fingers slid together till they interlocked tightly. 'A superb irony, don't you think? The Keepers could have come as golden gods, had they chosen; but then of course they would have had the limitations of gods. Which might or might not have been considerable...'

'Look,' I said. 'Just take it slow. Are you trying to tell me—'

He lifted his hand. 'The Keepers are dying,' he said. 'The ... ah ... invasion is ended. They were forced to attempt mastery of ... ah ... disciplines foreign to their natures. In the interests of their survival, they desired bombs and guns and tanks. But wasps cannot understand bombs and guns and tanks.' He tittered suddenly, and instantly repressed the noise. 'They were at a disadvantage,' he said. 'A disadvantage...'

Pete said huskily, 'Bill, dearest...' I should have been warned by the tone of her voice. I didn't look up. I could see now the fatal drawback of a group mind. If one individual was a genious, the race became a superspecies. *But if one went mad* ... I said, 'That's it, isn't it, Harmon? They had to try to study. Because they knew we'd whip them one day. And they couldn't understand...'

'Yes,' he said gently. 'The ... ah ... derangement is spreading. Very soon they will be incapable of coherent action.'

Yet it still didn't add up. I said sharply, 'But you reckoned these ... energy knots, whatever they were, floated in from space and studied us. They were logical, they had all knowledge, they knew what they were doing. They chose the sort of brains they wanted, the brains that could dominate the earth. They knew they'd have to deal with machines...'

He watched me steadily and it seemed the answer came into my mind of its own accord, rooted there and grew and flowered absurdly. I tried not to start laughing, I knew I'd have a job to stop. 'Harmon,' I said. *'When did they come . . .?'*

His hands trembled momentarily. 'That's difficult to answer,' he said. 'Time did not ... ah ... manifest itself to them in a way we can understand. To them their birth was the work of what we might call an hour. Or a thousand years. When they first observed us there were no machines. Vespasian was the ruler of Rome—'

Pete's chair spun across the chamber. She turned in the doorway, half-crouched with the knife in her hand. 'Well look at you, Bill,' she said. 'Sittin' soakin' in a load of mush ... They're crackers, you know that? He's crackers. Out of his tiny mind . . .'

Harmon hadn't moved. He said tiredly, 'Put that thing down, will you? Believe me, I understand how you feel . . .'

Pete grinned at him. 'I wonder if you do,' she said gently. 'I wonder if you do, symbo . . .' She used the word caressingly, as if it was an endearment.

Things happened fast. The man who had driven the truck appeared behind her in the tunnel. She saw my face change and tried to turn but he'd already got her wrist. I yelled at her and tried to get up; somebody caught me a thump that sent me sprawling. The chamber rocked; I got to my knees and saw Pete struggling. Two men were holding her while she wrenched and lunged; John shifted his grip and she ducked her head and bit like a cat. He swore, and somebody cracked her across the face. Pete spat and brought her knee up viciously; the symbo dropped sprawling and I landed across him. I gashed my knuckles twice on his teeth before I realized he wasn't fighting back.

I looked up, panting. There was the barrel of an army revolver. The hand that held it was very steady. Harmon spoke greyly from across the chamber. 'Get up,' he said. 'Or that man will kill you . . .'

I got up, and went to Pete. She was glaring, sweat glinting on her face. Harmon stood up and leaned back on the desk. His wrists vibrated as they took his weight. The man who was holding the gun swore disgustedly. 'Take 'em back where we got 'em,' he said. 'Let the bloody wasps pick 'em over. All they're fit for . . .'

Harmon shook his head, rubbed his hand across his eyes. 'No,' he said. 'There's been killing enough already.' He came round the desk to us. I hadn't realized he was such a small man. 'As I told you,' he said, 'the next few days will be difficult. Within hours the wasps will have lost all control. When that happens, anarchy will result. Our people won't be held under indefinitely ... Fighting is already going on in this complex; should the ... ah ... wilder elements gain control your lives and mine would be equally forfeit. We must confine you for a brief period at least, for your own safety. I guarantee you won't be harmed...' He moved closer and his hands were gliding over each other as though rinsing themselves with invisible soap. When he spoke again his voice was indistinct. 'I did what seemed to be best,' he said. 'From the start. You ... ah ... understand that. What seemed to be best...'

We were hustled away down the corridor.

The chamber to which we were taken was low and dark, a mere knotty excrescence in the pulp wall of a tunnel. The one opening into it was closed by a human-made grille of iron; in lieu of windows, a single ten-watt bulb burned dimly. Beneath it was a niche in the wall; blankets had been spread to form a bed. Pete lay down on it. The swarm-noise still roared round us; I'd been hearing it for so long now it seemed it had become a part of me.

They brought us a tray of food. There was a bottle of water, a couple of rough loaves, some cheese and hand-made butter; and miraculously, rolling tobacco, papers, and matches. Pete drank a little but she wouldn't eat. I made a couple of cigarettes, lit one for her. Then I went to the grille. Outside, a few feet away a symbo stood stolidly, gun in the crook of his arm. He gestured me back from the bars; I went and sat by Pete, lit my cigarette. I smoked it through and stubbed the butt; then I laid my head against the pulp wall and let my eyes drift shut. I felt dead tired, unable to think any more. I listened to the hypnotic sound of the swarm for a while, then I slept.

When I sat up the noise of the wasps had lessened. I blinked and rubbed my face. I thought I'd merely dozed for a few minutes but some change in the lighting outside the grille told me it was night outside. Just above me the bulb still glowed sickly yellow; under my feet the pulp vibrated slightly, transmitting the rumbling sleeplessness of the huge nest. As I sat I heard something that sounded like firing a long way away. The sound came to me queerly distorted by the tunnels. The fighting was still going on; I wondered why, what anybody could hope to gain now. I thought about Harmon and the others like him. People who'd risen from nothingness to power unlimited, and the unearthly confidences of the wasps. What would there be for them, when it was all through? How would we treat them, as traitors or heroes?

I shook my head. It was difficult to believe, even after what I'd seen, that we'd won back our birthright by default. I turned and looked at Pete. Her eyes were open, watching me. One hand lay slack. I reached across and took it, rubbed the knuckles slowly with my thumb. Her fingers felt cold. 'Pete,' I said. 'You OK now?'

'Yeah.' Her voice was flat, disinterested. 'Yeah, I'm OK. Why shouldn't I be?'

'You're not. What's wrong?'

'I told you, mate,' she said. 'I'm all right . . .'

I got up and sat on the edge of the pulp shelf. She lay quiet, watching me over the blankets. 'It's done, Pete,' I said. 'The wasps are through. It's all over.' I didn't know what else to say.

She moved restlessly, turned her face away. She muttered, 'Over for some . . .'

'It's over for you. Pete, do something for me.'

Silence.

'Pete?'

'What . . .'

I said, 'Nothing. Do nothing. Just play it quiet till we get out of here. OK?'

No answer. Her face was in shadow; I brushed the hair back from her eyes, dropped my hand to the side of her throat. She felt smooth, and warm. I said, 'You're a crazy bitch, you nearly had the pair of us chopped back there . . .'

She made a little noise, halfway between a laugh and a sniff. Her fingers moved up to curl on the edge of the blanket. I watched her. I was at a loss and she knew it. I said, 'Say something, if it's only drop dead.'

She made the snorting noise again. She said, 'It's funny, y'know . . .'

'What's funny?'

'Everythin'. You, me ... it's a right ruddy laugh when you think about it, ain't it? We just go round, an' round ... Don't get no farther, none of us.'

'What do you mean?'

'Ahh, nothin'. Nothin' that matters.'

'Tell me.'

Her voice was thin and flat, the words slurred by sleep. She said, 'I lay here thinkin'. All sorts o' things. Right back to when I went on the streets. Funny the way things keep goin' round, sometimes. Like you got a tune in your head. No reason for it, really ...'

I waited.

'Funny time that was,' she said. 'I wadn't no age. Fifteen, sixteen, can't remember. Had a bloke then, nice sort o' bloke. Young an' all that, you know ... But he was all right. I'd been goin' with him a few months. Dead serious we was, savin' up to be married an' that. The whole caper ...'

She was quiet again. The long muscles in her throat moved as she swallowed. I said, 'What went wrong?'

'He had to go in the Army. He got real cut up about it. Tried all sorts o' things to get out of it ...' She grinned faintly to herself, head still turned away. 'Had somethin' up with his shoulder,' she said. 'The right shoulder it were, the joint was weak or somethin'. Used to swing his arm round his head a few times and it'd all swell up like a football. He reckoned that'd get him out. Only they still had him ...'

I touched her hair again. Some faint scent came from her; not sweat and not perfume, just her own special smell. The past year had sharpened my senses; I realized I'd been able to tell for a long time, without turning, if she was near. She said, 'It were the night before he went off. We'd bin to the flicks. You know, try an' get his mind off it an' all that. He were real cut up. "I wanted you," he says. That was afterwards, when we was walkin' home. "I wanted you,' he says. "I di'n't want to wait no two years or three, I wanted you. You don't know what it's like," he says. "It's all right for you ..." He was cryin' a bit, you know. Christ, poor old Col ... He wadn't no age see? Neither of us were ...'

I said, 'Take yourself apart, Pete. Like a picture puzzle.

207

Find out what makes you tick. Confessions of a street-walker . . .'

She turned her face into the light. She looked haggard; dark lines showed under her eyes, the scar curled to touch her lip. 'I'm not confessin',' she said. 'Nothin' to confess.' She paused. 'I saw a film once on the Box. They were talkin' to these kids, you know, tarts. Askin' 'em all about it, why they was on the streets, that sort o' thing. They couldn't none of 'em say. It were just the way they lived, that were all.'

'Do you know why you did it?'

'Yeah,' she said. 'I know.' She spoke carefully, squeezing the words out as if each one was a little pain. 'I done it 'cause I liked it,' she said. 'It was a good life, most o' the time. I met some nice blokes. Sounds funny don't it? But I was high-class. Good at me job . . .'

'Why didn't you marry your boyfriend?'

She sneered. 'Marry him' she said. 'Cor, stroll on. He hated my ruddy guts . . . I did his, for a while. Then it didn't matter no more.' She licked her lips and frowned, watching me with her odd wide eyes. 'I was tryin' to help see?' she said. 'It di'n't matter to me, not the way it did to him. "Christ," I said to him, "don't go on like that," I said. "Here, come here, it's all right. I don't mind . . ."'

'But it wasn't all right.'

She looked derisive. 'What?' she said. 'First time? It never is mate. Only in the story books. I'd got it all to learn . . .'

There was a lot I wanted to say to her but I still didn't know how to phrase it. Maybe it was just reaction but in a strange way I was scared for her. She was beside me and close. I could touch her, but I couldn't stop her drifting away in a hopeless grey sea. Like Jane in *Enchantress* . . .

I reached down and gripped her shoulders. I know I dug my fingers in; her eyes opened in surprise then she frowned because I was hurting. Suddenly the words came; I could see what I wanted her to understand. The logic was wild and misty; I spoke quickly, stumbling through what I had to say before I forgot it. 'Pete,' I said, 'this thing about the wasps. About you wanting to die. In the caves, and out on the heath. And now . . . you're hurting yourself now because you can't find anybody to do it for you. You've got to stop, now. It's too

208

late, it doesn't matter any more. You missed your chance . . .'

She brought her hands up and tried to shove me off. I tightened my grip. I said, 'You are going to listen, this time. You wanted to be a martyr, you wanted to go out with a bang. You told yourself you brought the Furies, you killed your mother and your father and your family, you had to die to make things right. But you were lying, that wasn't the reason. I'll tell you what was wrong. You were sorry for yourself. Before the wasps ever came. You were sorry for what you'd turned into, you were sorry for what you'd done. You never wanted that boy. You were too young, all the rest was a way of getting out of it. You couldn't forget that, you tried to give yourself away to make up but it wasn't any good . . . Pete, it's all in the past, the Furies are nothing to do with you. Nothing to do with any of us, can't you see that? You can't keep fighting now, *you can't die because the Romans conquered Gaul* . . .'

She'd been arching about, trying to push me away. She stopped squirming suddenly, lay looking at me. The queerest expressions chased across her face; frowns, wincings, little quirky smiles. Her eyes flickered from side to side; she shook her head, grinned again. But what she was thinking, or what she would have said, I never found out.

The chamber swayed as if a hammer had struck it. The floor groaned, shock waves thrilled in the walls. The movement came again, more violently; and from somewhere under our feet there was a long hollow roar. Abruptly, the light went out.

I stood up convulsively, still holding Pete's wrist. I heard shouts and screams and the firing again, unmistakable now and close. For a second I couldn't think. I'd half turned to face the doorway; I saw the tunnel beyond the grating flash bright and darken again. Then the light was back but redder now and flickering. A dull booming replaced the sharper noise of the wasps; a gust of heat blew from somewhere, lifting my hair. Understanding came shockingly. The complex was on fire.

I ran to the bars. The tunnel beyond, sketched by a wavering orange glare, was empty. There was no sign of our guard. I put my shoulder to the grating. The iron groaned and stayed put. An acrid tang of burning drifted round me, smoke stung my eyes. I heaved again, violently. The catch gave, tore a chunk from the pulp wall. Pete grabbed my hand and we ran, slipping and skidding. No time for thinking any more.

A gale of heated air was blowing through the complex, bringing with it the roar of the flames and the musketry-crackle of burning pulp. The tunnels twisted and branched in a deadly sameness, swooping, crossing, splitting a hundred ways. In some, lights still burned; others were black as pitch. I stumbled along them, falling against the girder supports that pierced their walls. I tried to remember the route we'd used before but it was hopeless. The firing sounded again; it echoed weirdly, flinging back mockeries of itself till I couldn't tell whether the noise came from in front or behind. We were caught in a holocaust; through pulp windows I saw the sky glowing red, side tunnels panted heat at us. From some of them came the glaring light of flames. The symbos, cooped and watered and fed like animals, were taking a crazy revenge; nothing left now but to kill, and burn.

We reached an intersection. Pete was panting and holding her side. I was half blinded by smoke; I felt the floor trending downwards and followed it. I realized my mistake in seconds; the tunnel began to sway sickeningly, surging to my movements. I pulled up somehow, feeling colder air on my face. The fibrous tube had been severed; the unsupported tip moved slowly like the cut head of a worm. Across a tinged circle of night sky the opposing complex swayed raggedly, dropping gouts of orange cinders. Beyond it a dome had become a huge volcano; flame and brilliant flakes whirled up from its roof. I turned away pulling Pete behind me. She was holding an arm across her face; she screamed something but I didn't hear what it was. The noise inside the tunnels was deafening now; the firing was continuous and mixed with a thousand yells and screams. Bells and klaxon hooters added their raucousness to the din.

We got back to the fork, climbing towards the heat of the flames, and took the other tunnel. A few yards on it opened out abruptly; a spidery metal catwalk showed, spanning the void beyond. We pounded over it, crossed above a vast red-lit comb. From the far wall a dozen tunnels spurted flame on to the close-packed tiers of cells; I saw wasps, apparently oblivious of the heat, hauling grubs from the racks and dispatching them with quick snaps of their jaws. Pete squeezed my arm and yelled again, pointing; I saw a steel ladder spiralling down beside the comb. I ran to it; I was half a dozen steps down when a file of symbos ran across the earth floor below. One stopped and pointed, there was a shout, and bullets splashed flakes from the pulp over my head. I jerked back desperately, colliding with Pete; we were off the catwalk in a dozen strides, into the opposing tunnel and clear.

It seemed we ran through the nightmare for an hour, trying all the time to work our way down to ground level. Very slowly we left behind the worst of the heat and din. My lungs started to labour; each breath came as a separate sharp pain. Beside me Pete was reeling, still trying to clutch her side. Neither of us could run much farther.

We were in a wide, down-sloping tunnel lit sparsely by low-wattage bulbs. I pulled up. Air, sucked in to join the firestorm behind me, soughed past me. My ears were buzzing from the din we'd passed through but I could still dimly hear the rumble of the flames. They would spread to engulf the complex; it was only its vast size that had saved us till now. I'd given up all hope of finding my way out; we might stagger half the night through that huge coiling maze and never reach open air. We'd run into the symbos first, or the flames would cut us off.

In front of my knees ran one of the brightly painted girders. I pulled Pete across it out of harm's way and went back. We had to be near ground level. There was only one way of finding out; I clung to the girder, put my heels together, and jumped, bringing my weight down on the pulp floor. At the third or fourth try the fibres parted with a snap, leaving me clutching the support with my legs half through a yard-wide hole. I peered down, sweating. Below me was earth, maybe twenty feet away. I shouted to Pete and pointed. She understood; she swung down through the hole and dropped, I saw her land and roll aside. I let go the girder, trying to keep my body slack. My shirt tore on something; then the ground hit me, driving my knees up to my chin. My teeth cracked together; for a moment I was half dazed then Pete was pulling at my shoulder. I got up and stared round.

We'd fallen between two of the smaller domes; the flames

211

were behind us, I could see their reflections dancing on the weird hills of pulp. By sheer luck our flight had taken us almost to the edge of the nest area. We started to run again, keeping to the shadows. I sensed movements round us in the darkness and once a truck passed, headlights glaring, wheels churning desperately for a grip in the crumbling soil, but we were not challenged. A few minutes more and we were clear of the perimeter, the last of the nests bulking behind us. Somewhere a dome exploded with a drawn-out roar; the column of fire that rose from it lit the country for miles around. We ran again, impulsively; when we stopped, a shoulder of downland had almost hidden the conflagration. Above, the cloud reflection from the burning nests glowed orange, lighting a hemisphere of sky.

We moved away again, walking now and picking our way, feeling fresh air move against our faces. We were both too tired to talk; it was enough just to be free again, sensing the space and openness round us. In the first light of dawn, we reached the sea.

It was totally unexpected; it reared between two shoulders of hills, a great grey plain, immense and cold. I stopped unbelievingly and stared, one hand on Pete's shoulder. After so long, and so much effort, the sight just didn't mean anything to me any more. I'd put the tobacco we'd been given in my pocket; I squatted down and rolled a couple of cigarettes. Pete took the light silently, cupping her hand round the match; then she collapsed on the wet grass beside me, lay leaning on one arm and looking out at the quiet, dully twinkling vastness. After a while she turned back expressionlessly. 'Ain't altered much, has it?' she said softly.

We walked across the down. As we descended, the horizon rose until the sea ahead looked like an endless vague hill. A breeze blew up off the water, strong and cool. We reached a steeper path, irregular steps weathered in the rock; at the bottom we stopped for breath. We were in an amphitheatre. Dimly seen cliffs rose rough and weathered on three sides. There was the entrance to what looked like an old quarry; left and right were headlands, rocks showing beneath them. The sea was still some thirty feet below us, swilling and sucking round long ledges of stone. It was a gaunt, dangerous little bay, a spot where no boat would ever try to land.

The instinct to hide was still too strong to ignore. I walked to the quarry mouth, pitched in a couple of lumps of rock. Nothing stirred. I edged inside. It was a mournful place. Water splashed and banged intermittently, formed puddles and rivulets that ran towards the entrance, lost themselves in banks of shale. Here and there the flat roof was supported by drystone pillars. Behind the biggest of them was a raised alcove; Pete curled herself into it. A moment later she spoke from the near-dark. 'Bill,' she said. 'About what you was sayin' . . .'

'Forget it. It wasn't important.'

'No,' she said. 'There was somethin' in it. Funny . . .' she didn't speak again; I sat by her, rolled another cigarette. When I offered it to her there was no answer. She was asleep.

I dozed again myself, fitfully. When I woke it was full light. The sky was a translucent blue and the sun touched the rocks of the bay with a cool gold. I walked quietly to the quarry entrance. Out over the Channel, smoky in the distance, hung a congregation of monstrous shapes. Triangles, cubes . . . and another, repeated over and over into farthest perspectives. The looped cross, the Ankh, life-symbol of the old Pharaohs. The thunder from the swarms just reached the land, faint and evocative as the midsummer hum.

Pete was still asleep, tawny hair mussed up. I roused her. She knuckled her eyes, yawned, scratched and shivered, stood up and tidied her shirt. Then she followed me outside silently. We pulled up and stared. On the stone ledges at the edge of the sea stood a solitary figure; an old man, clothes ragged, painfully thin, face half covered with a silver stubble of beard. One hand was raised and pointing and I could hear the rise and fall of his voice. As we got close I made out the words.

'Babylon the great is fallen, is fallen, and is become the habitation of devils, and the hold of every foul spirit, and a cage of every unclean and hateful bird . . .'

Pete put her arm across his shoulders and grinned at him. 'Take it easy, ole dad,' she said gently. 'It's all right . . .'

I was staring out over the water. Right at the end, it was going to be easy. Far off, tiny and brilliant in the sunlight, was a helicopter. It was edging towards the mainland, moving cautiously, trailing a saucer of greenish foam. I started to shout, and wave my arms.

The old man seemed to become aware of us for the first time. 'Come out of her, my people,' he said quaveringly. 'That ye be not partakers of her sins, and that ye receive not of her plagues . . .' His arm was up again, pointing at the Furies. 'For her sins have reached unto Heaven, and God hath remembered her iniquities . . .'

The chopper was close now, nearly overhead, the engine noise slamming back from the headlands, startling gulls from the rocks. The down-draught tore at my clothes, whipped Pete's hair round her face. I saw the ladder descending and the hoist. We got the old man into it, followed him. I pushed Pete ahead of me. I was buffeted and deafened; then I was aboard, and the hatch was closed. The machine spun on its tail and fell away towards the open sea.

The winchman dogged the trap shut and straightened up, a blond boy wearing Fleet Air Arm insignia on a civilian sweater. He shouted, 'Under orders, pick somebody off the mainland. What the ruddy hell's gone wrong with the wasps . . .'

We were overtaken by a glittering triangle a hundred yards on a side. It swung away, its base nearly brushing the wave-tips. I said, 'They're crazy.' I tried to explain what had happened, pitching my voice over the noise of the engine. I don't know whether I was believed or not. We skirted the Isle of Wight, long since overrun, and headed for the Channel Islands. 'Daren't get too close,' explained the airman. 'Bastards fly into the rotor . . .' Another half-hour of racing sea and Guernsey showed up ahead. We landed on a pad built out over the water. The pilot killed his engine and the whick-whick-whick of the blades stopped at last. I got down feeling stiff and the boy helped Pete out elaborately. She smiled at him like a duchess.

It was queer to see traffic and pedestrians moving normally. There were Army vehicles everywhere, we were met by a jeep and an ambulance. I turned to the winchman. 'Look, we've got to get to your CO. It's vital.'

He looked doubtful. 'Actually we're a dual command, Navy and Army. Job to know who the ruddy boss is half the time . . .

The big white chief's on Jersey anyway, I think you'd better see our chap first. We've got a sort of organization set up for refugees, he'll fix you up after you've had a chat...'

I fumed but I had to give in. I got in the jeep with Pete and we moved off. Twenty yards away I was yelling to stop. The MP who was driving us braked, looking surprised. I ran across the pontoon. A collection of small craft was tied up alongside. One biggish cabin-cruiser stood out from the rest. She was painted blue-grey all over, decks, brasswork, everything, with a big stark number seventeen on her side, but I knew her. On her bow the raised letters of her name were still readable. She was *Enchantress*.

Staff HQ for the island was in a big hotel just off the sea-front. We were hurried in, made to give our names a dozen times over. Orderlies and MP's chivvied us from desk to desk. I started wondering how long it would be before I tapped one of the brassbound so-and-so's between the eyes. Then we were left alone in a room with two or three shabby chairs, a table piled with magazines. I picked one up. Some ersatz Army production called the *Island Gazette*. I leafed through the larityped pages, sneered over one or two bad cartoons, and chucked it down again. Finally another messenger arrived. The Rehabilitation Controller would see us at once.

We took a lift, stepped out into officer country. We were hustled through an anteroom, the orderly opened a door, closed it again behind us. I saw a wide desk, a bank of tele-phones. A man in a worn, neatly pressed uniform sitting writing. He looked up as we came in, and started to smile. I said, 'Good God...' and walked forward in a daze.

He came round the desk and gripped my hand. He said, 'Over a year ago, on the Plain... Last I saw of you, you were nose down in a ditch with a top-load of bloody wasps. Never expected to see you again...'

I nodded. 'I could say the same for you, Neil...'

There were lines on his face that hadn't been there before, and his hair was greying prematurely. He saw me looking at his sleeve and laughed. 'Nothing like a nice brisk war to step up the ruddy promotion... Well, grab a chair. What've you been doing with yourself, old boy, you look like Tarzan of the apes...'

For a moment I'd nearly forgotten Pete. She was still standing by the door, looking a little lost. I went to her and took her arm. 'This is ex-Lieutenant Connor, love. Remember, I told you about him...'

She caught Neil looking her up and down. She was scruffier than I was; long hair, beaten-up shirt and jeans. 'Sorry, dearie,' she said. 'But I just di'n't have time to powder me nose...'

I described our meeting with Harmon as briefly as I could. Neil heard me in silence. As I finished, one of the phones rang shrilly. A report from a spotter aircraft; off Saint Alban's Head the Furies were throwing themselves into the sea in millions. There was a carpet of them, floating on the waves.

Neil put the handset down and sat for a moment watching me. Then he picked it up again. He said, 'Bradley, get on to the old man will you? Yes, immediately ... What? I don't care what he's doing, tell him it's the biggest thing since they beached the bloody Ark...'

The wires were humming within minutes. A staff conference was fixed for fourteen hundred hours; Neil warned us after that we'd probably be flying to Jersey. Then he called in a stenographer. He said crisply, 'Right, both of you. Start again from the beginning. Better have it cut and dried, to a large extent this is going to be your party...'

It took another hour and several cups of coffee to get out of us all he wanted to know. Then he told us something of what had been happening in the Islands. After the first panic the civilian population had settled down well under the military, and a combined force had been organized from what units had managed to leave the mainland. Most of their efforts had been directed to feeding themselves and the Islanders though they'd done what they could to hit back at the wasps, flying reconnaissance and mounting the odd sortie against coastal nests. They had a couple of destroyers still operational and a pack of helicopters but supplies had been too short for anything like a real offensive. They had almost no bombs and ammunition and very little fuel. It had in fact been a unit from the Channel Island Command that had brushed with us at Chill Leer the previous winter. 'The human situation's chaotic all over the mainland of course,' said Neil broodingly. 'Rehabilitation's go-

g to be a major problem even without the wasps...' He
urned, looked at Pete quickly then back to me. 'What hap-
ened to the girl, Jane was it? The girl you were looking
:ter?'

I stared. 'But she's here. I got her on a boat, she's here
•mewhere...'

He narrowed his eyes. 'How do you know, old boy?'

'Because I saw it. The boat. On my way in. *Enchantress*.
ou've got her in camouflage... number seventeen.'

He pressed the intercom. 'Connie, get me the file on
uxiliary Seventeen will you? Make it snappy.' He lit a cigar-
:te. 'Minor part of my job. We've kept records on all the stuff
e took over in case we ever got a chance to hand it back.'

A girl came in, laid a slim folder on the desk. He skimmed
hrough it, frowning. Then he put it down, spread his hands
at on the cover. He said, 'She's a good boat. One of our best.
•one over two dozen provision runs to France.' He looked up
uddenly. 'She was found drifting about ten miles out. Nobody
n board. I'm sorry...'

I felt Pete's hand on my arm.

We walked along a beach of fine white sand. To our left was
small headland; the sun was setting behind it, turning the
uiles of water to a glittering cloth of gold. It had been a hectic
ay on the islands; an advance unit had already established a
eachhead in Dorset, they reported the coast nearly clear of
vasps and most of the dome cities in flames. Pete and I had
eard our report read over and over, been questioned across
alf a dozen conference tables. My shoulder was aching from
alf a dozen jabs and I had an uncomfortable feeling I was
oing to suffer worse in the morning but we were due to go
ack to the mainland sometime that night. The Army people
vere drafting in everybody they could lay their hands on for
ie first tidying-up operations. We'd managed to escape for
alf an hour; we moved slowly, savouring the quietness. Now
had time to think again Jane was haunting me. I said, 'I
in't imagine what happened to her. If ... if the wasps got to
er there'd have been signs. She must have been taken off, she
ouldn't just have vanished...'

Pete didn't answer. A car pulled up on the road behind us; I

heard the door open and slam, the faint swish of footsteps.
looked round. There was a WRAC driver, a dark, pretty gir
smartly uniformed. She said, 'Major Connor's compliment
sir, and are you ready to embark?'

I nodded. 'Thanks, we'll come at once...' I took Pete's arm
and turned for the staff car. She stopped suddenly an
wrenched away. I said, 'Hey, what's the matter?'

She wouldn't look at me. 'You go on, Bill. I'm not com
in'...'

'What?'

She said, 'You jus'... keep lookin' for that girl o' yours
You'll find her. Like you said, she ain't dead. I expect the
picked her up, some boat picked her up. That was what hap
pened, p'raps she's in France...'

'Pete, what the hell are you on about?'

She was trying to walk but she wasn't getting far because
was holding her back. She said wildly, 'Anyway I wouldn't b
no good to you. Silly idea, don't know what got into me ... B
a joke, wouldn't it? Right joke, scarred ole Granny, tell th
kids how we beat the wasps up. An' anyway I done that blok
in, don't forget I done that...'

'Pete,' I said. 'Pete, *shut up*...' I don't know how it hap
pened but she was in my arms and I was kissing her hair, he
cheek, the long scar, and she was crying. The first tears I'
ever seen from her; they matted her eyelashes, ran down he
throat. I didn't think she'd ever stop. The WRAC had turne
away; I held Pete till she was quiet. It took a long time. Ove
her head I could see the ocean and the distant horizon. On th
horizon, nearly invisible, a line of dark dots. The boats of th
second wave, heading out to the mainland. And beyond them
tiny and faint, a darker shadow against the northern sky. Th
ghost of a looped cross.

I've thought a lot about Jane. She obviously didn't land on
the Isle of Wight; she didn't lose her head, she held off care
fully, saw wasps, changed course for the Channel Islands
There would be maps somewhere aboard *Enchantress*, she wa
quite cool enough to navigate by them. But she never made i
Was it like Pete said, a Navy vessel saw her and took her off
left the cruiser to drift? Or did a lone Fury, miles too far from

land, spot the boat, and turn lazily against the blue, and dive
... For a time I was sure I'd see Jane again; there'd be a
knock on the door and a graceful woman would be standing
there, and it would be her. But now I'm not so certain. What
happened to her is a mystery only the sea could answer.

And the Furies of course. They knew ...

I've turned into something I never thought I'd be. A farmer.
Many of the survivors did the same; God knows there was
enough spare land, and every yard that could be cultivated was
valuable. Pete and I live on the Mendips, not very far from the
site of buried Chill Leer. The Agricultural people gave us a lot
of help when we were getting started but even so we had to
earn as we went along and the first two or three years were
fairly hectic. But we've got things better organized now, our
figures are well up to the area norm; last year we even managed to show a profit. The Mendips have come into their own
again; most of the great urban centres and the manufacturing
belts of the Midlands are still unapproachable but the hills
have taken over, they're supplying the new economy with what
they've always supplied, time out of mind; milk and cheese,
wool, butter, strawberries; coal and lead and calamine. It's
four years now since the last Fury died and the population of
England is still hanging round the two million mark but we
shall make out. After all there weren't many more of us in the
time of the first Elizabeth. People everywhere are picking up
the reins, starting over. This year we managed some small-
scale exporting to France and the Low Countries, and last
summer two ships slid into Plymouth flying the Stars and
Stripes.

When the newly constituted Department of Records
approached me to write this book I was uncertain about a lot
of aspects. I was going to leave Pete out altogether but after
the passing of the Act of Amnesty, designed to cover cases like
hers, she insisted I put everything down exactly as it happened. I'm glad now I did; it fulfilled an ambition of mine.

I've got one other. I want to wall off the shattered mouth of
Chill Leer and set in a plaque with the names of the people
who lived and died there. I'd like them to be remembered, for
a while at least. I can't do it yet, concrete still isn't plentiful
enough to waste pouring into holes in cliffs; we'd have to get

an authorization from the South-Western Supply Board and so far that hasn't been forthcoming. Pete says Dear Heart talks a load of mush, but she's working on it as hard as I am.

Several of the great steel-frame domes have been preserved as national monuments. The *pogrom* that followed the death of the wasps was nearly universal but prompt and farsighted action by the military saved a handful of nests for study. None of the symbo leaders survived; those that weren't torn apart by the people they'd controlled died in the burning domes rather than face us and answer for what they'd done. I'm sorry for that; like the rest of us, they were victims of circumstance. As Harmon said, they did what they thought was best ...

I don't think the wasps will ever be wholly forgotten. In an odd way they're more alive to us now than before; they've passed back into folklore, but they're still the bogys that haunt our worst dreams. They're the things that rattle doors on nights of wind, the faces that watch half-seen from the deepest woods. Gales boom in our chimneys, and we hear the noise of great narrow wings ... We're still fighting to re-establish ourselves, our towns are small and the roads between them bad, we barricade our houses after dark. We don't know yet what form our New World is going to take; but we know whatever we build from the wreckage of a culture, in some way it's got to be better, we've got to try a little harder to justify what could be the finest intelligence left in our galaxy. The Keepers still haunt the conscience of mankind; I think in the end they justified the name we gave them so lightly. To us, they were the Furies.

MORE ABOUT PENGUINS, PELICANS
AND PUFFINS

For further information about books available from Penguins please write to Dept EP, Penguin Books Ltd, Harmondsworth, Middlesex UB7 0DA.

In the U.S.A.: For a complete list of books available from Penguins in the United States write to Dept DG, Penguin Books, 299 Murray Hill Parkway, East Rutherford, New Jersey 07073.

In Canada: For a complete list of books available from Penguins in Canada write to Penguin Books Canada Ltd, 2801 John Street, Markham, Ontario L3R 1B4.

In Australia: For a complete list of books available from Penguins in Australia write to the Marketing Department, Penguin Books Australia Ltd, P.O. Box 257, Ringwood, Victoria 3134.

In New Zealand: For a complete list of books available from Penguins in New Zealand write to the Marketing Department, Penguin Books (N.Z.) Ltd, P.O. Box 4019, Auckland 10.

In India: For a complete list of books available from Penguins in India write to Penguin Overseas Ltd, 706 Eros Apartments, 56 Nehru Place, New Delhi 110019.

THIEVES' WORLD

Edited by Robert Asprin

Sword-play and Sorcery ... Murder, Mayhem and Mystery!

Thieves' World is what happened when the world's top science-fiction and fantasy writers got together to create the amazing new world of *Sanctuary* where you will mix and mingle with *Lythal the Star-browed*, whose magic is questionable, his sword-play not, *Jubal*, ex-gladiator and slave, now a respected citizen (he made his money selling slaves), *One Thumb*, the crooked bartender at the Vulgar Unicorn ... and even more fantastic characters!

TALES FROM THE VULGAR UNICORN

Edited by Robert Asprin

Continuing the fantastic fictional game begun in *Thieves' World*, here is a second collection of stories set in the amazing city of *Sanctuary*, where you can enjoy the quiet elegance of Ambrosia House; sample bizarre pleasures at the House of Whips; sip ale in the Vulgar Unicorn, and listen to some of the most strange, dangerous, magical and deadly tales ever told.

LYNN ABBEY, POUL ANDERSON, ROBERT ASPRIN, JOHN BRUNNER, DAVID DRAKE, PHILIP JOSE FARMER, JOE HALDEMAN, JANET MORRIS, ANDREW J. OFFUT, and A. E. VAN VOGT have dreamed up a world of wonders – a fabulous reading adventure!

DARKCHILD
Sydney J. Van Scyoc

Who was Darkchild and for what purpose had he come to the valley?

Khira was a barohna's daughter destined to wield the power of the sun over her peaceful people. Her way was hard, but she knew her heritage and her future . . .

Then, in the dead of winter, a ship brought Darkchild. He was not of her race, he had no memory. How could he pose the threat to her people that the Arnini assured her he did? Was Darkchild all that he seemed?

'Extraordinary . . . *Darkchild* is the best kind of science-fiction writing which transcends its genre and demands attention' – Stephen Donaldson

THE DAY IT RAINED FOREVER
Ray Bradbury

Stories by Science Fiction's most lyrical writer

Ray Bradbury is one of the few speculative writers to have created an identifiable and unified world of his own: from the nostalgia, mystery and romance of the mid-West, to the new colonies uneasily settling on the sands of Mars or the sinister tension of post-holocaust Mexico, his stories are a haunting evocation of the Gothic and the fanciful.